When had Whitney MacNair ever done what he'd expected of her?

A smile blossomed on Whitney's lips. "I'll help you."

"No."

"Yes."

"No!" Vincent's breath seeped out on a weary sigh. She looked so vulnerable and beautiful. So young and full of hope. He didn't want that look changed by the world he lived in.

Completely ignoring his decision, Whitney turned to retrace their steps back up the mountain. "We lost them back there. That's where we should start."

"MacNair, get your rear back down here." That cute, curvy little rear.

She continued to climb. "You need my help."

Vincent clenched his jaw. Whitney was a danger to herself, completely oblivious to just how dangerous and desperate a terrorist on the run could be. It was up to Vincent to save her from herself.

But who would save him from her?

Dear Harlequin Intrigue Reader,

Need some great stocking stuffers this holiday season for yourself and your family and friends? Harlequin Intrigue has four dynamite suggestions—starting with three exciting conclusions.

This month, veteran romantic suspense author Rebecca York wraps up her special 43 LIGHT STREET trilogy MINE TO KEEP with *Lassiter's Law*, and Susan Kearney finishes her action-packed HIDE AND SEEK miniseries with *Lovers in Hiding*. Julie Miller, too, closes out the MONTANA CONFIDENTIAL quartet with her book *Secret Agent Heiress*. You won't want to miss any of these thrilling titles.

For some Christmastime entertainment, B.J. Daniels takes you west on a trip into madness and mayhem with a beautiful amnesiac and a secret father in her book *A Woman with a Mystery*.

So make your list and check out Harlequin Intrigue for the best gift around…happily ever after.

Happy holidays from all of us at Harlequin Intrigue.

Sincerely,

Denise O'Sullivan
Associate Senior Editor
Harlequin Intrigue

SECRET AGENT HEIRESS
JULIE MILLER

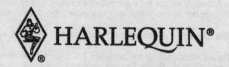

TORONTO • NEW YORK • LONDON
AMSTERDAM • PARIS • SYDNEY • HAMBURG
STOCKHOLM • ATHENS • TOKYO • MILAN • MADRID
PRAGUE • WARSAW • BUDAPEST • AUCKLAND

Special thanks and acknowledgment are given to Julie Miller for her contribution to the MONTANA CONFIDENTIAL series.

ISBN 0-373-22642-X

SECRET AGENT HEIRESS

Visit us at www.eHarlequin.com

Printed in U.S.A.

ABOUT THE AUTHOR

Julie Miller attributes her passion for writing romance to all those fairy tales she read growing up, and to shyness. Encouragement from her family to write down all those feelings she couldn't express became a love for the written word. She gets continued support from her fellow members of the Prairieland Romance Writers, where she serves as the resident "grammar goddess." This award-winning author and teacher has published several paranormal romances. Inspired by the likes of Agatha Christie and Encyclopedia Brown, Ms. Miller believes the only thing better than a good mystery is a good romance.

Born and raised in Missouri, she now lives in Nebraska with her husband, son and smiling guard dog, Maxie. Write to Julie at P.O. Box 5162, Grand Island, NE 68802-5162.

Books by Julie Miller

HARLEQUIN INTRIGUE
588—ONE GOOD MAN*
619—SUDDEN ENGAGEMENT*
642—SECRET AGENT HEIRESS

*The Taylor Clan

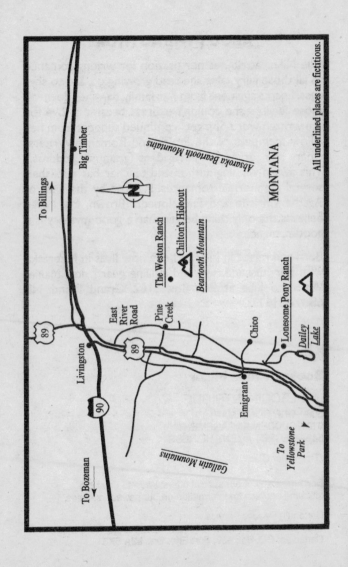

MONTANA

All underlined places are fictitious.

Absaroka Beartooth Mountains

Gallatin Mountains

To Billings

Big Timber

To Bozeman

Livingston

90

89

East River Road

Pine Creek

89

The Weston Ranch

Chilton's Hideout

Beartooth Mountain

Emigrant

Chico

Lonesome Pony Ranch

Dailey Lake

To Yellowstone Park

N

CAST OF CHARACTERS

Whitney MacNair—Touched by scandal, shunned by her powerful political family. Does this garrulous golden girl have what it takes to help Montana Confidential through its darkest hour?

Vincent Romeo—NSA agent with one mission—keep Whitney safe. Does this dark, brooding man of secrets hold the answer to her salvation?

Dimitri Chilton—The leader of the Black Order is alone and on the run.

Senator Ross Weston—He's facing the biggest contest of his political career.

Margery Weston—How far will she go to support her husband?

Warren Burke—Weston's campaign manager. How many dirty little secrets can one man hide?

Alysia Two Crows—More than just a maid?

Brian MacNair—Whitney's big brother has always taken care of her.

Daniel Austin—Will he have to choose between his family and Montana Confidential?

Gerald MacNair Sr.—He has the power to make or break a campaign for the presidency. But would he help his only daughter...?

I would like to thank my critique partner,
Sherry A. Siwinski, for sharing her expertise
on horses and ranch life with me.

This book is for her horse, Silver, a cantankerous
old character who lives with pain every day. And it is for
all the brave and loyal animals who touch our lives.
May they all live with peace and kindness.

Prologue

"Jewel?" Whitney MacNair's bay Appaloosa danced beneath her on the rocky path. A sure sign of trouble. "Your grandpa did say the rattlesnakes would be in hibernation now, didn't he?"

She glanced up the steep rock wall to the autumn golds and greens of aspen and lodgepole pine trees growing on the plateau above her. Sometimes a coyote would come out of the woods and follow along, just to check the new scents of horses and riders in his domain. The deceptive mix of light and shadow in the trees played tricks on her vision. Maybe something moved up there. And maybe she'd better keep her focus on the narrowing path.

The twelve-year-old girl on the sorrel gelding ahead of her turned in her saddle and shoved her hat back on her honey-blond hair. "It's too cold in October, Whit. Gramps said that if there are any snakes left, they won't come out to heat themselves on the rocks until this afternoon."

Whitney tugged at the neckline of her frost-blue cashmere sweater. It was warm enough by her standards. She'd already shed the matching wool jacket and tied it to the back of her bulky western saddle. She'd endured three months in this godforsaken wilderness, and she still couldn't get used to the rapid fluctuations in temperature.

She didn't really mind it so much today, though, she

thought, letting a satisfied smile curve her lips. Sure, the
nearest thing that passed for a town was a good fifty miles
away in Livingston. And it was another hundred more beyond that to reach anything she'd classify as civilization.
But her boss, Daniel Austin, had given her the sweetest
compliment earlier today.

Nice job, Whit, he'd said.

It wasn't so much the words, but the fact that he'd recognized her contribution—however small—to the smooth
running of Montana Confidential, a covert branch of the
federal Department of Public Safety. Under Daniel's direction, they'd set up a command center, beneath the guise
of a working ranch, to handle the threat of terrorists sneaking into the United States across the unpopulated Montana–Canadian border.

The Black Order, as the terrorists called themselves, had
attempted to destroy a research facility, sabotage a public
water system, even kill the governor of Montana, trying to
get a foothold of control in the U.S. But Montana Confidential and its diverse team of agents had turned them back
each time.

Whitney was no agent. She had the thoroughly ungla-
morous title of executive assistant. Glorified secretary was
more like it. Cum laude graduate from the best schools in
the East, sentenced to a job well beneath her talents and
experience.

But today, after nearly three months in the boondocks
of Montana, far away from her family—states away from
a proper department store—the isolation hadn't mattered
quite so much.

Nice job.

Her smile broadened. She'd been working day and night
fielding calls from law enforcement agencies all over the
state, reports of sightings of Dimitri Chilton, the leader of
the Black Order terrorist group, who was still at large.

It wasn't the kind of work she'd trained for at Smith College. But Daniel had needed her to fill that role, and she hadn't let him down. She'd been more than window dressing. More than a kid sister anyone needed to baby-sit. She'd rolled up her sleeves, sat her butt in the chair and kept the top-secret war room running while the field agents completed an undercover sting designed to expose and capture the Black Order.

Though some of the operatives had nearly lost their lives, they'd saved the Montana governor, and rounded up or eliminated every terrorist except one.

Dimitri Chilton had escaped.

Whitney shivered, feeling a sudden chill despite the trickle of sweat that gathered at the small of her back.

"What are we supposed to do if we meet this bear of yours?" she asked, diverting her thoughts back to her friend. She wondered if Jewel really had spotted a black bear this late in the year, or if this trail ride was just an excuse to discuss the pitfalls of puppy love with Charlie Korbett.

"I want to take a picture of it to show at school." The girl's small shoulders rose and fell in an adult-size sigh. "Besides, I had to get away from the ranch. C.J. wanted to take me shopping in Livingston. If she invites me to go on one more dorky outing with her…"

Ah. Cecilia Jane trouble. Jewel had a serious crush on C.J.'s new husband, Frank Connolly. Almost three months had passed since their August wedding in Las Vegas, but Jewel just couldn't forgive C.J. for "stealing" the man of her dreams, despite several efforts from Frank and C.J. to reach some sort of truce with her.

"She's just trying to be friendly, you know," Whitney commented.

"Well, she should stop trying. I'm not interested. I'd rather hang out with you any day. You are way cooler—"

The snap of a twig from above cut short the teen-angst tirade. Jewel glanced up as her horse danced beneath her. "Did you hear that?"

Whitney's heartbeat quickened. "Yeah." She racked her brain for the proper way to defend herself against a bear attack. Trouble was, they didn't get many bears back in Martha's Vineyard or Washington, D.C. But avoiding narrow alleys was a good technique to escape muggers. She applied the big-city logic and nudged the heels of her leather boots into the Appaloosa's sides. "Let's pick up the pace and get to the top of the plateau. There's not much space to turn the horses around here."

Jewel urged her mount into a trot and Whitney followed close behind. Something was out there. Snake or bear, perhaps. Something big enough and bad enough to spook the horses.

The Appaloosa's ears flattened against its skull. She leaned forward and stroked its neck, trying to ease the wary tension radiating from the horse into her legs and straight up to the warning bell dinging inside her head. "Easy, boy."

She scanned down the tree-studded slope to where Crooked Creek wound through the bottom of the valley. This steady climb into the Absaroka-Beartooth Mountains at the eastern edge of the Lonesome Pony Ranch suddenly seemed hundreds of miles away from the house and outbuildings where she and the Confidential team lived and worked.

"Whitney!"

A black, stocky figure leaped from the rocks above, caught Jewel by the shoulder and knocked her from her horse.

Bears didn't leap.

They didn't wear leather gloves and black baseball caps, either.

"Jewel!"

Whitney dug in her heels and charged the Appaloosa straight at the girl's attacker. The man bounced to his feet with Jewel clutched in his arms. But every ounce of tomboy and spitfire kicked and punched. He dropped Jewel on her rump in the dust. Whitney pulled her right foot from the stirrup, held tight to the saddle horn and kicked out just as he turned.

She caught him square in the jaw and sent him flying backward. Tugging hard on the reins, she jerked the Appaloosa to a halt.

Whitney spun around in the saddle to see Jewel going after her hat in the tall grass. "Jewel, get on your horse!"

The added height and a thousand-plus pounds of frightened animal would give her an advantage over the man. Jewel abandoned the hat and ran for her panicked sorrel.

The man in the short black coat scrambled to his feet. He paused long enough to flash Whitney a taunting smile. With the back of his gloved hand, he wiped the fresh blood from the corner of his mouth. He pulled the bill of his hat low over his forehead, masking his eyes.

Whitney knew a dare when she saw one.

He turned away. His brisk, long stride carried him quickly, methodically closer to Jewel.

The girl caught one rein on the sorrel's bridle. The horse's eyes rolled, and he reared up, pulling her off her feet. Jewel held on, but the man closed in on her.

"No!" Whitney screamed the warning. The man never broke his stride. Jewel tried to calm her horse, but her own desperation was too easy to read. Whitney tugged on the Appaloosa's reins. But she'd boxed herself in at the narrowest point of the ascent, leaving her no room to maneuver the skittish horse without tumbling down the side of the mountain.

Pulling her feet free of the stirrups, she swung her right

leg over the horse's neck and jumped to the ground. The impact of the hard, dry earth jolted her legs. But she absorbed the shock through her shins and knees and took off running.

Jewel had gotten close enough to wrap her fingers in the sorrel's mane. The man in black snatched the back of her denim jacket in his fist. Jewel pulled, he tugged, and Whitney charged.

Boot first, she kicked him in the side, aiming for a kidney. He lost his grip, flew three feet and dropped to his knees.

Whitney grabbed Jewel's left leg and lifted. "Get up."

Jewel swung her leg over and snatched at the reins. "Whit, look out!"

A thick black-clad arm closed around her neck from behind, choking her. The man lifted her away from Jewel. But boredom alone wasn't the only reason she'd signed up for those kickboxing classes in Livingston.

As soon as her feet touched ground, she shifted her balance and brought her elbow back into his gut. Once. She fisted her hand, squeezed her muscles into steel and struck a second time. The elbow jab loosened his grip and she twisted around. She rammed the butt of her hand up under his nose, and his head jerked back.

Whitney planted her left foot, and with every inch of her long legs stretched up to kick the heel of her boot in the very same place.

A slew of foreign obscenities bespoke his pain as he sank to the ground. She didn't wait to translate. She spun around and ran for her horse, shouting commands to Jewel behind her. "Get out of here! Get back to the ranch. Get help. Go!"

"Whitney!"

Glancing back at the frantic warning was her mistake.

The man was on his feet in hot pursuit. She braced for his attack.

She shifted her weight to her left and kicked with her right. But he was ready for her this time. He caught her ankle and twisted her knee, pulling her off balance.

Pain shot up past her thigh and she hit the ground hard, flat on her back, knocking the wind from her chest. The clear blue sky swam above her. She squeezed her eyes shut against the dizzy sensation and tried to suck in precious oxygen, but the effort seared her throbbing lungs.

A heavy weight fell on top of her, crushing her back into the uneven jabs of small rocks beneath her. Her eyes shot open in a breathless cry of pain and she saw the man in black above her. His forearm pressed down on the base of her throat. She was vaguely aware of lifting her hands and trying to push him off her.

Her mouth opened and closed, struggling to bring air into her deprived lungs. The sky above her swirled into a blur. She blinked her eyes clear and tried to move her legs, but the weight of his body trapped her. Her fingers turned to mush and lost their grip on his coat. A hammering sound pounded in her ears. Jewel's horse? Or the erratic pulse beat of a body fighting for air to breathe?

A drop of blood from her assailant's battered face hit her cheek and singed her skin. But she couldn't turn away from the grim touch with his arm anchored at her throat. He was choking her, she realized amid the gray haze that drifted into her mind and robbed her of rational thought.

She was going to die on the side of a mountain in the middle of nowhere, far away from family and friends and any chance of rescue.

With one final surge of energy she punched her hand up and knocked the cap off his head, exposing the shaggy length of his black hair. But it was the even blacker void of his familiar, spiritless eyes that snatched the last lingering breath of air from her throat.

She'd seen that face a hundred times, plastered on the walls and transmitted over the data screens in the Confidential war room.

Dimitri Chilton.

With nothing left inside her, no fight, no breath—no hope—Whitney surrendered to the blackness that consumed her.

Chapter One

"We're here, Romeo."

Agent Vincent Romeo opened his bleary eyes and studied his surroundings before ever lifting his chin from the pillow of his chest.

The Lonesome Pony Ranch looked pretty much the way his pilot escort had described it. Low, sprawling hills nestled between two mountain ranges. Horses grazing in snow-spotted pastures. A log house perched on top of a hill, surrounded by ranch buildings and guest cabins. Clear blue sky.

And not a skyscraper in sight.

Vincent unfolded his long legs from the tight confines of the chopper and stepped onto the concrete helipad. He rolled his cramped shoulders and tested the air by inhaling deeply. Nice. No trace of smog. His city-trained lungs would probably rebel.

He swiped his hand down his face and jaw, trying to shake the lingering fatigue. He could use a shave and a few hours of uninterrupted sleep.

But when the President of the United States summoned you at one in the morning for a special assignment, you didn't say no. Even if twenty-four hours earlier you were finishing up a weeklong stakeout that ended in a messy gun battle, leaving one agent wounded and a hit man dead.

That could have been you, Vinnie. He could hear Melissa's tearful voice in his head, even five years after she'd dumped him at the altar with that grand speech. Yeah, his job was dangerous. He put his life on the line every time he strapped on his badge and gun. But somebody had to walk the line between the good guys and the bad guys. Somebody had to make the world a safer place.

His father had walked that line. He'd known the risks long before that bullet had claimed his life.

Vincent knew the risks, too.

He strapped on his badge and gun, anyway.

"You coming, Romeo?" The dark-haired pilot who had picked him up at the airport, Frank Connolly, was already striding down the hill to a battered tan pickup truck.

Obviously fit and strong, Connolly's uneven gait piqued Vincent's curiosity. Like his father, had Connolly, too, been struck down in the line of duty?

Vincent didn't ask. He wasn't here to indulge his curiosity or to make friends.

He was here to do a job.

Tucking memories and philosophizing neatly away where they couldn't distract him, Vincent reached behind his seat to retrieve his gear. He traveled light. He already carried the important stuff, either on his person or inside his head. But it paid to be prepared for any contingency. He slung the black nylon duffel bag over his shoulder, and joined Connolly in the truck.

As they pulled up in front of the ranch house, a blond-haired man opened the screen door and stepped onto the porch. The weight of authority he carried on his shoulders easily identified him as the boss of this operation. He crossed to the top of the steps and waited for Vincent to approach.

By the time Vincent had set his bag on the wooden bench beside the front door, the boss had been joined by

Connolly and two other men, who introduced themselves as Court Brody and Patrick McMurty.

The boss introduced himself last. "Daniel Austin."

Vincent unzipped his black leather jacket and reached inside. He pulled out the wallet that carried his badge and ID and flipped it open. "Vincent Romeo. National Security Agency."

Daniel glanced at the identification and returned it. His firm handshake welcomed him and urged him to get down to business all at the same time. "The war room is downstairs, but I think we can do this right here."

Vincent handed him an envelope sealed with a stamp marked POTUS. "President of the United States, huh?" Daniel recognized the eagle logo, then slipped his thumb beneath the flap. "He wants to oversee this mission personally, is that it?"

"The hostage is of personal importance to the president."

Daniel paused. His clear brown eyes sent an unmistakable message. "She's important to *us*. And we call her Whitney around here."

Vincent acknowledged the warning with a silent nod. He folded his arms across his chest, distancing himself from the palpable urgency of this unusual business meeting. He made no apology for studying the group of men as closely as they scrutinized him. Each man seemed at ease with his surroundings, at ease with the type of job they'd been asked to do for their country. Daniel, Frank, Court—even Grandpa McMurty.

Patrick McMurty was some kind of retired sheriff or military officer. The upright carriage and balanced stance of an alert man ready for trouble were recognizable to Vincent's trained eye. According to the briefing he'd received on the plane, McMurty had been recruited to run

the ranch and provide the cover necessary for the operatives to blend in with this part of the country.

Montana Confidential had put together a pretty fair team
of counterterrorist agents. Having outside help to retrieve
one of their own probably wasn't sitting well with any of
them.

Vincent shrugged off the observation, only momentarily
concerned about treading on another man's turf. His job
was to rescue Whitney MacNair, not win any popularity
contest. He focused his attention back on Daniel, who had
finished reading the official letter. "Everything clear?"

"We're to provide you with whatever backup you need.
But you're point man on this mission." Daniel stuffed the
papers back into the envelope. "Name it and you've got
it."

Vincent knew his list already. "I need a map of the
terrain and I need to talk to the girl. I have everything else
I need."

Frank Connolly shook his head and stepped forward.
"You mean we have no part in this? Kyle Foster's cutting
short his honeymoon to help get Whitney back. He and
Laura will be here by this afternoon."

Vincent recognized the name of another agent and his
new wife, who'd been recruited to help expose collusion
between the Black Order and an American contact who
worked at her father's research facility.

The Black Order was no ordinary adversary. Like any
terrorist group, they despised the United States and its
global domination. But their insidious attempts to influence
and undermine the American government, as well as corrupt and frighten its citizens, weren't his concern at the
moment.

He had to bring home a kidnapped society girl. Let
Montana Confidential handle the terrorists.

Daniel Austin understood that. He laid a placating hand

on Frank's shoulder. "President's orders. The Confidential group is to play a support role only. Gerald MacNair, Sr., Whitney's father, seems to be an old family friend. This is being handled out of Washington."

Court Brody swore, clearly as frustrated by the red tape as Frank. "This is our territory. We know it better than any hotshot from the East Coast."

"Chicago," Daniel corrected him. Court, a former FBI man who probably understood the politics of Washington better than anyone there, seemed unimpressed. "And you do know this land better than any of us." The command was clear.

Vincent absorbed the brunt of Court's steely-eyed glare before he excused himself to do Daniel's bidding. "I'll draw up a map."

Frank, seemingly a respected voice of reason among the men, turned his argument to Daniel. "You're letting him go in solo? Chilton's a desperate man. No telling what he's willing to do."

Vincent handled his own defense. "There's one hostage, one kidnapper." He added the next without false modesty. "I only need me."

Daniel pocketed the orders. "What Frank's trying to say is that Chilton's unpredictable. He may be on his own right now, but he still has a U.S. contact we haven't been able to uncover. If he somehow managed to make that connection, he may not be alone. You could be walking into an ambush."

Just like Dad. His father had gone into that warehouse to save a little girl's life. And because of his sacrifice, his partner had been able to bring the girl out alive.

Without betraying the wandering path of his weary brain, Vincent acknowledged Daniel's advice. "Thanks for the friendly warning. But I've been briefed on Chilton."

Daniel swept his gaze across the rugged skyline of

snow-tipped mountains to the east. "Court's right. This is Montana wilderness we're talking about. You don't strike me as a country boy."

He'd had enough survival training and experience to handle just about any weather and terrain. But he wasn't interested in sharing his résumé at the moment. Time had been wasted already. He pushed up his sleeve and checked his multitask field watch. "She's been gone twenty-four hours. I think one night in Chilton's company is enough for Ms. MacNair."

Frank raked his fingers through his hair and turned away, taking the length of the porch in his measured stride. Daniel's acceptance of the situation was more amiable. "If you need breakfast, Dale's in the kitchen." He shifted his glance to Grandpa. "Patrick?"

Patrick McMurty straightened from the porch rail where he'd taken a seat and adjusted his straw cowboy hat on top of his head. "Jewel's at the corral. I'll take you to her."

Vincent followed him down the steps. When they rounded the corner, out of sight of the others, the older man wrapped his fingers around Vincent's forearm and stopped him. "You hurt my granddaughter—you scare her in any way—I'll turn my wife, Dale, on you with her frying pan."

Gray eyes waited with deadly serious intent. Vincent could respect a man who guarded his family so zealously. He had brothers and sisters of his own he'd fought to protect. And nobody, but nobody, could say a thing to hurt his mother and not receive a visit from him.

"I have to do my job, Mr. McMurty." Vincent made a rare concession. "But you can stay and give me a high sign if I overstep your boundaries."

The older man released him. His sun-weathered face

crinkled into a smile and he winked. "You could outrun Dale, anyway. C'mon."

Vincent lengthened his stride to catch up with Patrick. He filed away that last remark to be laughed at later.

DANIEL AUSTIN WATCHED Patrick and Vincent Romeo until they disappeared around the side of the house. Romeo acted like a big bad loner and looked as if he should be guarding the door at the local tavern. What he lacked in verbal skills, he made up for in intimidation factor. In jeans and leather, he looked more at home on the back of a motorcycle, roaring down the highway, instead of hiking deep into the mountains.

But he checked out. He had to be the best, or Washington be damned.

Whitney might have been an annoying pain in the butt at first, with her self-indulgences and pouty moods. But she'd grown on Daniel like a kid sister these past months. She'd proved that she had some real gumption beneath that superficial veneer. He didn't know what made her hide behind that bored society girl routine. But something was hurting in that big heart of hers.

Daniel didn't like to see anyone in his family—real or adopted—hurt in any way. If he couldn't fix it himself, then he'd do whatever was necessary to make things right. He'd walked away from his wife and son to keep them safe, to keep them from worrying and wondering if he'd come home in a box after one of his missions.

And he would step aside and let Vincent Romeo bring Whitney home. Because he was the best man for the job.

He looked to the far end of the slatted pine porch and saw Frank Connolly standing with both hands braced on the railing. He understood the kind of tension radiating from his shoulders, that inability to let go when you wanted to take action instead. This particular *family* crisis he could handle with a bit of older-and-wiser advice.

Daniel knew the sound of his boots revealed his presence, even though Frank continued to stare at some distant point on the horizon. "Don't stress about this, Frank. We'll get the job done. We'll get her back. Why don't you go home and check on that pretty new wife of yours. Don't let this job come between you and C.J. the way I let the work consume me when I still had Sheridan."

"Had?" Frank straightened and turned, the frown on his face reflecting his concern. "I thought Sherry and your son, Jessie, were coming from Maryland to visit you this weekend."

Daniel propped his foot up on a bench and leaned forward, resting his elbows on his knee. "I called and canceled this morning. There's no sense bringing them here and talking second chances when I can't promise her the time we need to work things out."

"You still love her, don't you."

"I'll always love her. I loved her when I married her, and I loved her when the divorce papers came through." Just thinking of her long chestnut hair and sweet, trusting smile brought an ache to his chest. Frank had found the real happiness he deserved with C.J. Daniel didn't want him to lose that. "I screwed things up with Sheridan. Don't make the same mistakes with C.J. We'll handle things here. Go home."

WHEN THEY REACHED the circular corral, Vincent could understand Patrick McMurty's concern. His granddaughter, Jewel, looked petite enough to blow away in a strong wind. Dressed in denim from head to toe, she stood just inside the fence, brushing the already shiny coat of a gray mottled horse. When she turned to greet her grandfather, he saw the unmistakable signs of red, puffy eyes. The girl had done her fair share of crying already.

Patrick climbed the fence and took a position on the opposite side of the horse, giving Vincent some space to interview the girl, but staying close enough to keep an eye on things. Vincent stayed outside the corral, suspecting his big size might frighten the girl. After an initial introduction, Jewel turned and kept her gaze glued on the horse, named Silver.

"Can you describe the man who attacked you?"

"I already picked him out of a book Daniel showed me."

"Could you tell me?" he prompted. Surprisingly enough, the girl answered his question. Like a runner finding her stride, she warmed up to the idea of talking to him, and soon had no trouble carrying on a conversation. Her detailed description of the man and the attack fit the information he'd been faxed on Dimitri Chilton.

Good. If Chilton matched his profile, then Vincent's plan was sound. "Why were you and Ms. MacNair up that far in the mountains?"

Jewel continued to brush the horse. "Whit and I like to ride. She's good at it, though she says she prefers an English saddle. I saw a bear up there a few days ago. But mostly I wanted to talk."

The quick shift from one topic to the next left Vincent with a need to pause to catch up. "What did you want to talk about?"

She looked up at her grandfather, seeking a reprieve on having to answer that question. Then she turned and climbed to the second rail of the fence, putting herself at eye level with Vincent. "It's my fault Whitney's gone. He couldn't catch me, so he took her, instead."

Vincent's heart went out to the girl. She seemed to be carrying an awful heavy weight on those slim shoulders.

He stated the truth, hoping to reassure her. "His intention was probably to kill you, and take Ms. MacNair, anyway. There was nothing you could have done."

Patrick McMurty cleared his throat. A high sign. Vincent stepped back and tried to think of a better explanation. But he'd already missed his chance. Jewel's eyes flooded with new tears. She jumped down from the fence and returned her attention to Silver's bony hip.

Vincent took note of the way the horse balanced his weight on three legs, with the left back hoof barely touching the ground. From his inexperienced perspective, it looked as if Silver was standing on tiptoe.

"What's wrong with your horse?" he asked.

"He's old, almost thirty." Jewel punctuated her words with a sniffle. "Oh, you mean his leg? He got hit on a farm road a few years ago. He has arthritis real bad. Gramps says I'm going to lose him soon." Her shoulders lifted with another drawn-out sniffle. And then she buried her face in the horse's side to hide her tears. "I don't want to lose Whitney, too."

She turned and wiped her tears away with her dusty fingers, leaving an endearing streak across one cheek. "You'll bring her home, won't you?"

Vincent looked over the back of the horse to her grandfather. Patrick's grim expression challenged Vincent to hurt the girl any further. Vincent reached through the fence and stroked the horse's nose, in lieu of touching the girl.

He'd do his job for his country, and for the twenty-six-year-old hostage he'd never even met. But most of all, he'd complete the mission for this tearstained girl who cared so much for her missing friend.

His promise was simple.

"I will."

"I'M NOT DEAD."

The observation squeaked through the parched ache in

Whitney's throat as she woke up. She tried to reach up to massage the bruised tissue at her neck, but a rough reminder pinched the skin at her wrist.

She breathed in stale, undisturbed air and opened her eyes to the dim morning light before remembering the source of the pain. Several layers of wide gray duct tape bound her wrists to the arms of a warped hardwood chair.

But knowledge didn't necessarily bring comfort. Like a condemned woman strapped in for a primitive electrocution, her wrists and ankles had been taped to the arms and legs of the chair. She had no fear of being electrocuted, though. The ramshackle, one-room cabin where she'd spent the night hadn't seen electricity or running water for years—if ever.

She breathed in deeply and winced at the burning in her chest. Combined with the rapid pounding inside her head, her achy body felt as though she'd been hit by a Mack truck…or thrown from her horse…or…

"Good morning, Miss MacNair."

Whitney's senses snapped to full alert at the crisply articulated greeting. The man in black.

Dimitri Chilton.

He lounged across the room from her in a battered recliner upholstered with ratty, mildewed plaid, with one leg draped carelessly over the arm of the chair. The front of his wool coat gaped open, revealing the steel gray butt of an oversize handgun sticking out of a holster beneath his left arm.

She'd attacked a man carrying that kind of firepower? Even the Department of Public Safety agents who worked at Montana Confidential didn't walk around wearing weapons that looked like some sort of handheld mini cannon. The pockets of her jeans held nothing more dangerous than a tube of lip balm and a tissue.

Her pulse rate kicked up a notch. He could have killed her on the spot with that thing. He could have brought down Jewel McMurty and both horses, too. God, she was an idiot. No wonder her parents and brothers, and the men she worked with, thought she couldn't look after herself.

With very little effort, she'd made a mess of things again.

A flash of white teeth in the shadows, and the bemused laugh that accompanied the smile, brought her back to the present. Whitney forced herself to breathe calmly, in and out through her nose.

Second-guessing herself now wouldn't help. She had to keep a clear head. She dredged up the stiff-lipped pride that had seen her through tough times before. She refused to bend her spirit to her captor, even though he clearly had the upper hand.

"Where are we? What time is it?" She squinted through the shadows, trying to bring his face into focus. "Have you called my father yet? I know who you are."

"I know you as well." His crisp Mediterranean accent bespoke a man of education and culture. But the bruises on her body gave testament to his penchant for violence. "Your father will be contacted when the time is right. He paid good money to silence your embarrassing little scandal, no? You were whisked away from an important job in Washington to become a ranch hand in Montana. And you had such a promising career ahead of you."

Whitney withered at the false sympathy lacing his voice. So much for pride. Even a terrorist from the other side of the world had heard of the pampered rich girl's shame. "So you read the newspapers, too."

"I wouldn't be doing my job very well if I wasn't informed, now, would I. I must make sure your father wants you back before I ask for ransom money."

Chilton had hit her at her most vulnerable spot. For the moment, she conceded victory to him.

"Then what do you want with me?"

He slowly unhooked his leg from the chair and leaned forward into the dusty shaft of sunlight streaming in through a lone, cracked windowpane. Dark, intelligent eyes studied her with superior indifference. She relished a brief satisfaction at seeing the dark purple blotches beneath both those eyes. She'd broken the bastard's nose with one of those kicks yesterday.

But satisfaction was brief. Something about his unblinking stare made her suddenly conscious of how vulnerable she was.

"You are my ticket to freedom and…revenge."

"What?" For a few breathless seconds, she pitied whoever had been foolish enough to cross him. He spoke so matter-of-factly, as if he had already planned his enemy's death a thousand times, in a thousand different ways.

And then she began to wonder just who his target for revenge might be. Montana Confidential? Her family?

Whitney sank back into the chair, unable to ward off the chill that assailed her. Every bruise and scrape on her back and arms cried out, each wound a tiny little voice reminding her of who she was and what she was supposed to be. Gerald MacNair's little girl. She was simply a pawn in this madman's game. Not Whitney. Not a woman. Not even a human being.

A pawn.

The first sting of tears pooled in her eyes. She turned her chin into her shoulder, not wanting to give Chilton the satisfaction of seeing her succumb to his taunts.

But he held all the cards. She could hide nothing from him. When she heard his footsteps on the dry, warped floor, she quickly blinked and tried to erase any signs of crying.

With the tip of his finger he touched the point of her chin and traced a line around the curve of her jaw. She cringed at the provocative touch. Violence encased in butter-soft leather was still violence. Her chest rose and fell in quick, panicked breaths. She felt the skin at the top of her breasts burn beneath his knowing gaze. "Is something not to your liking?" he asked.

Standing this close, she could smell the smoke and pine on him. She even detected a hint of musk and sweat. He'd been living outdoors for a few days, away from anything resembling soap and a shower. She gritted her teeth against the smell, and tried not to squirm beneath his scrutiny.

Whitney searched for an appropriate comeback, one that would make him remove his hand and gaze and smell without triggering his anger. Since she couldn't very well ask for her freedom, why not try the next best thing? Escape. But she had no chance unless she could get herself free from this chair. The full discomfort in her bladder suddenly felt like a blessing.

Her heart still pounded, but now a surge of hope instead of fear spurred it on. "I need to go to the bathroom."

He took his hand from her face and gestured around the cabin. "Do you see any facilities here?"

"I'm not too proud. I can go behind a bush outside."

"Not too proud?" He laughed, a mocking, derisive sound completely at her expense. "I never thought I would hear that from an American. Very well. I will take you."

He pulled a long, slender knife from inside his boot and slipped it between the bottom of her right wrist and the chair. With just the slightest shift in position, he could slit her veins wide open. Whitney sobered a moment. She wasn't free yet.

But in a swoosh of gentlemanly style, he flicked the blade neatly through the tape, releasing her arm. As she flexed her fingers to bring circulation back into her hand, he snatched the loose end of tape stuck to the top of her arm and ripped it off, taking hair and skin with it.

"Ow!" she screamed, instinctively dragging her arm into her chest to protect herself from further pain. Purplish red welts immediately popped up on the top of her wrist.

"I'm sorry," he mocked. "Did I hurt you?"

"You bastard," she seethed.

But his dark eyes danced in gleeful retribution above the marks of pain she had inflicted on him. "I have been called worse. *You* may call me worse before our time together is done."

With that ominous promise to dull her temper, he repeated the sadistic release on her other arm. Her leather boots protected her ankles from a similar fate, so she was able to stand without much difficulty. Walking out the door ahead of him proved a greater challenge. With the knife slipped neatly into his boot, he pulled the gun from beneath his coat. Square-angled and lethal-looking, it fit the length of his forearm and tucked into his armpit. With its snub-nosed tip jabbing Whitney between the shoulder blades, she lurched to the door and stumbled down onto the gravel that passed for a front porch outside.

Regaining her balance, she followed the point of his gun to a nearby bush. Once outside, she could see that the dilapidated cabin had once been a pioneer's homestead or a miner's shack. An area around the house had been cleared of the towering lodgepole pines that surrounded them. Over the years, brush and smaller trees had grown into a wild garden of sorts, covering any path or road that might indicate the way off this small rise.

Whitney rubbed her hands up and down her arms, adjusting to the damp morning chill, and made an easy decision. Anyplace was better than here. When she got the chance, she would simply take off. It couldn't be more than twenty yards to the woods. She could easily lose Chilton in there. Then, once she was beyond the range of his knife or fist or gun, she would worry about finding her way back to the Lonesome Pony Ranch.

"Do you mind?" she asked, turning her back to him and unhooking her belt. He had stopped her at a shoulder-high stand of scrub pine.

"Yes. I know what you're thinking. I will not take my eyes from you."

The blood rushed from her head down to her feet. Whitney wondered if her shock at the accuracy of his guess reflected on her face. So much for escape. Holding on to what little dignity he'd left her, she dropped her jeans and took care of business, feeling the blush of embarrassment flood heat into her cheeks.

But while she zipped her jeans and tucked in the hem of her jewel-necked sweater, a new opportunity presented itself. The pocket of his coat chirped with a telltale ring. A cell phone! And if it was ringing they weren't as close to the middle of nowhere as she originally thought. They had to be near a cell tower for Chilton to be receiving a call. Whitney slowed her movements and took great care to snap her jeans and fasten her belt.

"Yes?" The other party seemed to be equally brief and to the point. "I have her."

Whitney snuck a peek over her shoulder, as if seeing him on the phone would help her understand his conversation.

"You'll make the arrangements, then?" What arrangements? she wondered. She watched his nostrils flare with an impatient breath. Sensing his growing distraction, Whitney quickly finished dressing. "Fine. No. I'll call you." With the next pause, she sized up the shortest route into the trees. "We have an agreement, you and I." Chilton's voice rose with tightly controlled anger. "Don't cross me in this."

The instant he turned his face into the phone to make his point, Whitney took off running. She dashed through the bushes and clambered up and over a pile of rock before she heard the rapid fire of bullets behind her. She dropped to her haunches and scooted off the other side. Either he was a lousy shot, or he hadn't been aiming directly at her. She doubted the first was true.

"Stop her!"

Chilton's command made no sense. But she'd hit the low brush now. She hurdled a shrub and lengthened her stride, closing in on the treeline. More shots jarred her eardrums. The bullets slapped the earth beside her feet. Whitney stumbled, touched her fingers to the dirt and righted herself.

She pulled up short as another man, taller and thinner than Chilton, emerged from the woods, holding the same type of boxy gun, pointed directly at her.

Whitney heard her own startled breath rasp in her lungs. She shifted direction, splitting the distance between the two men, and ran the way she had in high-school track. She pulled away from her pursuers, hearing the static of bullets, coming close but never hitting her, like shouts from the crowd, urging her on.

She could see the big trees now, rushing closer. She put her hands up in front of her face and shoved her way through a stand of baby pines.

And smacked into the unyielding chest of a third man. Short and stocky. Dressed in black and armed like the others.

Feeling the burn of muscle in her thighs now, she backed up into the pine branches, spun, and returned the way she'd come. Five strides. Ten.

Another man in black rounded a granite boulder and blocked her path.

Four men!

Her abductor was not alone in his abandoned hideout.

Tears of shock and unwilling surrender mixed with her panting gasps, making deep breathing impossible. She turned. The stocky man walked through the pines. She jerked another ninety degrees. The tall man. One more turn and she faced Dimitri Chilton.

The circle closed in on her. Whitney's gaze darted from one man to the next. Helpless as a rabbit trapped in a snare, she could only wait for her inevitable demise.

With a wall of men surrounding her, Chilton snatched her under the jaw, lifting her up onto her toes. His hard fingers dug into her cheekbone on one side, while his thumb left its bruising imprint in the other side.

"I grow tired of your defiance." The refined breeding she'd noticed in his voice earlier was eclipsed by the thick accent of his native tongue. "I am not always a patient man."

He threw her to the ground. The wrench on her jaw and the impact of dry, hard dirt left her ears ringing.

"Tape her and gag her."

Whitney gathered her senses long enough to realize what was happening to her. She was aware of every hard touch and unkind word. One man bound her wrists, another taped her at the ankles. The third shoved a handkerchief into her mouth, thrusting her tongue back and pinching her lips against her teeth. He rolled her face into the dirt and tied the handkerchief behind her head, catching a few strands of hair in the knot and plucking them from her scalp.

"Wait." Chilton punched in a number on his cell phone and knelt beside her. He ripped the gag from her sore mouth and pressed the phone to her ear. "Say hello to your father."

Fearing some kind of trick, but brutally aware of the

four guns trained on her, she obeyed his command with a dutiful whisper. "Daddy?"

"Whitney? Is that you?"

Hope surged through her at the sound of her father's voice. "Daddy!"

But hope was snatched from her as quickly as it was given. Chilton shot to his feet.

"Mr. MacNair. It's so nice to finally meet an American powerbroker like yourself. I think I have a deal you will be interested in…"

With a succinct hand signal, Chilton walked away, carrying all thoughts of rescue with him. Before Whitney could make a plea, the gag was shoved back into her mouth.

Without the blessing of unconsciousness, she endured the gut-wrenching dizziness of being tossed over the stocky man's shoulder and carried back to the cabin. Inside, he dropped her with an unceremonious plop onto a dusty mattress in the corner.

Moments later, Chilton filled the doorway, an ominous shadow blocking out the sunlight. He snapped shut his cell phone and smiled at her in a way that made her skin crawl. "Your father sends his best."

Then he looked to his men. "Return to your post." Chilton gave the word and they disappeared into the vast and varied camouflage of Beartooth Mountain.

More fearful than ever, too confused to do otherwise, Whitney didn't move away when Chilton knelt on the floor beside her and spoke. She decided she preferred his anger over this deceitful guise of civility.

"Now, if you are very good, and do not defy me again, I will give you water at sundown and take you outside to relieve yourself." She closed her eyes against the hateful caress of that soft glove on her cheek. "But, if you make a noise, if you move without permission…I will kill you."

Whitney nodded her understanding. When he slammed the cabin door behind him, she turned onto her side and buried her nose in the moldy ticking. She curled up into a fetal position, and let her own silent tears keep her company.

Chapter Two

Though she hadn't expected it, Chilton kept his word. As the sun faded and darkness claimed the cabin, he came to Whitney and helped her sit up. He loosened the gag and let it hang around her shoulders like a necklace. While she worked her jaw to restore feeling to the muscles in her mouth, he opened a canteen.

He held it up to her lips and let her drink her fill. A slop of excess water dribbled down her chin and pooled on the front of her sweater. But Whitney was too smart to mind. She'd had an entire day to do nothing but think. Chilton had to ransom her sometime. He had to trade her for his freedom or revenge or whatever purpose this kidnapping served. But she intended to keep her strength up. She intended to be ready and able to run again, in case he changed his mind about letting her live.

"Rashid will take you outside." The short, stocky man she'd seen before materialized like a shadow in the creeping darkness. Chilton freed her feet, but left her wrists bound together. Before she left, he whispered one last warning. "Do not provoke him."

Though she could speak, she chose a submissive nod to answer him. Rashid and his gun escorted her to the far side of a pile of ancient rocks. She made no effort to ask for privacy. She allowed him to undo her belt buckle and zipper, then turned her back to him and dropped her pants.

She heard a thunk and a shuffle of feet behind her. Either Rashid was impatiently shifting from foot to foot, or he was angling around to get a better look at her derriere. Though she could feel the heat creep into her face, she bit her tongue to stifle the crisp retort she had in mind for his blatant voyeurism.

Whitney pulled up her panties when she was finished, but with her hands bound, her jeans proved to be more of a challenge. She could pull them up over one hip, but when she'd reach for the other side, the weight of her belt would make them slip. She tried twice, and ended up with the denim pooled around her knees.

Swallowing what bit of pride she had left, she turned back to Rashid. She blinked twice, and looked again.

Not Rashid.

Though this one, too, was dressed in black from head to foot, the man who stood guard over her now held a different gun. Something sleek and compact that fit into his fist. So Chilton had called in another thug. In the dawning light of the moon she could see his black eyes, the shadow of black stubble on his jaw, the short, shiny crop of inky-black hair that molded to his head.

The thing that frightened her most about this man was his size. He stood bigger and brawnier than any of the others. Well over six feet tall, the breadth of his shoulders strained against the leather jacket he wore. He fit the dimensions of the mountain itself. Even his legs, encased in black denim, looked as solid as the pine trunks that towered around the cabin clearing.

She definitely didn't want to cross this one. Whitney raised her hands in surrender. "I'm not trying to escape this time, I promise. I just…" She didn't want to say the wrong thing. She'd been warned not to speak at all. But necessity dictated taking this risk. "I need some help with my pants."

"Ms. MacNair?"

His deep, raspy voice held no trace of the accent the other men shared. He buried his gun inside his jacket and closed the distance between them. She was too stunned by what she'd just heard to make any protest when he reached down and pulled up her jeans.

With swift, spare movements, he zipped and snapped, and buckled her belt. With him standing so close, she had nowhere else to look but at the controlled flex and give of his broad chest beneath the jacket and a wool turtleneck. He smelled different than the other men. Clean. Leathery. She tipped her chin and looked him in the eye. "Who are you?"

From somewhere behind him he pulled out a switchblade knife and punched it open. She recoiled from the razor-sharp point. But he grabbed both her hands within one of his and pulled her to him. He slipped the knife between her wrists and slit the tape. He'd freed her. Whitney's confusion must have reflected in her face. He closed the knife right before her eyes so she could see he didn't plan to slit her throat as well.

"Relax, ma'am. I'm here to rescue you."

"Right. And I'm the tooth fairy." Vincent narrowed his gaze and watched the changing emotions play across Whitney MacNair's upturned face. Her creamy skin reflected the moonlight, revealing fear, distrust, anger. But not once did the classic contours of her oval face soften into anything resembling joy or relief. "I'm tired of playing these games. Just take me back. I won't run away. I promise."

He knew an uncharacteristic moment of indecision when she walked around him and headed for the open ground of the clearing. Few things surprised him, yet her straight-backed refusal to accept his help did.

But he wasn't a man to let anything rattle him for long. Before she reached the end of the rocks and the sight line from the cabin, he snatched her by the belt and pulled her up against his chest. He backed them both into the shadows. "Where are you going?"

"Back to the cabin." The crown of her hair barely reached his chin, but she squiggled in his grasp as if she had a chance of escape.

His grip held firm. "You can't."

"I can and I will." She reached back and swatted at his hand. "I won't have your boss take away what privileges I have left. Now let me go."

Vincent knew of hostages who became attached to their kidnappers, who became loyal to the keepers who terrorized them if they stayed together long enough. But Whitney MacNair had been held for fewer than forty-eight hours.

Maybe she hadn't understood him. She might be injured or brainwashed or just too frightened to listen. He spun her around and clasped her by the shoulders. "I'm Agent Vincent Romeo. I'm here to take you home." He scrunched down to her level and looked her straight in the eye. "Do you understand?"

In a shadowy trick of the moonlight her eyes appeared colorless. Gray, her file had said. But much paler than he'd imagined, as airy and light as quicksilver.

The expression in those eyes was unmistakable, though. Simmering anger. Pure rebellion.

Her wide mouth tilted into a sarcastic line. "Romeo, hmm? Romeo, 'Romeo, wherefore art thou, Romeo?'"

Shakespeare? Like he'd never heard that joke before. All right. So he'd never heard it while he was in the middle of an incisive, undetected strike into enemy territory to retrieve a spoiled society dame who had fluff for brains.

"Come with me now, or I will take you by force."

Though he never raised his voice above a whisper, he snapped the directions with a clear-cut authority that was rarely challenged.

"I said I'd go back." She twisted her slim shoulders within his grasp. "Just don't touch me anymore."

Giving her the benefit of the doubt, he released her. She stumbled back a step in her haste to get away from him. Her heel caught and she staggered backward. Her arms flew out like twin windmills, but her left foot hit on the same impediment and her balance was lost. She landed with a soft thump on her backside.

On top of the man he'd taken out two minutes ago.

Dazed by the proof of his mission, she touched her fingers to the dead man's face. His skin would still be warm, but his lack of a response to the woman sitting on his chest should clue in even her stubborn brain to the truth.

Vincent checked his watch while she studied the man. He scanned the clearing for signs of the other guards when she looked up at him. He unholstered his gun when she looked back at the corpse and met her questioning gaze when she looked up at him again.

"Is he…?"

"Dead."

She scrambled to her feet with reflexes rivaling his own. In an instant she was behind him, her fists gripping handfuls of his jacket.

He had her full attention now.

She poked her head around his shoulder. "Did you do that?"

"Yes."

"How?"

"You don't need to know."

He could feel her chest expand and press into his back as she dealt with the shock. The pictures he'd seen of Whitney MacNair had given him the initial impression of a woman of above-average height who needed to put some meat on her bones.

His introduction to her tonight, though, had provided an unexpected glimpse of a nicely rounded bottom. And the stretch of her body against his back indicated an athleticism to her build that decried her klutzy maneuvers thus far.

"Let's go," he ordered, setting aside his awareness of her physical attributes. When he turned toward the high ground, he expected her to follow.

But what else had gone as he expected tonight?

Whitney moved in the opposite direction, back toward the terrorist's body. "You jerk." She kicked the body's crumpled legs. "You hurt me." She collapsed to her knees, grabbed the front of his jacket and shook him, as though his ears could still hear. She raised her voice to a level that would certainly catch the attention of any living ears. "And don't think I didn't see you look..."

"He's dead."

Vincent wrapped his arm around the waist and lifted her clear off the ground. He clapped his hand over her mouth to stifle her startled yelp and carried her back to the cover of the rocks. She beat at his arm with her fists and writhed within his grasp.

The gun he still held in his hand made it difficult to keep hold of her. Persistent as a fish on a hook, she nearly slipped free. He twisted around and pushed her back against the boulder, trapping her there with his body, absorbing the force of her blows until her energy was spent.

Until he felt the drop of hot moisture hit his hand where it covered her mouth. *Oh no,* he prayed. She wouldn't do this now. She couldn't.

Great. Maybe the reason MacNair had shuffled his daughter off to Montana was because she was crazy. An absolute dingbat without a single survival instinct in her bones.

But she had the most unusual eyes. Sad eyes, he thought. Wounded eyes that seemed to catch and reflect even the dimmest light without allowing anyone to see inside. Right now they brimmed with tears that spilled silently down her face. Vincent peered through the shadows and saw the bloodstain on her cheek. Acting on instinct, he shifted his hand to touch his thumb to the injured spot.

"Are you hurt?"

She shook her head, stirring her cheekbone beneath his touch. The blood came away on his thumb, revealing unblemished skin. She must have put up one hell of a fight to draw someone else's blood.

Somewhere inside, his confusion shifted and was replaced by an old familiar calling. To protect. Crazy lady or not, Whitney had been taken by force, degraded, and possibly even abused. She had a right to cry. A right to pummel the corpse of a man who had terrorized her. She needed a kind of emotional help that wasn't in his power to give. But he could keep her safe. He could get her home in one piece.

If she'd let him.

"If I take my hand away, will you be quiet?"

She took a deep, steadying breath and nodded. Slowly, watching for any sign of verbal protest, he removed his hand. He stepped back to put some physical distance between them, and thought through the next series of moves he had to make. The light brush of her hand on his chest diverted his attention.

"I thought...I'm sorry." Her voice was little more than a husky whisper. "You look just like the others." She pointed to the dead man. "The black outfit... Do you have some ID?"

Vincent allowed himself one choice succinct curse.

He supposed her initial distrust was justified. With his dark coloring he could pass for one of Chilton's men. But hadn't he identified himself already? Hadn't he gotten to her when no one else could? Didn't she have a lick of common sense?

He dropped his face down to her level and articulated each word so she would understand. "We are twenty yards from Dimitri Chilton and his hired help, and we have to be at the rendezvous point in less than ten minutes. Do as I say right now, or you won't get the opportunity to ask another question."

She puffed up like some wounded debutante who was about to run off and tell Daddy what the mean old man had dared to say to her. Vincent stared her down. His menacing silence brooked no argument. After a charged moment, her shoulders dropped and her chin fell to a subdued angle.

Finally, she'd do as he said.

She followed his lead and crouched behind him when he moved to the edge of the rocks and knelt down to spy through the brush and locate the other two patrol guards he'd spotted earlier.

But the silence was too precious to last. He felt a tap on his shoulder before her warm breath whispered in his ear. "What about Montana Confidential? Does Daniel Austin know I'm here? And Jewel? Did she get home okay? What about my horse?"

He looked over his shoulder and stared at her in disbelief.

"There is a time to run, a time to fight and a time to shut up."

Vincent held her gaze until he was sure she understood which time this was.

Though he was quickly learning not to trust her silence, he couldn't afford to waste any more time. He had to get them out of there. Now.

He shifted his weight to the balls of his feet and held the gun with both hands in front of him. He stilled his breathing and concentrated on the sounds of the night around them. The darkness would be their ally. He had to time their dash across the open terrain with the sweeping currents of cloud cover. The moon would be hidden for only a few seconds, but that would be all the time they...

The snap of a twig jarred him. He pushed Whitney back against the rock, shielding her body with his, automatically covering her mouth with his hand. He held his breath and waited for the guard to pass by.

The man walked past at a leisurely pace, indicating no alarm about his missing comrade or the length of Whitney's trip to relieve herself. Vincent considered taking this guard out, too. He could do it in a matter of seconds. He could do it without making a sound.

But he couldn't trust Whitney to keep her mouth shut or to follow his orders without an argument.

When the sound of footsteps faded, Vincent eyed the sky and counted off his own internal clock. The time to move was now, or they'd never reach the old mining road where his Washington contact was due to arrive soon. The driver couldn't park and wait for fear of detection. And with the short turnaround time necessary for a hostage retrieval, he couldn't spare the days needed to abandon the truck and let it sit long enough for Chilton's men to disregard its presence.

The plan was to reach the rendezvous point and radio his contact to pick them up. If he couldn't reach the site, he'd call in a bypass so the truck would drive on without alerting the terrorists to the location.

Whitney's delays had already endangered the mission. Soon he would be left with plan B. Instead of bringing MacNair's daughter home, he'd simply keep her alive until a second rendezvous could be scheduled.

If she didn't screw that up, too.

"This is the time to run." Gambling their lives on her cooperation, he released her and scooted to the farthest end of the rocks. "Stay right behind me." She was already clinging to the back of his jacket when he turned to give his next command. "Don't fall down."

Ignoring the questioning look on her face, he took her hand and sprang to his feet. Keeping low to the ground, he sprinted for the trees, drawing Whitney along behind him. After only a few steps she extended her legs to match his stride, and Vincent quickly realized he had no need to compensate for her speed. She very nearly outdistanced him.

They had barely reached the cover of the trees when the alarm sounded.

"Rashid!"

Three shots fired, followed by a rapid discussion shouted back and forth in Chilton's native language.

Inside the treeline, Vincent shifted directions and headed up the mountain. He felt the jerk of Whitney's arm at the sudden alteration of course. But within moments she fell in step beside him again. The confusion and shouting from the cabin bought them precious seconds.

He found the path he'd marked earlier. It led to a boarded-up mine shaft. The slope steepened by several degrees and Vincent leaned forward to take the climb without breaking his pace.

"Where are we going?" Whitney's breathy query broke

the frantic sound of stamping feet and scrabbling bits of gravel breaking loose to roll down the incline behind them.

He released her hand to leap across a three-foot-wide crevasse that split the path. He paused and turned, waiting for her to make the same jump. She balked at the other side. Her chest rose and fell, breathing deeply, in time with his own strained breath.

Vincent swore as she planted her hands at her hips and demanded a response. "I asked where you were taking me."

He had no time to explain his plan. He spared her an answer before turning his attention back to the zigzagging climb to the top of this crest. "Away from Chilton."

They were at least ten minutes out. He had to cut time somewhere. He hit the trail at a faster pace. He heard her make the leap behind him. Good. She was moving.

"That's not much of an answer."

"Don't talk. Save your breath."

A heavier tread in the underbrush below them caught their attention. Chilton's men had found their trail.

"Is that—"

"Move it."

He went back to grab her hand and pull her along at his speed. They doubled back on a hairpin turn and her slick-soled riding boots slipped on some loose gravel. She went down hard on her knees and left hand. With his help, she quickly regained her footing. A spot of creamy white on her pant leg indicated she had ripped her jeans, and probably cut her knee in the process.

But with Chilton closing in, they had no time to stop and play doctor. "Hang in there, Ms. MacNair."

He wasn't a big one for encouragement, but he needed her to keep up. The brightness of the moon worked against them in the woods. Its iridescent light created deceptive shadows that assailed them from all directions, playing havoc with Vincent's own internal compass. But Chilton's men had no such handicap. The beam of their flashlights bounced through the trees, illuminating leaves and rocks and even their path like all-seeing eyes.

But the mine shaft should be close now, almost straight above them. *Yes.*

Changing his strategy, Vincent spun around and retraced their last few steps. He pulled out night-vision goggles from his jacket pocket and slipped them over the top of his head. He had the original trail memorized, could probably find it with or without a light. But covering new ground required he be able to see.

He went back to the steep sheer slope that went straight to the top of the plateau. Looking up, he saw that a few small trees managed to cling to the rocks. And traces of abandoned birds' nests indicated tiny ledges and crannies in the rock itself. About twenty feet to the top. The drop-off below them was another hundred feet or so. But with Chilton's men closing in, he decided they had little choice.

Whitney tugged at his jacket and pointed to the swaying lights coming up the path. "Hello, spaceman. Bad guys coming."

Vincent wrapped his hands around her slender waist and lifted her off the path.

"What are you doing?" He set her toes on a four-inch ledge, and she automatically grabbed hold of the tree root in front of her face so she wouldn't fall. "Romeo?" Her voice held hardly any tone, an indication of her shortness of breath. He'd pushed her hard and she'd hung in there with him.

He was about to push her harder.

"Climb."

With his greenish night vision through the goggles showing him the way, Vincent guided Whitney's hands to the sturdiest grips, and slowed his pace to make the climb beside her.

He changed his grip to her shoulder to keep her from moving when Chilton and his men ran past directly below their feet. Chilton shouted orders in his native tongue and his two men responded with clipped words and phrases. The terrorists continued up the winding path that took them farther away from their position. They'd reach the top about the same time, but Vincent would be closer to the road. That still left him with a slight advantage.

He urged Whitney to resume the climb. "Do you know what they're saying?" she asked.

Damn, but the woman loved to talk.

"Chilton doesn't want you dead."

"That's nice."

He didn't want her dead *yet.* Vincent didn't share what other promises of violence Chilton had in mind for her in the meantime.

"He wants me dead, though."

"Not so nice, hmm?"

A third of the way from the top she slipped. The root she clung to began to peel away from its thin layer of dirt. Vincent nabbed her by the wrist to keep her from falling. She cried out in pain, but quickly turned her face into her upraised arm to muffle the sound.

Vincent bided his time while she hugged the rock, alternately wanting to hurry her along and to ask what he'd done to hurt her.

"Whit?" Maybe by now she was too weak and too frightened to answer.

After a moment she wrapped her fingers around a more secure grip and pulled herself up to the next ledge. When they reached the end of the steep shortcut, he hoisted himself up and over to the top of the plateau. He was winded from the exertion, but reached out to pull Whitney up beside him.

She rolled over the top edge and curled into a ball, her energy totally spent. Her breathing came in shallow gasps that echoed in the night air. He needed to quiet her down. Chilton's men would be close now. But when he knelt behind her and touched her shoulder, she winced. She pulled her hands into her waist and curled up even tighter, making it impossible for him to assess her condition.

"You *are* injured." She clearly needed time to rest if she was to go any farther. He listened for the sound of Chilton's men in the distance. He could give her a minute. "Stay here."

A nearby break in the trees hid the entrance to the boarded-up mine shaft. Vincent pried off a board at the bottom and tossed it aside. He reached in and pulled out the black nylon duffel bag he'd hidden there. He dropped his goggles inside and set it at his feet. Then he took out his knife to loosen the nails of the next board. He was pulling loose the third board when he heard a soft voice at his shoulder.

"Are we going in there?"

Vincent rose to his feet and turned. Whitney had come up behind him undetected. Not an easy feat for a grown man trained in covert experience. The irony of this talkative amateur pulling it off wasn't lost on him.

She huddled inside her thin blue sweater with sleeves that barely came past her elbow. She looked cold and exhausted and not much older than that Jewel girl back at the ranch. That distracting urge to protect trickled into his thoughts again.

He'd planned to go back for her. But Whitney had found her way here.

Vincent pushed aside the impulse to swallow her up in his arms and warm her with his own body heat. He didn't have time to deal with the hostage's needs right now. He had to get her to freedom. That meant making the rendezvous that was fast approaching.

Besides, Whitney had more resiliency than he'd expected for a pampered society girl from a privileged family back East. He had to give her credit. She might lack common sense, but she had stamina and determination to spare.

"No." He reached out and took her by the elbow, more gently this time, and led her up the rise to the top of the shaft. "Decoy."

"So Chilton will think we've gone in there?" She crouched behind the rocks where he pointed.

"I hope. Stay here."

He slid back down the slope to grab his bag and cover their path. When he returned, he held out his hand to help her to her feet. She studied his hand with the same trepidation she might use if he'd stuck a gun in her face.

"It's not much farther." Distancewise, he spoke the truth. But he couldn't promise that Chilton and his men would make this an easy trip.

Her shoulders lifted with a determined sigh and she reached up to fold her hand into his. The ground was flatter up here. Still rocky and dotted with trees, it provided less cover, but they could move more quickly. Vincent broke into a loping run, and Whitney kept pace behind him.

When they reached the road, they ducked behind a pile of decaying tree trunks that had burned and fallen to the ground after a recent forest fire. Whitney leaned back against the wood and seemed to concentrate on her breathing. Vincent pulled the two-way radio from his pack and called in.

"The hawk has his prey. Repeat. The hawk has his prey. Over."

A blip of static answered, then cleared. "Understood. Hawk's nest on the move. Out."

"I don't think I like being referred to as prey." She breathed in quick, shallow breaths, but her voice sounded stronger. "Chilton's a smart man, you know. That's not much of a code for him to break."

"He'll have us in his line of sight any minute. He doesn't have to eavesdrop."

Preparing for that certainty, Vincent pulled out his gun, checked the clip and reloaded. In the light from the moon, he saw those quicksilver eyes of hers pool up like saucers.

But was it the gun, or Chilton's imminent arrival that frightened her?

"Is there something I should do?" she whispered.

"Shh."

"Of course. Always with the shush thing."

Thankfully, she settled in beside him to do her brooding in silence and no doubt think of the next line of questions she wanted to ask. Vincent squeezed his eyes shut. Fatigue was starting to tell in the protest of his muscles as he knelt behind the cover of the trees. But his senses were working just fine. He fine-tuned his ears and listened for the crunch of footsteps in the underbrush.

He heard the order to spread out and widen the search first. Chilton hadn't taken long to discover his ruse, and was closing in. Vincent opened his eyes to check his watch. Their ten-minute flight had taken twelve. "Where are you?" He breathed the urgent wish between clenched teeth.

Right on cue, the roar of a four-wheel-drive engine echoed through the rocks of the plateau. But Chilton heard it, too.

A black pickup topped the crest and bounced down the mining road toward their position.

"There he is." Whitney popped up and pointed at the truck.

"Get down, dammit!" He palmed the top of her head

and pushed her down to the ground just as the first bullets hit.

The rapid fire of semiautomatic weapons flashed like fireworks in the darkness. Vincent braced his elbow on the top rotting trunk, took aim and fired at each burst of light.

A spatter of bullets hit his position, splintering the wood and sending chunks of bark flying. Vincent ducked to the ground, pinning Whitney beneath. With his hand on her head, keeping her flat in the dirt, he rose again, pointed his gun and fired.

He hit his mark. The flash fire of one weapon sank to the ground and went out. But the bullets kept flying.

The truck engine gunned and picked up speed.

Two of the terrorists were close enough to make out their shapes as they dodged from cover to cover, spraying bullets in their direction.

The squeal of brakes behind him gave a small measure of reassurance. "Romeo! Get in!"

Vincent grabbed his bag, pulled Whitney up by the arm and pushed her toward the open door of the waiting truck.

"Go! Go! Go!" he ordered.

The driver stomped on the accelerator. Whitney had climbed in, headfirst. Vincent flattened his hand on her butt, pushed her across the seat and tossed his bag into the bed of the truck. The wheels spun on the gravel and dirt, giving him time to get his feet on the running board before the truck sped away. Clinging to the open door with his left hand, Vincent turned back and fired at their pursuers.

A spray of gunfire hit the truck. Bing. Bang. Thunk.

The truck lurched and Vincent fell inside. They'd hit the back window and shattered it. "Gun it, Carl!"

Whitney sat in the middle of the bench seat, brushing the broken glass from her shoulders.

"You hit?" he asked, keeping his eye on the side-view

mirror, mentally calculating the distance before they'd be out of range of Chilton's weapons.

"No."

The truck continued to pick up speed.

"Romeo?"

Whitney's fingers dug into his thigh.

"Romeo!"

"What?"

He pried her grip from his leg, then looked up to see why she'd cried his name.

Carl was slumped forward. A tiny hole leaked bright red blood from the back of his head.

He was dead.

Chapter Three

"What is it with you and dead bodies, anyway?" Whitney didn't know which way to move. She was crunched in the cab of a truck between a killer and a corpse.

And the dead man was driving.

Vincent leaned across her and grabbed Carl by the shoulder. When he pulled him back, the body's limp fingers released the steering wheel.

"His foot's still on the accelerator. Grab the wheel."

Grab the wheel?

She understood what he wanted her to do. She just wasn't sure she had the desire to do it.

"Whitney."

Fine. Nothing like an order in that crisp, low-pitched voice to make her kick it into gear. Her father had that same kind of voice. He never asked, either. He just expected her to do whatever he commanded.

She wedged her shoulder between Carl and the steering wheel and took hold. Vincent threw his considerable weight across her lap and reached beneath the dashboard. The engine whirred in protest and the truck immediately dropped speed.

"What are you doing?"

He grabbed her left ankle and placed it on the accelerator. "Drive."

For a few awkward moments, she simply acted on instinct. She pressed down on the accelerator and tried to gauge the upcoming curve in the road from her vantage point. With Vincent pinning her legs, she couldn't sit up any higher. And with Carl's weight on her shoulder, she stooped beside the wheel, looking between the wheel and the top of the dash to guide them along the dark road.

When she entered the curve, the headlights picked up a stand of boulders that had claimed that particular spot for untold millennia. Whitney moved her foot to hit the brake and slow them down, but Vincent moved it back to the accelerator.

"Don't stop."

"But—"

"Drive."

And then she realized what he was doing. He reached across her and opened the driver's-side door. The ground rushed past at an alarming speed. "Oh my God. You can't do that."

But he already had. He pulled Carl's legs from the floor of the truck and shoved them out the door. Then Vincent sat up, latched onto her arm to hold her in place and pushed Carl out from behind her.

The body hit the ground with a horrible thud. She couldn't help but look in the rearview mirror to see his limp body roll to the side of the road. "I can't believe you did that."

"Whitney!"

All at once his hands were on the wheel with hers. He cranked it a quarter turn to the left, jerking it from her grasp.

The rocks she'd seen from a distance rushed up in front of them with frightening speed. She stomped on the brake. Vincent turned the wheel.

But with gravel and speed they had few options.

Vincent wrapped his arms around her, turning so his body shielded hers from the impact. The truck spun out and slid madly through clumps of rocks and brush until it slammed with a deafening crunch into the rocks.

Vincent's body lurched forward, then crushed her against the seat.

And then it was still.

Whitney slumped within the cocoon of Vincent's body until she could hear something besides the pounding of her heart in her ears.

His weight on her chest didn't stir. "Romeo?"

She flattened her palms at the front of his chest to push some space between them. She felt the reassuring tattoo of his heartbeat beneath her hand. But she needed to see his face. Find out if he was conscious or injured.

He was a bigger man than she realized. Solid muscle filled out his large frame. She took a deep breath, put her shoulders into it and managed to push him over into the seat next to her.

His eyes were closed.

An instant panic quickened her pulse again. "Romeo?" She touched her fingers to his parted lips. His regular breathing warmed her fingertips, but did little to reassure her. "Romeo?"

She climbed up on her knees in the seat to bring her up to eye level with him. She cupped his face between her hands and shook him gently. "Romeo? C'mon. Wake up."

The rasp of his beard growth tickled her palms, sending inappropriate shivers of awareness straight up her arms. She might be reacting to his rough brand of charm, but she seemed to be having no effect on him.

For an instant she wondered if Dimitri Chilton had heard the crash. How far behind was he? Did he still pursue them? Her pulse quickened with renewed urgency.

Vincent Romeo was her only ticket off this mountain. The big brute had to be okay.

"Romeo." She called his name right in his ear and gave him a light smack on the cheek. Nothing. She tapped him again. "Dammit, will you—"

Faster than the panic rising within her, his eyes popped open. He snatched her by the wrists and twisted her flat on her back in the seat with his larger body trapping her there.

Whitney's breath whooshed out in a startled gasp. She stared helplessly up into eyes that were black. Black as coal and filled with deadly intent.

"Romeo?"

His eyes narrowed between sooty lashes. His gaze traced the shape of her face, lingered on her neck, then seemed to fix on the small jut of her breasts. To her horror, she felt the tips tighten into pebbled beads beneath the intensity of that look. Pinned beneath his crushing weight, she felt more exposed than she had been behind that rock with Rashid.

"Um—" She licked her parched lips. "Are you okay?"

His gaze darted back to her mouth, drawn to the movement there.

And then he blinked.

He squeezed his eyes shut and shook his head. The raspy groan in his throat told her the movement hurt. He released one of her wrists and touched the back of his skull. The succinct curse he chose revealed just how much it hurt.

"I took a blow to the head. Things were fuzzy for a minute there, but I'll be all right."

"Good. Because you're hurting me."

As quickly as he had pinned her to the seat, he released her and scooted to the far end of the truck's cab. It was almost embarrassing to see how quickly he could move away from her. Whitney sat up much more slowly, nursing her wounded pride and massaging her sore wrists.

"Is that where I caught you?"

The ugly purple welts that encircled her wrists were visible, even in the moonlight. Vincent thought he'd done *that* to her? She found the energy to summon a rusty smile. "No." He'd probably saved her life.

Her smile was eclipsed by the memory of Dimitri Chilton's eyes, laughing at her expense. "It's from the tape they used to tie me up. Chilton thought inflicting a little pain would keep me in line."

Vincent said nothing, but she could feel the atmosphere in the truck change. He was past recovering from his knock on the head. Agent Romeo had returned. And the man who had made her body tingle with awareness, even in the face of danger, disappeared.

"Let's get you home." He tried to get out, but the truck frame had bent and the door was jammed.

Whitney obeyed his silent command and climbed out the open door on her side ahead of him. She couldn't help peering up the road behind them, wondering if she could see Carl's body. One man's life sacrificed for her own.

The shock of the discovery hit her and robbed her of breath. The Black Order wasn't just out to hurt her or her family. True terrorists, with a cause she couldn't begin to understand, they possessed a ruthless determination to get what they wanted.

Heaven help anyone who stood in their way.

A feeling of absolute shame retched in her stomach, turning it sour.

She'd felt shame before.

The shame of accusations she couldn't defend herself against.

The shame of public scrutiny damning her reputation.

The shame of hearing her parents' teary voices filled

with disappointment as they boarded her on a plane for Montana.

But none of that could match the knowledge of one man trading his life for hers.

"Did Carl have any family?" she asked.

Vincent had crawled beneath the truck to inspect the damage. When he came out, he stood and dusted his hands off on his jeans. He was giving her that crazy look again, the look that said he wondered if she had any sense. "I didn't know him," he answered. "He was just a voice on the radio. A contact."

"Don't you care that he's dead?"

He climbed into the bed of the damaged truck and picked up his duffel bag. He tossed it over the side and climbed back down. "He was doing his job. Like I'm doing mine."

He opened the bag and pulled out a folded piece of paper and a heavy-duty flashlight. When he knelt down and unfolded it, she could see it was a computer-generated map.

She hugged her arms around herself, feeling a chill from within far colder than the crisp mountain air. "That's a callous attitude."

He absorbed her accusation with no reaction other than to stand. "Dimitri Chilton has a pretty callous attitude toward life and death. He had to have heard the crash. If he has reinforcements to call, he's doing it right now. If not, I expect him to show up here any minute."

Whitney shivered. "If you're trying to scare me, the job's already been taken." Forget trying to wheedle an emotion out of Vincent Romeo. The man had ice in his veins. The sooner she cooperated, the sooner she could get back to Jewel and Daniel and people who might actually care. "Let's just get in the truck and drive out of here."

"Can't. The axle's shot." He folded up the map and stuffed it back in the bag.

"Great."

"Let's go." He slung the bag over his shoulder and shined the light up into the woods to the east.

"What's your plan now?"

"Call in. You're safe for now. We'll set up a second rendezvous for tomorrow."

She spread her arms wide and asked him to look at the trees and rocks and nothingness surrounding them. "Where are we going to spend the night?"

"If your friend Court Brody knows this mountain the way I hope he does, there should be an old prospector's cabin about two miles away on the other side of that ridge. You up for the hike?"

"Do I have any choice?"

He was already walking. "No."

"You like those one-word sentences, don't you?"

"Yes."

"Yes?" she repeated under her breath. Was that a joke? Or merely proof of a stated fact?

Whitney shook her head and pushed her weary body into step behind him. She still had another two miles to try to figure out Vincent Romeo.

VINCENT ENTERED the cabin first and scanned for signs of unwanted tenants and wildlife. The temperature was dropping rapidly outside as night deepened into midnight. The damn-fool woman traipsing along behind him didn't have a coat. She wasn't even wearing a heavy sweater. What kind of simpleton went horseback riding in the mountains without wearing more rugged clothes?

Probably back in Martha's Vineyard, she had a servant to run along behind with a jacket or shawl when things got cold.

Vincent immediately regretted the unkind thought. She hadn't asked to be kidnapped. And Dimitri Chilton didn't care whether she suffered or not. From Whitney's brief explanation in the truck, the bastard probably got a kick out of seeing her suffer.

She hadn't complained about the grueling hike, the perilous rock climb, the flying bullets, the wrecked truck. Not once.

The only thing she'd criticized was his own behavior. Yeah. He hated to see a fellow agent go down. He hated the call he had to make to report his death. He hated the thought that anyone had to die. But those were the risks. Job one was keeping Whitney MacNair safe. Carl Howard would have understood.

Why couldn't she?

When he heard her boots on the boards that passed for a front porch, he turned around. "It looks sound enough. None of the windows are broken. There's no furniture, but we can make do on the floor."

She pushed her way past him and inspected the ten-by-twelve-foot hideaway for herself. "As long as the roof doesn't leak and I can warm myself up, I'll be happy."

Vincent closed the door behind him and dropped his bag to the floor. She had already crossed to the cobwebby stone fireplace and dropped to her knees to brush out the crumbling remains of broken plaster and charred wood.

"We can't build a fire."

The shock on her face when she looked up at him reminded him of the Christmas Eve when he snuck downstairs and discovered his father was filling in for Santa Claus. "No fire?"

"Chilton could spot the smoke."

He pulled a black T-shirt and a spare set of jeans out of his bag. "We can black out the windows, though, and leave a lantern going through the night."

She had no response to that. She stayed where she was, looking small and defenseless.

Vincent made no false promises, so he had nothing to say to cheer her up. He busied himself hanging his clothes over the windows, setting up the lantern, and pulling two granola bars and a water bottle out of his bag.

"Here. Before you fall asleep." She hadn't moved from in front of the empty fireplace. But when she took the offering of food and drink, she uncurled her legs and rose to her feet.

"Thanks."

When she turned his way toward the light, he swore. Five dark bruises, fitting the span of a man's rough hand, dotted her cheekbones. Against her pale, peaches-and-cream skin, the marks stood out like a crude attempt at finger painting.

She cowered back a step, startled by his curse. "What's wrong?"

He remembered her wrists. She'd mentioned pain there twice before. He reached for her fingers, water bottle and all, and pulled her wrist up into the light. The duct tape had left angry welts the size of thick yarn, curling like bracelets around her bruised wrist. "Son of a bitch."

"So you said." She pulled her hand away, as if embarrassed by the marks.

"Get something in your stomach," he ordered. "I'm giving you some aspirin and we'll doctor those up."

Her immediate protests fell on deaf ears. He spread a tarp on the floor and set out aspirin, alcohol swabs and antibiotic ointment. He could sense her fatigue because the arguments didn't last for long. When he told her to have a seat, she crossed her legs like a ballerina and folded herself, pretzel-style, to sit on the tarp.

Vincent brought the lantern close to illuminate his work. He bathed her face with water and dabbed the bruises with alcohol. She had such fine pale skin. Clear and smooth, like cream to the eye. And down the bridge of her nose, spilling onto her cheeks, a sprinkling of dusty freckles reflected the reddish highlights in her hair.

He pushed aside the red-gold locks that fell in waves past the top of her shoulders and tended the thick bruise across her neck. He recognized that kind of marking. She'd been choked to unconsciousness. Applying that kind of pressure a few inches higher or lower would have fractured her larynx or crushed her sternum. Either wound, left unattended, could have killed her.

Damn Chilton. Vincent didn't know Whitney beyond the dossier her father had sent. But Jewel McMurty thought the world of this woman. Daniel Austin and his men were chomping at the bit to get her back. And though she'd already complicated the hell out of his well-laid plans, she'd proved herself to be more than a pretty face or a rich bank account. She didn't deserve this kind of abuse.

No one did.

It was Vincent's job to stop the bastards who preyed on innocent victims. Melissa Stamos, his high-school sweetheart, couldn't see that calling. She'd bashed his heart and his pride on the altar of Saint Stephen's Church in front of family and friends, condemning him for putting his life on the line for people he didn't know.

He hadn't known Whitney MacNair twelve hours ago, either. But he was damn glad to have her sitting in this abandoned cabin with him, enduring the clumsy doctoring of his big hands, instead of reading her name in the paper as another senseless victim of the Black Order's killing spree.

"So what goes on in that head of yours?" Whitney asked.

Lost in his thoughts, her soft voice startled him. Lord,

the woman liked to talk. And he still had nothing he needed to say to her beyond, "Let me see your wrists."

Her frustrated sigh sounded a lot like Melissa just then.

He pulled her wrists into his lap and gently cleaned the wounds. She flinched at the mere touch of salve to the damaged skin, but didn't cry out. An unforgiving fist tightened in his gut with each bit of pain he grudgingly inflicted. But Whitney endured the healing touches without a word of complaint.

However, it seemed nothing could stop her questions.

"You give new meaning to the cliché, 'strong, silent type,' you know that?"

Vincent continued his work, focused on the task at hand. He drew his fingers along the slender sculpt of her forearms, turning and inspecting them for further injuries. Her skin felt smooth, supple beneath his hands—softly pampered, as he expected, but with sleek muscle beneath the surface that indicated some honest work—or workouts, at the very least.

"Ow." Without thinking, he'd pressed his thumb into a toned band of muscle, testing the refined strength of her arm. She tilted her head, studying him with a curious pout. "You don't do this much, do you? I mean, the doctoring part. I imagine you do a whole lot of running around, shooting your gun, rescuing damsels in distress."

Now how did he respond to that?

"Where else?" he demanded. Whitney's bright eyes suddenly shuttered. He heard the harsh sound of his words echo in the cabin, and that fist squeezed even tighter inside him. She pulled her hands from his lap and reached for the bottle of water. He waited patiently while she took a drink. But he knew she still hadn't answered. He dropped his voice to a raspy pitch, trying to soften its tone. "Are you hurt anywhere else?"

"My back. We wrestled on the ground, and I scraped it

up a bit.'' The forced lightness in her tone didn't fool him. ''It's nothing serious,'' she insisted. ''I'll be fine. Thanks for doing the rest, though.''

He tilted his head and asked her to turn around. ''Let me see.''

''I tell you, it's nothing.''

She scooted around on her bottom, giving him a good look at the back of her sweater. Cashmere didn't lie. The tight weave had pilled and snagged and caught bits of leaves and dirt in the soft, furry nap.

But the two spots of dried blood at her right shoulder blade weren't part of the material's design.

Vincent tucked his index finger beneath the hem and lifted. ''Son of a bitch.''

Whitney laughed. ''You repeat yourself a lot, you know.''

She reached behind and plucked the sweater from his hand. But he easily overpowered her protests and pulled the sweater up to her shoulders. ''You call this nothing?'' He focused on the deep cut right above her bra strap. ''At least one of these marks needs a couple of stitches.''

''You're no sweet old country doctor, are you?'' she accused. The sharp bite of her voice might have something to do with the certain stinging he caused by cleaning the scrapes and bruises with alcohol. ''You really need to get a bedside manner.''

Maybe he should say something about her grit. Her class-act determination. She hadn't complained about her injuries though she had to be in obvious pain. Not once. Was that a by-product of East Coast breeding? A stiff upper lip? Or was it a sign of something more substantial inside this garrulous daddy's girl?

Vincent gave it a shot. ''You're a tough cookie, MacNair. I know men who would have caved under the kinds of injuries you've sustained. You haven't complained once.''

''Why should I?'' She winced as he taped a bandage over the deepest cut. ''I'm alive, aren't I? People are dying all around me. Believe me, I have nothing to complain about. After all, what's a little pain when you're Whitney MacNair, blacklisted daughter of the MacNair dynasty?''

Whatever happened to a simple thank you? He pulled down her sweater and boxed up the supplies, not understanding the hysterical rise in her pitch.

''I don't care where you're from.'' He shrugged the confusion from his shoulders. ''You're a human being. You feel pain like the rest of us.''

HUMAN?

No. She was Whitney MacNair. She wasn't allowed to feel pain or fear or betrayal.

Whitney scrambled to her feet, unnerved by the surprisingly gentle ministrations of Vincent's hands. Unnerved by the sudden reminder that he had risked his life to take her home—but they didn't want her there.

She was an embarrassment to the MacNair name. Never mind that she'd done nothing wrong. Her family had overreacted when they'd read an inflammatory story about her flirtation with her married boss, and about the expensive gift he'd given her. They hadn't even asked for her side of the story. Instead, they'd banished her to rural Montana.

She paced to the window, then settled for reading the label on his jeans when she remembered she couldn't look outside.

It unnerved the hell out of her to hear this stranger with the midnight eyes pinpoint exactly what was wrong with her.

A human being?

Not until all hint of her scandal with Senator Ross Weston died down.

Vincent moved around the cabin with spare, sure ease, repacking his duffel bag and opening the door to check outside. When he came to the window where she stood to check the woods in that direction, she bolted to the opposite side of the cabin. He'd bull's-eyed the vulnerable weakness in her don't-care armor, and she desperately needed to get it back into place.

"Chilton's an idiot, you know." Vincent glanced her way when she spoke, but said nothing. "If he wants to raise money for his cause, or blackmail his way out of the country, he picked the wrong girl to ransom. I mean, even he knows about the scandal. There's a very good chance my father wouldn't pay to get me back. He doesn't want to see the family name splashed in the headlines again.

"I have four big brothers. Gerald, Jr., William, Derek and Brian. All in politics. Gerry's running for attorney general of Massachusetts. The election's in a couple of weeks. If it gets out that I was stupid enough to get kidnapped by a group of terrorists, that'd be even more bad press. Who knows where Dad would send me next?"

She felt the question in Vincent's eyes when he crossed to the other window and secured it as well. But he didn't ask it.

Whitney answered it anyway.

"That's right. I'm not here by choice. Out of sight, out of mind. Out of the headlines. I'm used to the big cities. I mean—" she spread her arms wide "—there is just way too much scenery here. No cabs. No coffee shops." She sought out his gaze across the room and found him still watching her. The eerie blackness in his eyes seemed to swallow her up, making her feel raw and exposed. She clutched her arms in a tight hug around her body, warding off a chill that caught her unawares. "I just wanted to make a difference..."

How many times had she said that? To her father? To Daniel Austin? To herself?

How many times had she been denied the chance?

"I know you think I'm crazy. That I just babble on for no reason, but—" Whitney's breath caught on a strangled gasp and she realized she was about to cry. Not those silent tears that had put her to sleep last night. But a really big, bellowing cry that would leave blotches on her face and her sinuses plugged.

"Look. I've got some nervous energy I need to work off." She pressed her fingers to her lips to stifle a sob. "I could use a little conversation to distract me."

"We need sleep," was all he offered.

Maybe that's all it was. She was just too damn tired to fight off the shock of the trauma she'd been through.

"I'm the one who's scared here. I'm the one who got kidnapped. I'm the one who's been shot at and ogled and threatened. The one who's wounded and bruised and humiliated. I'm the one who's been pushed around by some big bully with a badge, who won't talk, who throws dead buddies out of trucks and doesn't even care—"

She fell silent, surprised by her own words. She walked over to Vincent, her hands held up in supplicant apology. "I'm sorry. That wasn't fair. You've done a lot for me."

Still nothing.

She reached out farther, touched his forearm. The steely bulk of muscle there flinched beneath the brush of her fingertips, then went still. Unsure of how welcome her touch might be, she looked up.

He focused those black-as-night eyes on her, but said nothing.

What in the world made a man so quiet? Like stone.

As imposing and forbidding as the mighty Beartooth Mountains surrounding them.

She didn't know if she'd ever get used to the silence of the mountains. No steady stream of traffic, no hum of voices and music until early in the morning, no whirl of energy.

Just—quiet.

She didn't know if she could ever get used to Vincent's silence, either.

Whitney curled her fingers into her palm, embarrassed by the rejection of both her touch and her apology. "Fine. I'll talk to myself." She hugged her arms around her middle and crossed to the empty fireplace. "So, Agent Romeo, how long have you been in the business? What? Forever? Carrying on a family tradition, I bet."

"Leave my family out of your rambling."

She whipped around, surprised to hear him speak. "Oh! He talks!" On the heels of embarrassment came a defensive burst of anger. "Tell me about your family. You've got a beautiful blond wife named Juliet, I bet. And a trio of little black-haired boys who don't talk much, either. Let's see, their names are Paris and Mercutio and—Friar Lawrence."

"MacNair—"

"They probably don't mind you traveling the world, seeing all the finest places, like this lovely, abandoned shack a thousand miles away from nowhere. You've probably risked your life hundreds of times. Saved diplomats and royalty. Blown up buildings and broken men's necks. And here you are, stuck baby-sitting a 'tough cookie' like me."

That's when the first crack broke in her control. Her eyes burned with the fear and hurt and shame she'd endured. She clasped her hand to her mouth, but it was too late.

"I'm sorry."

She tried to atone for going off the deep end. But the words opened the dam, and the tears became sobs that wrenched her body.

She hugged herself tighter and sank to her knees, too exhausted to endure the emotions buffeting her.

"Stop that."

The hesitant command barely registered. She looked up through the veil of her tears, and saw Vincent close the distance between them. He stood over her a moment, tall and strong, and frowning with confusion.

After a moment he seemed to make a decision. He shrugged out of his jacket and knelt beside her. Without a word, he wrapped it around her shoulders.

She clasped the leather collar together and buried her chin inside. The weight of it felt like a hug. The silk lining still held Vincent's warmth and his scent.

Her tears faded to silent sobs, but indicated no signs of stopping. She lifted her gaze and tried to show him her thanks. His mouth opened and closed, as if he was searching for words that eluded him. Whitney wasn't going anywhere soon. She waited for him to speak.

Vincent shrugged helplessly, stretching the seams of his turtleneck beneath the black leather shoulder straps of his holster. He was such a big man. So hard. So purely masculine.

So completely out of his element at this moment.

"Don't. C'mon."

His distress reached out to the part of her that could still think clearly. "I'll try not—" A hiccup cut her short.

"Hell." He tucked his hands beneath her elbows and lifted her to her feet. He pulled her into his arms and turned her head and cradled it against his chest. "You're just tired. Cold and beat-up and tired."

The heat from his skin seeped through his sweater and

into her cheek. The black wool tickled her nose, but she breathed in anyway, absorbing his clean, male scent like a soothing vapor.

He patted her head, unsure or unwilling to hold her tighter. "I'm not hurting you, am I?"

Hurting? She hadn't felt this safe and sheltered since— since ever. She sniffed twice, then lifted her head to see past the stubble on his square jaw. She wanted him to know that *he* hadn't hurt her. "No. You're doing just fine."

His dark eyes sparkled with some unnamed emotion. Whitney discovered she could get lost there. Lost in the mysterious depths of those eyes.

"In that case..." He pulled away. Oh no, he wasn't going to leave her? Not when she'd just said he'd been gentle with her. But he pried one of her hands from its death grip on his sweater and led her over to the tarp. "I haven't had more than a catnap in the past three days. And you're exhausted."

He knelt on the floor and pulled her down beside him. He sat with his back against the wall and guided Whitney to the vee between his legs. Then he pulled her against his chest and wrapped her in the snug circle of his arms and body.

With her cheek resting over the steady beat of his heart, Whitney sucked in a deep breath, and finally felt herself relax.

"It's gonna get colder before morning." She heard his words through the cavern of his chest. "We'll need to keep each other warm."

Practical words. Vincent Romeo seemed to be eternally practical.

Whitney nodded. A heavy blink took her by surprise. Her eyelids burned with the salt of her tears, but she discovered she was too tired to care. The weight of fatigue kept them closed.

Vincent was so warm. So strong. So sweet.

And she'd been so... Before sleep claimed her, Whitney summoned the strength to remember her manners. "I'm sure you have a lovely wife and family. I didn't mean to insult—"

"I'm not married." Vincent adjusted his position. He tucked his jacket up around her neck and pulled her hair outside the collar. His hand seemed to linger there, straightening the tangled length of careless curls. "I keep bad hours and bad company."

Whitney yawned and felt her body sinking into his strength and warmth. "Has there ever been anyone special?"

His silence tugged at her compassion. And made her curious enough to lift her head. "Romeo?"

She'd never again make the mistake of thinking his eyes were black voids that revealed nothing. He squeezed them shut to mask the glimpse of turbulence she saw there. When he opened them again, she could see they blazed with pinpoints of light, like tiny stars dotting the sky at night. And they were filled with sadness.

"Romeo?"

He cupped her cheek in his big hand and pulled her back to his chest. "Once."

"What happened?"

"She dumped me at our wedding."

That seemed like quite an admission from a man who had shunned all personal questions up until now. Whitney felt guilty for prying the information out of him. She snuggled closer, offering comfort even if it might not be appreciated. "Why?"

"The job."

So he was a big tough loner who killed bad guys and tended wounds with equal finesse.

Whitney wanted to tell him thanks. That she was glad he was on her side.

But sleep claimed her first.

Chapter Four

"Move it, MacNair."

Vincent shook Whitney by the shoulder and watched her curl into a ball in response to his summons.

He felt less like a heel for waking her so early when she found the energy to say, "Go away."

So she was mule-headed from the get-go, was she? He almost smiled, but common sense overruled. His Washington contact had promised a chopper on a burnt-out plateau a good two hours' hike from here. He needed to be there at noon for the pickup.

Vincent had every intention of being there. And every intention of arriving before sunrise so that Chilton and his men would have a harder time tracking them.

He couldn't afford the delays that had cost them their rescue last night. Or the distraction of another night as Whitney's bed pillow.

Even now he could feel the imprint of her on his body. Long, strong legs tangled with his. A small, firm breast and curvy hip pressed against his torso, softening into his harder angles, waking the interest of his body.

He could have dealt with that. He'd denied the needs of his body more than once while on a mission. When it came down to success and survival, he could turn off that prickling awareness in his skin and blood.

Like when he needed to concentrate on offering comfort and staving off shock—or guarding against a desperate terrorist whose hostage he'd stolen from under his nose.

He'd trained himself to ignore those little frissons of lust that charged his nerve endings.

But then Whitney had moved in her sleep. She'd stretched herself like a cat and snuggled closer, using his body as both bed and blanket. Her hair had caught in the scruff of his beard, and shaking loose, had released her scent. Anger had been his first reaction, when his nose detected the grime and violence of the Black Order's hands on her. But his own outrage had eased at the more delicate smell of Whitney herself.

Baby shampoo.

He'd expected her to smell like something much more pricey. Expensive perfume or champagne or a showroom Lamborghini.

The sweetness of her scent, the unexpected reality of the woman herself, snuck around his defenses. The practical reasons he'd had for holding her shifted into something more personal. He'd pressed his lips to the crown of that glorious fire-gold hair before he even realized his detachment had slipped.

He wouldn't let that happen again.

Chilton was out there. Searching. Waiting.

Vincent couldn't afford to be distracted by hair the color of a fiery sunset, or a scent as innocent and sweet as a baby's.

He bent down and snatched the collar of his jacket and peeled the garment off Whitney's shoulders. Still cocooned inside, she unrolled like a piece of candy and plopped onto the floor. "There's no limo waiting to take you home. You have to rise and shine all on your own."

Lying in a heap of legs and elbows, she pushed herself to a sitting position. "I see you got an A in rudeness at spy training school.'' She pushed a fall of warm russet curls off her forehead and tried to stretch some of the stiffness from her neck and back. "Is it even morning yet?"

He'd already packed everything in his bag, including the lantern, so the only light in the cabin came from the moonlight streaming through the dusty windowpane. While her eyes adjusted to the dimness, he reached for her hand and pulled her to her feet.

"I radioed my boss in D.C. this morning."

She squinted toward the window, interrupting before he could finish detailing their situation. "This isn't morning. I've seen morning. It's a lot brighter than this."

The frosty puff of air from her lips reminded him how cold the mountain air in late October could be. Just as he had the night before, Vincent wrapped his jacket around her shoulders, this time helping her stuff her arms into the sleeves and zipping it up to her chin. "You'll need this more than I will."

"Need it for what?"

"A two-hour hike."

Her slender form shivered inside the bulk of his jacket. The cuffs hung past her fingertips, and the hem hit her thighs. And when she tipped her face up to his, the moonlight touched her translucent skin, bathing it in a soft, cool glow that matched the ethereal mystery in her quicksilver eyes. Vincent's breath caught at the vision of angelic beauty. She looked so young and delicate and fragile. Her lips were finely sculpted, full, unpainted. So tempting. So vulnerable.

Those frissons of lust reacted before he could control them. The blood thickened in his veins. His skin heated at the possibilities. His lips parted for a breath of air, for the chance to taste hers.

She dispelled that idea with the next words out of her

mouth. "So what incredible journey are you taking me on today, Romeo?"

Her sarcasm kept him from forgetting his duty, kept him from bending down to stroke those aristocratic lips with his own. He shook his head and erased the tender impulse from his mind. He wouldn't allow a few errant hormones to interfere with getting the job done.

Vincent slung his duffel over his shoulder and anchored it so his gun hand would be free. "Taking you home. I arranged for a chopper pickup. I want to be at the rendezvous site before Chilton has the advantage of daylight to track us."

"Oh goody."

Following the gesture of his outstretched hand, she preceded him to the door. But instead of going out, she turned. Surprise, surprise. The woman had something she wanted to say.

But he subdued a sigh of impatience as she showed an uncharacteristic hesitancy in choosing her words. She seemed fascinated with some nub of wool on his chest, studying it for several moments before lifting her gaze to his. "About last night. I'm sorry if I made you uncomfortable. When I freaked out like that. That doesn't usually happen. I've been under a little stress lately."

That was supposed to be a joke, right? She wanted him to laugh, to admit to the intimacy they'd surrendered to last night by sharing body heat and trading secrets. And then she wanted him to dismiss it.

Instead, Vincent put himself on guard.

One thing he had learned from Melissa's humiliating speech at the altar—he could never mix his kind of business with a personal life. The woman or the job always demanded more of his time and focus than the other was willing to give.

Whitney MacNair was looking for someone to care.

He couldn't do it. He *would not* do it.

He'd keep her safe. But someone else would have to be responsible for mending her trust and healing her heart. His hormones could fend for themselves.

"Let's go."

He snapped the command instead of giving in to the urge to brush a careless tendril off her forehead and tell her not to worry.

It wasn't just a matter of his survival. Staying focused was necessary for her survival, too.

Her mouth dropped open to speak, but no words came out. Seizing the rare opportunity her silence presented, Vincent reached around her and opened the door. Then he took her by the elbow and guided her out into the frigid, moonlit morning.

WHAT HAD HAPPENED to the gentle giant who'd held her so tightly and soothed her fears throughout the night? The one who'd seemed to care that she was hurting, despite his gruff and brooding exterior?

Agent Romeo had returned in full force this morning.

She liked the other guy better.

Whitney trudged along in Vincent's footsteps, planting one aching foot in front of the other. She'd lost all sense of direction except for one—up.

He seemed undaunted by the darkness that was just now creeping into dawn. A shadow among the shadows, he'd set the pace of a drill sergeant and had explained his plan as thoroughly as a monk who'd taken a vow of silence.

Her slick-soled riding boots had been made for sticking into a pair of stirrups, not mountaineering. She'd slipped more than once on the smooth expanse of glacier-cut granite that formed their path. The bottom of her toes, where she gripped her feet, were starting to go numb. And a blister the size of Montana itself had rubbed onto her right heel.

The golden rays of the sun cut their way through the chilly morning mist, and Whitney took another shot at getting the nicer Vincent Romeo to come out and talk to her again.

"Are we there yet?" she asked. Even if he didn't laugh at the tired old joke, maybe he'd be annoyed enough to stop and rest for five minutes.

No answer.

Her foot hit a loose rock that rolled, smacking her heel against the ground. Whitney grit her teeth against the stab of pain as the blister broke open and her sock rubbed like sandpaper into the raw skin.

Damn, damn, damn the man, anyway! Whitney sank to one knee, debating whether to scream her head off in frustration or chuck the rock at his broad backside.

Deciding she wouldn't give him the satisfaction of either response, she grabbed the trunk of a pine sapling and pulled herself up. Stepping gingerly on her right foot, she concentrated on what she did best to avoid thinking about the pain.

"Where did you buy that wool sweater?" she asked. "You've got that whole black-on-black thing going, which is a little passé, but it works on you. Saks, I'm guessing. They have a great men's department."

What made the sweater so wonderful was the way it clung to the bulges and hollows of his shoulders and arms like a second skin. The design of the flat knit emphasized how his back tapered in to his trim waist.

She'd been watching that back for several miles now, and had memorized how his black jeans fit him snug, but not tight, cupping his tush with loving familiarity before expanding to cover the flexing strength of his thighs.

Something deep inside her clenched as her gaze lingered

on the masculine grace of his movements. Suddenly, her skin felt tingly. Flushed. Hot.

"Damn." She muttered the curse aloud, feeling betrayed by her body's dramatic rise in temperature. She wanted to stay mad at Vincent. She absolutely did not want to be attracted to him.

She'd made such phenomenally bad choices in men recently.

Users. Takers. Each had had an agenda of his own.

And she'd gotten hurt each time.

Anger she could handle. But hurt...

Shaking off that entire line of thinking, she returned to the easy distraction of her shopping skills. "I take that back. A man like you wouldn't be caught dead in a department store. That sweater's either Land's End or Eddie Bauer. Am I right?"

To her surprise, he stopped and turned. She braced herself for a scathing comeback. At the very least, a simple shushing.

But the opaque shadows in his eyes made her wonder if he had heard a word she said. "We'll cut across here." He took her hand and led her down into a washed-out ravine, away from the cover of the trees. His strong, sure grip gave her the balance she needed to dodge the bits of scrub pine and broken rocks that had settled at the center of the gully. When they turned to resume their climb, he released her. "Even though we're exposed, we'll leave less of a trail."

His simple explanation went a long way to lighten Whitney's mood. Not anxious to return to his brooding silence, she tugged at the hem of that well-studied sweater and stopped him. "There. Did that really hurt so much to have a normal conversation with me?"

The shadows in his eyes vanished for an instant, and

the darkness behind them seemed to reach out and swallow her up. "I'll talk when I have something to say."

The power behind that low-pitched promise trickled through her veins like warm syrup and strengthened her like a hearty meal.

"Thank you." Whitney smiled. The stretch of muscles across her face felt good. She tilted her face toward the sunrise, enjoying the warmth bathing her skin. It had been days since she'd even felt like smiling. Even longer since she'd dared to believe in a man's word. "I feel better."

When she tipped her face back to Vincent's she was washed in an entirely different kind of heat. She'd had admiring looks from men before. But no wink or smile or appreciative twinkle compared to the intensity of the fire blazing in Vincent's eyes.

But the shadows returned in an instant, shutting off his emotions so quickly that Whitney wondered if she had imagined his interest.

Self-conscious that she had misread his reaction, she pushed a wayward fall of hair off her forehead and shook it loose down her back. She shouldn't be disappointed that Vincent wasn't really interested in her. She must look a sight. No makeup. Wild hair. Bruised and dirty. Her dry lips seemed to crack beneath his blank scrutiny. She pulled lip balm from her pocket and rubbed a thin coat onto her lips. Then she dotted her cheeks and nose to protect her skin from the wind and cold, dry air.

Patting her pocket when she had finished, she managed to sound as if his look and his words hadn't affected her so profoundly. "Shall we go?"

But Vincent made no move. His eyes narrowed to question her. "I say a few words and you feel better?"

"Funny how that works, isn't it?" Assuming their course was up, as always, Whitney started the climb on her own. "C'mon, Romeo. I've got a hot shower and a hair dryer waiting for me at the ranch."

"You're limping."

"No, I'm not."

He clamped his fingers around her wrist and tugged her to a standstill. A faint memory of yesterday's torture doubled her hand into a fist and she resisted.

But, just as quickly, his grip gentled. So did she.

"Sit."

"The sun's rising. You said we had to be there by now." He knelt in front of her, his left hand running up and down her leg, squeezing at her ankle, her calf, her knee, her thigh. Whitney touched his shoulder to stop his search. "It's just a blister."

"Why didn't you tell me—" Vincent raised his head and their faces almost touched.

Whitney froze. The warmth of his hands—at her thigh, at her wrist—rekindled the fiery awareness of his blunt tenderness and unquestionable power.

What she had denied with the logical part of her brain blazed into an overload of sensations. He was so solid, so hard and warm beneath her fingertips. This close, she could see tiny lines of life and sunshine crinkling beside his eyes. She wondered if laughter had formed any of the creases there. She breathed in and savored his clean, simple scent. He wore no cologne or aftershave to give him away to the enemy or cover up his own musky identity. When she exhaled, Vincent's breath mingled with hers and she swallowed hard.

She wanted him to kiss her. She wanted to know how firm or pliant his lips would be on hers. Hard and straight and masculine, would they soften when he kissed? Or would he claim her? Take her? Would he ask her to be an equal partner in his embrace?

Spellbound, Whitney felt herself falling. Falling into

those incredibly unique eyes. Unblinking orbs of obsidian beauty. Full of untold secrets. Full of untapped strengths. Dark and sexy and…

"We'll stop here."

Like an unexpected gust of frigid mountain air, Vincent moved his hands to her waist and sat her down, pushing space between them. His words held a double meaning in Whitney's fevered mind. *Stop* drooling on me. *Stop* being so needy. *Stop* being such a pain in the butt.

Of all the adolescent…

The cold from the granite beneath her seeped through her jeans, chilling her skin. Chilling her heart and tearing her ego to shreds.

She'd practically thrown herself at him. That whole kissing fantasy had gotten way out of hand. He was here to do a job. To rescue her. To get her home in one piece.

Period.

Hadn't she adamantly argued against the same sort of injustice when Ross Weston had kissed her? She hadn't wanted his attention. Not like that. She'd wanted to do her job. She'd just wanted to do her job and not have to worry about whether or not the senator she worked for would keep his hands to himself.

She, of all people, knew better than to subject Vincent to that same awkward discomfort.

"Sorry." Her breathy apology sounded inadequate. She thought of the warning he'd given her at Chilton's cabin. "I know. There's a time to run, a time to hide and a time to shut up. Apparently, I'm having a hard time keeping those three straight."

Again, he failed to find the joke in her self-deprecating humor. Vincent shrugged his duffel off his shoulder and dropped it on the ground beside her.

He pointed up to a craggy overhang of rock some twenty feet above them. "The chopper's landing on that plateau.

I'll go on ahead and check it out. First-aid kit's in the bag. If you can fix it yourself, do it." He pulled his gun from its holster and popped out the clip. With deadly looking efficiency he checked the bullets, slipped the clip into place and snapped the barrel back, loading the first bullet into the firing chamber. "I'll be back in five minutes."

Whitney nodded and watched him take the last twenty feet in a few long strides, then shimmy up and over the rocky outcropping, disappearing from sight.

"That eager to get away from me, huh?"

Her chest heaved in a weary sigh. She gave up trying to figure out Vincent's moods and her reactions to the man. Better she concentrate on something more productive. Like getting back to the ranch and finding out if anyone there had missed her. Jewel would be upset, at any rate. The girl might even be blaming herself for Whitney being captured by Dimitri Chilton.

With that sobering thought to focus on, she reached for Vincent's bag.

VINCENT'S NERVE ENDINGS were on full alert. He crouched low to the ground and scanned the trees that surrounded the clearing.

Something didn't feel right.

It wasn't a sound so much as a lack of sound that made him suspicious. He should be hearing birds and rodents or whatever kind of wildlife awoke with the sun on this side of the mountain. He knew many animals migrated or hibernated in the fall. But something should be alive and moving out there.

Unless something—or someone—had scared them off.

He stared deep into the shadows beyond the open pasture, toward the rock face that rose behind the trees, looking for signs of any human animal. That slim stand of pines provided the only cover where Chilton and his men could hide up here.

Maybe fatigue was throwing his senses off. With the butt of his gun cradled loosely between his hands, he skirted the rim of the plateau for a closer look.

After circling the pockets of snow that clung to the shady interior of the forest, Vincent pressed his back into the trunk of an ancient pine and listened. He heard the wind whistle through the heavy boughs, and the limbs creaking and groaning as they swayed.

But there was no crackle of static that might indicate a radio. No grind of gears from a vehicle. No voices. No snap of twigs or crunch of rocks beneath booted feet. No birds chirping, no scrabbling of tiny paws in search of food, either.

Vincent made a quick trip around the perimeter of the clearing, waiting for the wary tension within him to dissipate.

Maybe it was the gentle scent of Whitney's hair that had him off kilter. Or the hungry look in her eyes that had made him want to kiss her a few minutes ago. No, *devour her* would be a better description of the sudden, rushing heat that had consumed him. He'd wanted to taste each tiny freckle across that creamy expanse of smooth skin that glowed cool in the moonlight and radiated warmth in the sun.

Vincent checked his watch. He had just under five hours left to guard her. He could last five hours without giving in to the primitive urges of his body. In five hours he could deliver her to his Washington contact, then check in to a hotel, take a long, cold shower and sleep for two days.

Or maybe it was the way his wary heart cracked open a little bit at Whitney's simple admission that he could make her feel better. He didn't even remember what he'd said. But he remembered her smile. He remembered her ''thank you.'' He remembered wanting to make her feel that way again.

Vincent dispelled those fanciful imaginings on an impatient breath of air. Oh yeah. His objectivity had been shot to hell on this assignment.

He couldn't do the relationship thing. Melissa had made that more than clear. And Whitney MacNair, with her blue-blood background and innocent eyes, wouldn't be interested in a one-night stand with the son of a Chicago cop. Nah. She'd want the flowers and champagne and pretty words. He just wanted to get her out of his system.

Bedding the hostage wouldn't exactly win points with her father and his buddy, the president, either.

Vincent shut down that whole distracting train of thought. If all he could do was his job, then by damn, he'd do it right.

Finding nothing in the trees to validate his sense of alarm, he struck out across the open grass of the plateau. He didn't holster his weapon, but he dropped his hand to his side. The five minutes of privacy he'd given Whitney were up. He'd better get her out of sight. Then he could worry about how to survive a few more hours in her company without completely losing his mind.

That's when he found what he'd been looking for.

Half a footprint in the snow.

He held himself completely still, moving only his eyes to analyze and identify the direction, size and age of the clue. His breathing was controlled. Silent. A disciplined energy curled within him, stealing out from his brain through the tips of his fingers and toes.

''Whitney.''

He mouthed her name, knowing he might already be too late. Adrenaline freed him from analysis to action, and he took off in a dead run for the edge of the plateau. He was a damn idiot for ever leaving her alone in the first place.

"MacNair!"

Right on cue, her head popped up over the ledge of rock. "I know, I know. I took longer than five minutes. But I really thought you'd come for me."

She disappeared for an instant and dread sank to the pit of his stomach. He had a good ten strides left to reach her.

"MacNair!" Shouting was risky. If Chilton's men had merely passed through, then he'd be calling them back to their position. But every cell in Vincent's body had tightened with suspicion. Chilton was here. Hiding. Vincent had to reach Whitney first.

The next thing he saw was the top of her bright auburn hair, shining gold and copper in the sunlight. A breeze caught its length and unfurled it like a banner.

As distinctive as a warning flag.

A beacon for anyone within a mile of this clearing to see.

A dramatic grunt preceded the dip of her shoulders, and then his black nylon bag sailed through the air as she hefted it over the top of the outcropping. "What do you carry in that thing, anyway? If it's a helicopter we can assemble, let's do it and get out of here. My feet are killing me."

Damn that woman. She made more noise than his entire family put together in one room at Christmastime.

Vincent reached the edge as she hooked one leg over the top. He grabbed her belt at the back of her waist and lifted her. With one glance, he scanned the washout below her. No one. Where the hell were Chilton's men?

"I put some ointment and a bandage on my blister. Took longer than I thought to get my boot—"

He clamped his hand over her mouth and rolled her onto the ground beneath him. "Not a word." He whispered the warning beside her ear. Keeping her still. Keeping her silent. "Understand?"

Her pale eyes blanched above his hand. When she nodded, he released her. She immediately whispered, "What's going on?"

"Dammit, MacNair."

And then he saw them.

They broke through the tree line on either side of the washout below them. Chilton, he recognized. There were three more men with him. Each dressed in black, each carrying a semiautomatic weapon.

Each charging up the mountain toward them.

There'd been four men at Chilton's cabin. Vincent had killed one, wounded or killed a second in their pursuit.

"Where the hell is he getting reinforcements?"

"Romeo. What are you—?"

He grasped Whitney's chin and turned it to the side. Her body flinched into his and he knew she saw them, too.

"Have they been following us?"

"They've been waiting for us."

Vincent propped himself up on his elbows and used a millisecond to weigh his options. Shoot or run. Whitney was out in the open.

Simple decision.

He rolled to his feet and dragged her up with him. "Run!"

He shoved her toward the trees. In one fluid motion, he aimed his gun and fired. Chilton's men were in the open as well. Easy targets without the cover of trees. When one went down, Chilton shouted an order. The others dived for the rocks, taking them out of Vincent's line of sight beyond the lip of the overhang. Having bought Whitney a few precious seconds, he turned to follow her, snagging his bag along the way.

God, that woman could run. Something like pride, maybe admiration or relief, gave Vincent a fleeting feeling of triumph. He pursued the flash of copper-gold hair where it disappeared amongst the trees.

Separate them. The order came in a foreign tongue. Chilton's men were scaling the rocks. Circling them. Herding them into the trees.

A hail of bullets pummeled the ground at Vincent's feet as he hit the tree line. Why hadn't they fired before?

Whitney. They wanted their hostage back in one piece. He was expendable.

Branches slapped at his face and chest as he raced ahead full speed. He needed more time, more distance before he could stop and establish a defensive position. His knees protested the punishing run after two hours of steady climbing. His lungs burned as he deepened his breathing to compensate for the thinner air of this altitude.

Just as easily as running or breathing, he popped the spent clip out of his gun and tossed it. Without breaking stride, he slipped a new magazine from his pocket and shoved it in.

Shift. Load. Turn. Fire.

Vincent staggered a step at the recoil. He hadn't expected to hit anything. But he'd expected to see a target.

"Damn."

The terrorists had separated. He slowed his pace a fraction. Now he could hear the voices shouting around him. Commands echoing off trees. Messages that stabbed him in the back like a knife. Cutting him off from Whitney. Leaving her at Chilton's mercy.

"Son of a bitch."

Whitney wouldn't understand what the terrorists were saying. But he did.

"MacNair!"

"Romeo—"

The clip of her plea struck him right in the gut. They had her.

Vincent shifted directions. Ran straight for the light. Straight for the clearing on the other side of the trees. Straight for the sound of Whitney's voice.

The pounding of his boots on the topsoil changed to a smacking sound as he hit bare rock. A rock slide had cleared a gully on this side of the trees. A deep V that cut straight through the mountain to the other side. That's where they'd taken her.

He entered the cutout. Sheer rock on either side, with piles of rock and snow at the center where the sun couldn't quite reach.

He's coming! The warning came from behind.

Good. He wouldn't have to face all four men to get her back.

Praying he knew Court Brody's map by heart and that he hadn't mistakenly run into a dead-end canyon, Vincent rounded the corner, gun raised in front of him.

And found Whitney.

One man had her. Sort of.

Vincent almost grinned as he slowed to a walk and regained a steady breath. The bastard had cinched his arm around Whitney's throat and was half dragging, half carrying her with him, making it impossible for him to keep his gun pointed at her head. She kicked and elbowed and punched her captor, refusing to be his shield, refusing to surrender.

"MacNair?"

Her beautiful eyes, darkened by fear, looked up and saw him. And flooded with hope.

"Get back!" The man in black shouted the order in English and trained the gun on him. Then he pointed the gun at Whitney, unsure which target provided a better defense.

Her captor's confusion would work to Vincent's advantage. He pushed aside his own fears for Whitney's safety and let a deadly calm fill him with renewed strength and strategy.

He'd taken her by stealth yesterday.

Today, he'd take her back by force.

He never broke his stride. He lengthened each step. He couldn't shoot, for fear of hitting Whitney, so he holstered his weapon.

"Get your hands off her." Vincent's low-voiced command bounced off the rock walls.

"Romeo, what are you—"

"Get back!" Her captor retreated, taking Whitney with him.

Vincent kept advancing, his eyes pinned to the man in black.

"Romeo?"

For a single heartbeat of time, he slipped his gaze to hers and said, "Fight him."

This would be a hell of a lot easier if she understood his message. She did.

He saw a flash of white teeth and heard a squeal of mortal pain. She'd bitten her captor's hand. He released her and Whitney ducked. Before the man's fist connected with her head, before he got off a shot at him, Vincent rammed him. Fist first. Knuckles to forehead. The man crumpled like a puppet whose strings had been cut.

"Let's go."

Whitney was already on her feet when Vincent took her hand. She latched on with both of hers and fell into step at his shoulder. They needed to get out of the snow, away from the trail of footprints.

"Where's your backup?" she asked, picking up the pace when he did. He headed on through the cut. Chilton and his men controlled the plateau now. There'd be no helicopter coming to pick them up at noon or any other time. "How come we're always doing this by ourselves?"

"We were set up."

"What do you mean?"

He heard the foreign voices shouting questions and obscenities behind them, closing the empty circle, searching for their prey.

Vincent took a detour before answering. He turned off the main path and jumped down a five-foot drop toward the western slope. It'd be a much steeper descent, but this way provided more brush and boulders to hide behind.

He reached up and wrapped his fingers around Whitney's waist, lifting her down beside him. Again he was struck by how delicate and slender she was, despite her sinewy strength and endless chatter. She could be hurt so easily. Not just by guns or hands or vicious words.

By betrayal.

They had both been betrayed.

With her hands still braced on his shoulders, she dug in her fingertips, demanding his full attention. "C'mon, Romeo. Don't go quiet on me now. So Chilton and his men were waiting for us. He's good. This guy has given Montana Confidential fits for three months. What makes you think it was a setup?"

He pulled her hands from his shoulders and clasped them between them.

"I speak Arabic."

"So? What did they say?"

"They called me by name."

Chapter Five

Vincent released Whitney's hand and slid down the embankment toward the stream below them.

"Chilton used the words 'Vincent Romeo' and 'NSA'."

Whitney slid down after him, and marched downstream through the leaves on the bank, following the direction of his pointing finger without stopping for a breath. "And the only way he could have known who you were and who you work for is if he was tipped off. Right?"

Vincent scanned the slope above them. They'd lost Chilton's men over an hour ago, and she'd been working this revelation through ever since.

Reassured their trail was clean, he fell into step behind her. Brody's map didn't cover this side of the range, but the terrain flattened out up ahead. Within a couple of miles they should reach the high pastureland used by one of the big ranches, if not an actual service road.

If his sense of direction hadn't failed him. And the weather held. And the Black Order didn't have any more tricks up their sleeves.

"You don't have any idea who told Chilton our plans?" He'd given Whitney a black stocking cap to wear, both for warmth and to hide her red telltale flag of hair. He missed seeing those tempestuous curls bouncing along her shoulders. The kind of hair that only a woman like Whitney could do justice to.

Hell. Exhaustion was kicking in. He was too easily distracted now. He needed some serious sleep. Otherwise, he could have resisted falling into this conversation with her. "Somebody in Washington gave us away."

She turned around and walked backward so she could face him. "You think your boss is linked to terrorists?"

"No."

"The chopper pilot, then?"

"No." With a firm hand on each shoulder, he turned her back around and guided her over a dip in the bank before letting her go. "Daniel Austin said Chilton had an American contact. I can't believe it's anyone inside the agency, though. More than likely, someone tapped into the call. I don't want to use the radio until I can run a scan on the equipment."

"Company man, huh? If not the NSA, then who?"

"I intend to find out."

"So we're going after Chilton?"

"No. I'm taking you home."

Whitney stopped in her tracks. Vincent went ahead and passed her, on the off chance that she'd keep walking if he did. "Then you're coming back?"

"Yes."

"But the trail will be cold by then. Chilton could be long gone. The Black Order clearly still has support here in Montana. You keep killing terrorists, he keeps showing up with more. He knew our location this morning long before we got there. You can't let him get away."

Vincent's breath seeped out on a weary sigh. Of course, when had Whitney done what he'd expected of her? He turned to face her. Even at this distance, his oversize jacket, her unadorned freckles and the expectant look in her eyes combined to sucker punch him in the gut. She looked so vulnerable and beautiful. So young and full of hope. He didn't want to disappoint her. He didn't want to see that look changed by the world of danger and suspicion he lived in.

"I won't."

A smile blossomed on her lips. "Then I'll help you."

Her reasoning was flawless, her patriotism admirable. But his job was to keep her safe. "No."

"Yes."

"No."

"We lost them at that big gully." Completely ignoring his decision, she turned to retrace their steps back up the mountain. She found a foothold, then stretched her arm to grab a larger rock for balance and pull herself up. "That's where we should start."

"You're not going anywhere but back to the ranch."

She continued to climb. "You need my help."

"No."

Vincent dropped his bag and jogged back up the bank. He would simply reach up, catch her by the ankle and pull her down to earth and to reason.

But now those long legs of hers were working against him. "MacNair." He swiped a gloved hand across his clenched jaw and started up the slope after her. "Get your butt back down here."

That cute, little curvy butt.

He had such a nice view from this angle.

Just as nice as that sweet freckled face and glorious mane of hair.

Vincent clenched his jaw as his thoughts moved to the velvety smoothness of her skin. He chastized himself with the jarring movement of their climb. He wasn't here to analyze her finer attributes. He was here to keep her safe. After two days in her company, he could understand the urgency of her father's request to the president.

Whitney was a danger to herself, completely oblivious to just how dangerous and desperate a terrorist on the run, like Dimitri Chilton, could be.

It was up to Vincent to save her from herself.

But who would save him?

"Do you have any idea where you're going?"

"If we find Chilton, we can eavesdrop. I know he made two calls from his cell phone when I was at the cabin with him. One was to my father. The other must be his contact."

He snatched at her foot, but she flicked his hand away, sending a shower of pebbles and dirt down on him. He waited for the rock slide to settle, then hurried his pace to catch her. "Don't you ever run out of gas?"

"Think of it, Romeo. This could be the break we need to bring down the Black Order. All we need is a name. Or a code word."

"It's not that easy to uncover a mole's identity," he argued, referring to the elusive traitor who'd revealed their whereabouts to the Black Order. "You'd need surveillance equipment. Skilled operatives. In some cases you have to work for days, weeks, even years, to find that one phone call or memo or computer disk that proves where the information leak is. You're not going to find him by eavesdropping on one phone call."

Whitney had drifted off course and reached a sheer rock face. Without ropes and pitons, she couldn't scale that kind of incline. But even that didn't stop her. Scooting to the side, she tried to work her way around it. "Don't you want to nail the bad guys?"

Vincent studied the course above and below her, and found a foothold on a different path. "My mission was to return you safely to your father. There was nothing in my orders about bringing in any terrorists."

"But they tried to kill you." The strain in her voice told him she was slowing down.

"They're not the first. They won't be the last."

Whitney made the mistake of looking down at him. "You live with that kind of threat every day, don't you?" Vincent kept climbing while she worked through her hesitation. He took advantage of the color draining from her cheeks and moved to cut off her ascent. "You don't always face the bad guys alone, do you?"

She sounded shocked, sympathetic even. Sort of like Melissa's reaction when she first learned the details of the work he did for the government. He wondered if Whitney's concern would turn into fear and resentment the way his fiancée's had.

Vincent berated himself for having such a thought at all. He had promised a lifetime to Melissa, giving her plenty of time to change the way she felt about him. His time with Whitney was limited to the duration of this mission. And the sooner it ended, the better. He'd turn her over to her father and be done with her. No more mishaps, no more endless conversations.

No more fascination.

"Home, MacNair."

He swung himself up and had her in his grasp. But she found a grip for her toes and pushed herself beyond his reach.

"Chilton's not interested in you." He detected an almost desperate tone as she switched back to her original line of reasoning. Why wouldn't the woman just give up this crazy idea and stop this reckless race up the mountain? "He wants me. If I show up, then he will, too. You can be hiding out, and track him while he follows me."

In Whitney's hurry, she grabbed at an exposed root. The shallow topsoil couldn't support her weight and the root ripped from the ground. She made the mistake of holding

on to the root instead of the rock and sailed backward.
"Romeo?"

"Hell."

The chain reaction happened too quickly for Vincent to
brace himself. As Whitney flew past, he snagged her beneath the arms and jerked her toward his chest. When she
hit, his foot slipped. He held the rock for a precarious
moment, but five fingers were no match for the weight of
two adults and gravity.

"Romeo!"

Her arms snaked around his neck. Vincent turned his
left shoulder into the rock and locked his right arm around
her waist as they slid and bounced down the unforgiving
wall of granite and dirt. He absorbed each jolt into muscle
and bone, shielding her from the brunt of their fall. As the
ground rushed up to meet them, he tried to turn. But it
was too late.

His feet hit the slick earth and flew out from under him.
They smacked into the cushion of leaves and dead grass
and rolled together down the bank. They crashed through
a tangle of deadwood caught at a curve in the stream, and
were saved from a drenching in ice-cold water when Vincent slammed into the one solid trunk of aspen in the pile.

He lay there stunned, breathless, his shoulder aching,
his eyes squeezed shut against the swirling world of trees
and sunlight above him.

"Romeo?"

A tender touch stroked across his cheek. A caress. A
query.

Vincent gathered control of his spinning world and focused on that touch. As oxygen returned to his lungs, he
became aware of other touches. Long legs tangled with
his, his thigh wedged in a crevice of soft heat. A delicate
weight sprawled across his chest, punctuated by two small
mounds pressing into him. A slender hand cupped his jaw,

and strong yet delicate fingers ran with concern along his cheekbone, the hair at his temple, the arc of his ear.

"Romeo?"

She'd touched him like this before, with concern. With care. When the truck had crashed and he'd been unconscious. That was the first time he'd noticed the willowy curves of her body. The first time he'd allowed himself to think of her as a woman. Not a hostage.

Damn her, anyway, for turning a routine mission into an unpredictable roller-coaster ride. One minute he was in control, the next they were tumbling down the side of a mountain. He did his job. He did his job. He did his job. Damn her for stirring up feelings that had nothing to do with that job. Damn her for complicating his life.

In the time it took him to open his eyes, he'd rolled over, pinning her on the bed of leaves beneath him.

"Nothing's simple with you, is it?" he accused.

Her eyes expanded, darkened. He watched the play of surprise, relief, and something like desperation dance across her face. Her hands swept down across his collar and balled in the front of his sweater. "I want to help. I work for Montana Confidential. I can——"

"Shut up." The frustrated order came out on a husky whisper. "You're going to listen to me. You are not volunteering for any foolhardy, unplanned strike——"

"I can do this." She moistened her lips in a nervous gesture, and his gaze dropped to the unconsciously erotic glimpse of her sweet pink tongue. Suddenly, Vincent's entire body felt parched. Starved for just one taste of her. "I want Chilton as bad——"

Easing his weight onto his elbows, Vincent lowered his mouth to hers. He lingered there a moment, simply touching her lips. He absorbed her taste, her scent, her surprise. And when she opened her mouth—to protest, no doubt— he angled his head and sampled her unintentional offering.

Soft. Firm. Feminine. He nipped at the aristocratic arch at each corner, and drew his tongue along the fine curve of her bottom lip.

Just a taste.

Just enough to get this distraction out of his system.

Just enough to detect a pulsing heat between his legs.

He needed to retreat. For sanity's sake. He needed to shut down his body's reaction to her.

She frustrated him, that was all. Annoyed him. She was headstrong and spoiled, and he deserved a kiss just for enduring her company in this rescue gone sideways.

Vincent lifted his head and inhaled deeply, enjoying the calming control that seeped into his limbs.

"Think about it." The breathy catch in Whitney's voice gave him a perverse satisfaction. The fact that she swallowed and continued on carved a chink in his contented armor. "Why does Chilton want me so badly? My father sent you instead of paying a ransom. And still he pursues us. There's something more going on—"

Vincent kissed her again.

He captured her lips and demanded her silence. No. He demanded her attention. On him. On them. On the way her long, lithe body fit so perfectly beneath his.

Her fists opened and she splayed her fingers across his chest. Yeah. He liked that. That false contentment became a slow, drugging heat that made the line between control and surrender hazy to detect. He wanted her to touch him again. His chest. His face. He wanted to feel her skin on his skin.

He made the request with his mouth, and somehow she seemed to understand. Her fingers crept up around his neck as his tongue swept into her mouth, seeking hers. She gave him a tentative welcome, touching the tip of her tongue to his.

He asked again.

To his feverish delight, she ran her fingers higher, along the curve of his head, and discovered the friction of her palms against his bristly short hair. She moaned in her throat, a sound as ragged and disjointed as his own thoughts.

She shifted beneath him, adjusting the cradle of her hips to support his heavier weight, drawing him nearer to her unique feminine heat. He slipped his hand down to cup the flare of her hip and hold her there as an urgent message rocked between them. Vincent's rational mind exploded with the need to answer.

Whitney joined her tongue to his in a move as bold as her auburn hair, and Vincent claimed her. He took. He gave. He asked. He received.

He was awash in the sensations of Whitney MacNair. Her taste. Her scent. Her touch. Such beauty. Such spirit.

He'd been too long without sustenance like this, too long without admitting, much less fulfilling, this consuming need.

"Whit—" He breathed her name along her cheek, tearing his mouth from her succulent lips to indulge an idle fantasy. He found one freckle. Then another. And another. A little touch of his tongue. A tiny press of his lips.

A long tendril of coppery hair had slipped from her stocking cap and fallen into his path. He reached up with one hand and swept the cap off her head. Handfuls of rich, sun-red waves spilled into his hand. He pulled them to his nose and buried himself in the fresh, wholesome smell of…

Sweat. Laced with a foreign spice.

And gunpowder.

A clarity of awareness spiked through him, as icy and sharp as the mountain stream beside them.

"Son of a—"

Vincent cut himself off. He was too close to her. This

was too perfect. He'd already spoiled the moment. He wouldn't shock her with a self-condemning curse.

He inched some distance between them, forcing cleansing air in and out of his lungs.

Confusion blanched the silver in Whitney's passion-clouded eyes, leaving them almost colorless. Unlike the flaming patches of pinkish red that stained her cheeks.

He should have known better. He should never have lost control like that.

He had no right to take advantage of her free spirit, her adventurous nature, or whatever it was that had allowed him to kiss her. That had made her risk taking part in an embrace like that.

Through sheer will alone he managed to stand and help her up. He led her to the top of the bank, then released her hand. He moved two steps away before shame and common sense sapped his strength and he sank to the ground.

With elbows on his knees, he swiped his hands across the rasp of his jaw. He steepled his fingers and pressed his lips against them, unable to dispel the aftershocks of Whitney's willing kiss.

From the corner of his eye he watched her hug her arms around her waist and pace. How could she possibly possess such energy when he felt completely drained?

She made three laps before coming up to sit beside him. She folded herself up inside his big jacket, making the determined thrust of her chin look somehow childlike and poignant all at the same time.

"Don't think you can just haul off and kiss me to shut me up. I'm not going to change my mind on this."

She tried to make a joke of it, but Vincent didn't laugh. In reality that kiss was a sad testament to how badly he had lost his focus on this assignment. Maybe it was time he put in for a leave of absence. Maybe he needed to do something new.

Melissa had warned the job would take a toll on him. She'd meant the physical risks. But clearly, by age thirty-five, in the midst of the Montana wilderness, it was beginning to take a toll on him mentally.

And that's when the other memories rushed in. Vincent pressed his face into his hands, trying to ward off the images. His dad in a coffin. His mother's tears. The incredible weight of becoming a father figure to his younger brothers and sisters.

He felt a brush of fingers on his forearm and sat bolt upright.

Whitney snatched her hand away. But she didn't retreat. "Do we need to talk about this? About what just happened?"

Talk?

What could he say? How could he explain the jumble of emotions he had no business feeling, anyway?

He turned to Whitney, wishing he had the words.

She wore the hint of a brave smile on her face, and her eyes sparkled with their quicksilver light.

But he saw her porcelain-smooth skin, roughened with the red marks from his two-day beard that lay side by side with the marks of Dimitri Chilton's abuse.

Vincent pulled the glove off his left hand and reached out to touch her chin. He tipped it first to the left, then to the right, inspecting all the damage she'd sustained these past few days. The violence written on her soft, freckled features sickened him.

A familiar fist of justice tightened in his gut. It made him strong, righteous and absolutely sure of his next words.

He turned her chin and looked her straight in the eye. "I will not use you as bait to draw out Dimitri Chilton."

With that final word, he found the strength to pick up his gear and start the trek downstream toward civilization and rescue.

Whitney, unfortunately, didn't understand final words. He heard her footsteps running behind him. "Dammit, Romeo. I am not some spoiled princess without a mind of my own. I know there are risks. But I know I can do this secret-agent stuff. I can help."

Vincent whirled around, planted himself, pulled himself up with every bit of might and muscle he possessed. Whitney skidded to a halt and backpedaled a step.

"My father was shot in the heart when I was eighteen. Died instantly. He'd gone into a warehouse to rescue an eight-year-old girl who'd been kidnapped by her mother's boyfriend. He drew fire while his partner got the girl out.

"He was a Chicago cop doing his job. He knew the *risks*.

"*He* was the *bait*."

His crude telling of the heroic, painful story had its intended effect.

He turned and marched on down the hill in silence.

"SON OF A BITCH."

After trudging along with a companion whose dark mood made even the light mountain air seem oppressive, Whitney was relieved to hear that single curse.

"You really need to expand your vocabulary, you know that?"

Funny, but she was actually beginning to read his silent signals. A slight nod to the right or left indicated she should follow and in what direction. The flat of his hand behind his back meant stop.

And that black-eyed glare over his shoulder meant to be quiet.

Though she craved some human interaction to help sort

out her thoughts, she was tired enough to obey. She sat where she was, curling her legs beneath her. The stream gave them plenty of fresh water to drink, but they'd split the last energy bar at lunch. Four hours later, her stomach was growling, her foot was throbbing, her head itched beneath the wool cap, and her mood was becoming more and more like her brooding escort's.

"What do you see?" she had to ask. He'd pulled a pair of binoculars from his duffel and was looking toward the northern horizon.

That stiff set to his shoulders blocked her out as effectively as one of his pithy no's. The more time she spent with Vincent, the more she learned about communicating without words.

Now if she could just figure out what that body-rocketing, mind-soaring, soul-stealing kiss had meant.

He'd turned her inside out with the coarse seduction of his hands and mouth. He was such a big man, so strong, so earthy. A little rough around the edges, even. And yet he'd been gentle. Patient with her as he tested her response. Had he been unsure of his welcome? Had he sensed her mistrust of a man's desire?

She was more than the sum of her parts. More than a pretty face or a blue-blood pedigree or a prize to be won.

She'd been wined and dined by society's finest. Wooed by men of wealth and power. Maybe it was the curse of an overprotective father and four older brothers, but she'd never experienced such raw, spontaneous passion before.

She'd given up her virginity on the sheets of one of the finest hotels in Martha's Vineyard. But lying with Vincent in a pile of leaves and mud had been more memorable by far. He shut out the world with his size and power and honest need, shrinking her universe to just the two of them. He made her believe he wanted *her*. Not Gerald MacNair's daughter. Whitney. Too skinny, too noisy, too headstrong. Just her.

That is, until he pulled away so abruptly.

Maybe he *was* just shutting her up. She had a habit of getting on people's nerves, she knew. But she only wanted someone to listen and take her seriously. She didn't want to be coddled and protected her entire life.

She wanted to find the man who'd kidnapped her and punch his lights out for degrading her so, for making her feel afraid. She wanted to complete Montana Confidential's mission and eliminate the threat of the Black Order in the United States. She wanted to be kissed like nobody else in the world mattered again.

Fat chance.

She blew out her frustration on a sigh and picked up a pebble to toss into the stream. The stone sank to the bottom of the clear water, and Whitney felt her spirits sink with it.

"How's your foot?"

Vincent's question startled her from her self-pitying reverie. It had been so long since he'd spoken, she almost didn't recognize the familiar deep-pitched rasp.

She wanted to ask him what had happened to his voice. Had it always sounded as if he had that trace of laryngitis? It gave him a weathered quality, the sound of a man who had forgotten how to be a little boy a long time ago. After losing his father so tragically, she imagined he'd grown up instantly.

But Whitney didn't indulge her curiosity. Conversation with Vincent was a precious thing, and she didn't want to jeopardize this opportunity by changing the subject. "It hurts like hell, but I don't need crutches yet."

"You got another mile in you?"

Was that a challenge she heard? She stood and brushed

the dirt and debris from her jeans, and her curiosity swerved in a whole new direction. "I might."

"We may not need to chance the radio, after all. Here." He held out the binoculars. While she put them up to her eyes, he stood behind her and angled her in the proper direction.

Whitney squinted and adjusted the knob until they were focused. She squinted again. Was that a gravel road? Steps? A sparkling white wraparound porch?

"It's a ranch." A very successful one, judging by the number of corrugated-metal outbuildings and the matching pair of black SUVs off to one side of the sprawling cut-stone residence. "My God, it's a house!"

A surge of renewed energy spun Whitney around. She flung her arms around Vincent's neck and hugged him tight. "Yes! We did it! We're going home!"

He snugged his arms around her and lifted her off the ground. She felt weightless, airborne high above the puffy cotton-ball clouds in the sky above her. And for an instant, she thought he was sailing up there with her. But all too soon her feet hit the ground and Vincent said, "Business before celebration, MacNair."

His hands settled at her waist and she made the awkward realization that he was holding himself perfectly still. Whitney quickly pulled away, feeling the sting of his rejection. But she refused to let embarrassment destroy her buoyed spirits.

"What kind of business are you talking about?" She reached up to push the hair from her face, but discovered everything was already tucked away beneath the nubby black wool of Vincent's stocking cap. Neatly controlled. Out of sight. Out of trouble. Nothing to mess with.

The symbolism wasn't lost on Whitney.

She kicked her pride up a notch and pretended Vincent's lack of an explanation didn't hurt. She concentrated her attention back through the binoculars and developed a sudden interest in studying the ranch's layout. "We *are* going home now, right?"

"As soon as I check it out."

Whitney jumped at the scrape of metal on metal. "What are you doing?"

Vincent held his gun as if the deadly piece of steel was as much a part of him as his own hand. He slapped the magazine of bullets up into the handle and tucked it into the back waistband of his jeans. "I'm down to three rounds."

Whitney frowned along with him. "We don't have to shoot our way in there, do we? Can't we just walk up and ask nicely to use their phone to call the NSA?"

"Not after the last setup. I don't know if it's my equipment or my contact that's been compromised. I'd like to get an independent line and call your friend Daniel. He'll have a secure line at the compound. We can call your father from there."

She liked the *your friend* part. Seeing Daniel again sounded good. Going home sounded even better.

"Let's go."

"Hold on." The steel-edged grip on her arm would have stopped her, even without the warning. "Someone's coming up the road."

A wary energy radiated from the broad set of his shoulders. The laid-back intensity of it filled the air around him, setting Whitney's nerves on edge. But she thought she understood his caution. "You think the Black Order beat us to it?"

With his hand still on her arm, he scrunched her close to his side behind a stand of gorse bushes. "I count two men in the truck cab, one riding in the bed." He released her and knelt to dig out something from his bag. "What do you see?"

He was asking for her help? He was including her in his *business?* A sense of importance straightened Whitney's spine. She held the binoculars up and spotted the telltale trail of dust spitting out behind the black pickup. The cloud settled to earth as the truck pulled to a skidding stop in front of the house. "I see two men standing beside the truck. They have guns." She lowered the binoculars just as she felt the blood draining from her face. "They're dressed in black."

Vincent squeezed her hand, sharing his strength. "I'm going in for a closer look."

"What? No." She snatched at the front of his sweater. "Shouldn't we be running the other way?"

He stayed calm as he hunched his shoulders to her level to look her in the eye. He stayed practical. He stayed Vincent. "There may be people inside. It might be Chilton's headquarters. It might be nothing."

"People?" Whitney swayed with memories of duct tape and taunts and a man's pleasure at inflicting pain. She squeezed her hand into a fist at his chest. "We have to help them if someone's inside. We have to warn them."

"*We* don't have to do anything." He unhooked her fist from the front of his sweater and pressed a tiny silver box into it. "I'll go up ahead and assess the situation. This a two-way radio. Shortwave. Too small to be detected by normal scanners. But you and I can keep in contact."

Whitney tried to match his composure. But her hand shook as he showed her how to pin the radio to her collar and hook a detached earpiece into her ear. "How does it work?"

"Just talk into it. It's voice activated. I'll hear every word you say."

"Will I hear you?"

"If it's safe to talk." He looked back over his shoulder. "One of them's at the door now. You watch through the binoculars and tell me anything you think's important. If I can't get to the house, I'll come back here and we'll leave. Understand?''

Whitney's gaze fluttered from the house up to Vincent's expressionless face. ''You said you had only three bullets.''

For an instant, a light warmed the cold black void of his eyes. ''I'll be back.''

''Promise?'' She remembered Carl Howard. She remembered Vincent's poignant story about his father's death. She shivered at the thought of a bullet silencing the heart that beat inside the big, warm chest that had cradled her so gently while she slept last night.

Vincent reached out and touched her cheek. The supple leather at his fingertips stroked her so tenderly she couldn't help leaning into the caress.

''Yes,'' he answered simply. No joke. No dramatic speech. Just a succinct promise she tried to believe.

And then he was gone. He slipped into the small trees and underbrush and disappeared before she could question the reassuring gesture. And before she could question her heart's aching reaction to it.

Chapter Six

Whitney breathed in deeply and set herself in position on the slight rise above the ranch. Vincent had paid her a higher compliment than any pretty words could have.

He'd asked for her help.

Feeling like an equal partner in this, at least, she didn't intend to disappoint him.

She reported everything she saw, from the men at the truck lighting their cigarettes, to the man in a blue suit who answered the door. The blue suit disappeared into the house and the man on the porch turned around. Whitney gasped. She'd suspected as much, but she'd hoped she was wrong. "The third man's Chilton."

"I recognize him from here." Vincent's voice sounded distant but clear from the tiny radio nestled inside her ear.

Whitney altered her scan and tried to find him somewhere on the grounds of the ranch. "There's at least one man inside. What should we do?"

"Watch the house, MacNair."

She glanced around at the soft-voiced rebuke. Was Vincent close by? Could he see her?

Could Chilton?

Alarmed by the possibility, and hoping that returning to her duty might help Vincent in some small way, Whitney lifted the binoculars and watched as the front door opened again.

Like a disgruntled neighbor who hadn't been invited to the block party, Chilton puffed up. He drew back the front of his coat and stood with his weapon clearly on display. She saw no mask of civility there, no pretense of culture.

Whitney's heart stuttered. Three terrorists, three bullets. Maybe helping the people inside wasn't such a good idea.

Of course, what kind of ruthless terrorist knocked on the front door and waited for someone inside to greet him? The hackles of suspicion she had started to develop over the past few months shot up.

A man stepped out onto the porch to greet Chilton and Whitney's stuttering heart stopped completely.

He was a big man with silver at the temples of his cocoa-brown hair, dressed to perfection in Montana chic— unscuffed brown boots, pressed jeans, a western-cut jacket of tan suede and a crisp white shirt. In the middle of his artificially tan face he wore a smile. A smile too white to be real, too easy to be trusted. A smile that never reached his sparkling blue eyes.

"It's Ross Weston," she reported to Vincent. "Senator Ross Weston."

He shook hands with a murdering terrorist as if the two were old friends. Friends who'd had a falling-out, judging by the heated exchange of words she could see but not hear.

"The guy running for president?"

How many senators from Montana were vying for that position? "Yes."

Vincent swore. "I'm at the back of the second building. I'll cut around and see—"

"No. He's not in trouble. They're arguing. They know each other."

Suddenly, the people inside the house didn't seem to be

in any trouble at all. Suddenly, she and Vincent seemed to be the only uninvited guests. Whitney crouched down, feeling exposed, though she knew she was well hidden. But Vincent was out there all alone. With three bullets. And a porch full of power and evil just a few feet away. "Vincent, come back." His name escaped on a whisper of terror.

"Easy, MacNair."

"I don't like this." The two men at the truck snapped their attention toward one of the metal buildings. They ground out their cigarettes beneath their boots and raised their guns. When they started walking, Whitney scanned the path ahead of them, praying she wouldn't see *her* scruffy man in black. "Vincent?"

Suddenly, she was back in that cabin on the mountain, taped and lying on that rotting mattress. Fighting the urge to beg or cry while Chilton and his friends pointed their guns at her. They laughed and promised to pull the trigger if she tried to escape again.

That same fear curled deep in her gut. It threatened to swell and consume her. But she fought against it. She pressed her lips together and nibbled on the inside. She breathed in deeply and pushed the fear to the shadowy recesses of her mind where she could pretend it didn't exist.

Daniel had once complimented her for remaining cool in a crisis. She could do no less when her own life might depend on it. Or Vincent's. She offered a quick update over the radio. "The thugs at the truck are moving toward the tan building farthest from the house."

"Good."

"Good?" A slice of panicked intuition threatened to undermine her attempt at control. "Please tell me you're not there."

The two men disappeared inside the building. She tried

to calculate the distance from her post to the barn. Could she run fast enough to get there in time to help Vincent? And once there, what could she do?

"Vincent?"

She heard a thunk. And a moan. Something falling.

"Vincent?" She stood straight up and pressed her hand to her mouth to stifle the urge to shout.

Silence.

"Vincent?"

Damn the man and his silence. She prayed this was good silence. Normal, annoying Romeo silence. Not dangerous, deadly, oh - my - God - now - I'm - all - alone - in - the - Montana - wilderness silence.

She swung the binoculars back to the front porch. Maybe, by some cruel twist of fate, she'd been dreaming.

No. They were still there. Still talking, though the discussion looked a bit more peaceful now. Not friendly, but businesslike. She hoped the fact they were still talking meant they hadn't been alerted to Vincent's presence.

She hoped.

They were the only two men visible now. Whitney rocked back and forth on her feet, feeling the need to pace, feeling the need to do something.

She'd give Vincent a minute. A minute to call in or show himself. "Dammit, Romeo, where are you?"

She reached up to her cap and pushed the black wool back far enough to thread her fingers into her hair and massage her scalp. Daniel had once told her that not knowing was the hardest part of waiting. The hardest part of sending a man out to do his job. He trusted his men, had faith in the skills of his team. But not knowing…

Whitney had stayed up late with him several nights when an agent was out on a mission. Popping popcorn in the kitchen, running needless tests on equipment down in the war room.

These few minutes were giving her an understanding of why her boss couldn't sleep well at night.

And an understanding of why he kept himself so busy, working either in the administrative office or with the horses out on the ranch.

Whitney returned to her post, trying to make sense of the connection between her kidnapper and her former boss.

Ross Weston.

Well connected in Washington, well loved in the heartland.

He'd won the support of agriculture and big business alike with his tough stance on foreign business. The hypocrite ran an antiterrorist campaign from his seat on the National Defense Committee.

America for Americans, he preached.

A catchy slogan suggested at a staff meeting over a year ago by one of his bright, up-and-coming former aides.

Whitney MacNair.

Heiress to a political dynasty in Massachusetts. An idealistic young woman who joined his staff because she wanted to make a difference in the world. She brought her family connections and fresh ideas to Weston's campaign.

The same bright young woman whose name had been scandalized across the country by an unauthorized picture leaked to the media. A simple thank-you kiss blown out of context. Her lips on his cheek, his hand on her bottom.

Rumors that blotted out the truth.

A bright young career ruined.

A randy old man cheered behind the scenes for still being able to "get it on" with a young beauty.

Whitney sank to her knees and tried not to retch at the implication of what she was watching on that front porch.

Negotiations for peace with the Black Order?

Not likely.

Whitney wasn't the only one betrayed by Ross Weston.

Her country had been betrayed as well.

"I knew I was in trouble when you called me by name."

The deep scratchy voice was right beside her, not in her ear.

"Damn you—" She jumped up and thumped Vincent on the shoulder. But punishment for sneaking up on her, for being gone so long, for frightening her, quickly became a needy grasp. The binoculars fell around her neck as she glided her hands across his chest and arms and down to his waist, checking for a wound. Checking for a bruise, a paper cut, any indication that he had been harmed by Chilton's men.

She framed his face in her frantic search, rubbed her palms against his beard, dabbled her fingertips beside his eyes. He caught her hands between his and pulled them down, holding them together, prayerlike, between them.

"I'm in one piece." He reassured her unspoken question with his quiet voice and dark-as-midnight eyes.

Trapped in the heat of his stare, she couldn't look away. If darkness had a fire, it was blazing there in the smoldering eclipse of his gaze.

"I thought something had happened to you. You didn't answer. I heard a sound. I thought there was a fight or you fell, or—"

The fire loomed closer as his mouth descended toward hers.

Whitney moistened her dry lips with the tip of her tongue. His gaze dropped to that same point and she felt a throbbing there. A shaking, a newly discovered need that only Vincent could assuage for her.

She closed her eyes as his lips touched hers, savoring the touch, the texture, the taste of him. She opened her mouth and welcomed him. His tongue rushed in and she met him halfway. He was safe. He was here. And for now, he was hers.

Touching only his hands and lips, she felt surrounded by him. Engulfed by his heat. Heartened by his strength. She leaned into him, wanting more, wanting this to be more than just gratitude or reassurance or shared relief.

All too soon, he pulled away, leaving her heart hammering in her chest and her lungs laboring for air. Her mind struggled to make sense of what was happening to her.

Vincent, however, seemed to suffer no ill side effects of that unexpected kiss. He bent down and retrieved his bag, zipped it tight and slung it over his shoulder. She had to know what he was thinking, if he was thinking anything at all when he kissed her.

"You were trying to shut me up, huh?"

"No."

The possibilities behind that single word triggered the tingling all over again. She pressed her lips together in an effort to control the sensation, and watched him walk away.

She was a healthy young woman, she reasoned. Maybe that was why she felt so drawn to him, because of his raw, enigmatic sex appeal. He'd rescued her time and again. She wouldn't be the first victim to fall for her savior. Spending nearly forty-eight hours alone with him on an untamed mountain was bound to lead to something.

And maybe there was nothing to that kiss at all. Maybe it was just a kiss.

One thing was certain. If Vincent Romeo held the answers to her questions, she'd never find out the truth.

He followed the stream back the way they had come, skidding down the embankment to obtain even more cover. Whitney hurried to catch up.

He pulled a cell phone from his pocket and held it up. "An independent line."

"Let me guess. The guy you borrowed it from won't be

needing it right now because he's passed out on the barn floor?''

"Something like that." He slipped the phone into her hand. "Call Daniel."

"Wait a minute." With the ability to get home literally within her grasp, she suddenly felt a surprising, nagging inclination to stay. She pointed her thumb over her shoulder toward Weston's ranch. "Shouldn't we do something?"

Vincent stopped. She translated the impatience behind his weary sigh and interrupted before he could give her the excuse she knew by heart. "I know, I know. *I'm* your first priority. But I'll feel pretty damn guilty if I'm home safe and they hurt or kill or corrupt someone else when I could have prevented it."

He dragged his gloved hand down his cheeks and jaw, trying to squeeze a little patience into his explanation. "We *are* doing something. We're going back to Montana Confidential and debriefing on what we discovered."

"And what, exactly, did we discover?"

Whitney tipped her chin to meet the black-eyed glare that had grown cold once more. "Chilton is a fugitive from the law. Not the kind of man a United States senator should be consorting with."

She didn't think it was terribly smart for Chilton to get involved with Weston, either.

"That's it? That's all we do?"

"Yes."

With her ever-vigilant giant casting his shadow over her, she bit back any further protest and punched in the number to the Lonesome Pony Ranch.

DANIEL AUSTIN FOLDED his arms across his chest and leaned back in the worn leather chair of his office. His relaxed slouch didn't fool any of the men in the room with him. He'd gotten little sleep in the past seventy-two hours. One of his own had been taken by the enemy. Put through hell.

And he'd been powerless to help her. His hands had been tied by the president himself. He'd had to put his faith in a man he didn't know. He'd had to count on Vincent Romeo to find Whitney. Keep her safe. Bring her home.

When she climbed out the back of Patrick McMurty's old station wagon, he'd swallowed her up in a hug, squeezed her tight. And he'd beat the snot out of anyone who repeated seeing a sheen of tears in his eyes.

Bruised and dirty, but chin held high, she'd been the one to tease him about caring. They were a family, she said. And Daniel believed her. An unlikely mix of men with a past, men with something to prove or something to hide—and a woman who wore her heart on her sleeve and her pain in her eyes.

Yeah, they were a family. *His* family. Not like Sheridan and Jessie, his ex-wife and his son, the family of his soul— the two people in the world who could make him whole again.

Whitney and the others—they were the family of his heart.

And Dimitri Chilton had made the mistake of messing with them. The president wasn't giving the orders this time.

Now the game was his.

"You think Senator Weston is Chilton's American contact?" He directed the question to Vincent, who sat across the desk from him.

With Whitney safely home, Daniel had grabbed a three-hour nap and taken the time to shave and clean up. He noted that Vincent had done the same. The big man looked surprisingly comfortable in the hot seat at the center of the room. Though he had no responsibility to the Department of Public Safety or the Confidential team, he had agreed to answer questions that would help them put Chilton and his band of terrorists on ice. More importantly, they could expose the Black Order's American contact—if it was, indeed, Ross Weston.

"It's a strong possibility. Circumstantial evidence more than anything. I couldn't do a thorough reconnaissance with MacNair there."

The big man had yet to call Whit by her first name. What was that all about? Romeo spoke of her the way an agent would refer to his partner. A bond of some sort had formed between them. Something only two people who had seen and survived hell together could understand.

Whit hadn't said much about the rescue. Romeo even less. Even if they gave him details, Daniel still wouldn't know all that had gone on between them. He mentally shook his head and moved on.

"Understood. You've given us a lot to think about. Gentlemen?" He opened up the floor to the others and settled in to watch his men work while he considered the big picture.

Whitney had been checked out by the doctor in Livingston. Then she'd gone upstairs to sleep and shower and fix her hair—or do whatever mysterious things a woman did to unwind.

Something was up with her, too. He couldn't put a finger on it, but if he was a gambler, he'd wager it had something to do with the man they were interviewing right now.

Romeo had earned Daniel's respect as a resourceful agent. But he still wasn't sure he should trust the man. Whitney had been too quiet this morning. And the tension between Romeo and Whitney had been as thick as Dale's sausage gravy.

What had happened to her up on Beartooth Mountain?

And what did Vincent Romeo have to do with it?

"What *did* you find out?" Frank Connolly leaned his hip on the edge of the desk and pulled Daniel's attention back to the discussion at hand.

"Three men, two women inside the house besides Weston. Two of the men were armed. State-issue Sig-Sauers—9mm. The second female had to be a maid or cook. She wore a uniform. Chilton and two men outside." For a man with little time, he'd been surprisingly thorough. "One of the outbuildings was locked. I didn't have time to get in. The second was a standard barn."

Frank glanced over his shoulder. "A presidential candidate would travel with bodyguards. That would explain the hardware inside."

Daniel shook his head. "This whole setup stinks. Why wouldn't *they* take out Chilton?"

Kyle Foster ran his fingers through his sandy brown hair and turned away from the bookshelf he hadn't really been studying, after all. "You don't think he's trying to bring in Chilton himself, do you? Come off as some sort of hero right before the election?"

"Blackmail?" Court Brody, standing straight and tall beside the open door, added his speculation. "A politician has to have dirty laundry somewhere. And Chilton still needs to get out of the country."

Vincent shook his head. "It looked like Weston was the one holding the cards to me."

Daniel stood and circled the desk. "A presidential candidate making a deal with the devil himself. Would he really risk it?"

"MacNair says he has the ego for it."

Daniel lowered his gaze to Vincent's. The man's unrevealing eyes would make him one hell of a poker player. He wondered how much of her association with the senator

Whit had revealed to him. He wondered if he knew the whole story himself yet.

The tension in the room tightened a notch. Each man had survived a run-in with the Black Order. Each man had been betrayed by someone on the inside—a fellow citizen. He couldn't blame a one of them for chomping at the opportunity to finish the job and take back a little of what had been stolen from them.

Vincent pushed himself to his feet, looking as if he, too, could feel the change in atmosphere. He struck Daniel as a smart man. A smart man should be on guard. "I can take you to the Weston place. But I've been ID'ed by at least one of the terrorists, so I can't go in."

"That's all right," said Daniel. "This isn't your beat."

"I want a piece of him, though. With his seat on the National Defense Committee, he has access to NSA reports. He has a redline to my superior. I was set up on this rescue. If Weston's the man—"

"We don't know that he's the contact."

Court moved in behind Vincent. "The FBI's information on state militia groups funnels through the defense committee. I'd pay good money to find out who leaked my name to the Sons and Daughters of Montana."

Kyle closed the circle. "The Black Order damn near killed my wife. If Weston's responsible for that—"

Frank made their opinion unanimous. "We suspected the governor was guilty, why not a man running for an even higher office?"

"Whoa." Daniel understood their need to take action. Their need to make someone pay for the bloody trail of heartache and death the Black Order left in its path. But it had to be the right man. "We're getting ahead of ourselves here. I need proof that this guy is Chilton's inside man. I don't want to go after Weston and find out he's just another pawn in this game."

Vincent shook his head. "There's only one way to find out what the connection between Weston and the Black Order is."

Daniel studied each man—each friend—standing in the circle. The look in their eyes was clear. "One of us needs to go in there."

A forced cough from the doorway interrupted them. Whitney stood there, hands perched on hips, the determined set of her features making her appear somehow older and wiser than her twenty-six years. With the full attention of every man in the room, she announced. "It should be me."

Chapter Seven

"You're not seriously considering this idea, are you?"

Daniel closed the door and waved Vincent's protest aside. "Let me hear her out."

Whitney clutched her arms around her and inhaled deeply, bracing herself for this unexpected kink in her proposition to Daniel.

One very big, very tense, very unsmiling Vincent Romeo.

Thankfully, Daniel had cleared the other agents from the room. She had a chance of arguing her case with him. He might actually listen to the logic of her idea.

The others would tease her, treat it as some kind of joke. They might mean well, but they could be as overprotective as her real big brothers. Whitney wanted to play the game with the big boys. Pretty little Whitney was great to flirt and pal around with, but she belonged safely tucked away at the compound where she couldn't get herself—or anyone else—into trouble.

Vincent was no different.

Except for the *brotherly* part.

With his fingers splayed at the waist of his jeans, and his brawny shoulders stretched to imposing proportions beneath his black ribbed knit shirt, he created an intimidating opponent. Apparently he still saw her as a hostage—to a lack of common sense.

"This isn't about you, Romeo." She tossed her hair back over her shoulders and tipped her chin up to meet his challenge. "It's a Montana Confidential matter, not NSA. You have no say in this."

He leaned in closer. "I am responsible for your safety until I hand you over to your father."

"Guard-dog time is over. I'm a big girl. I can take care of myself."

Daniel sat on the front edge of his desk, coolly refereeing the charged battle of wills. "He has a point, Whit. Your family wouldn't approve of what you're proposing. It's not in your original job description."

Whitney marched over to the desk. "My family connections are going to serve me well for a change. Weston would like nothing better than to have my father's endorsement for president. Dad's word could guarantee him the votes in New England. He's not going to turn away an opportunity to meet with me when an election's at stake."

"But you're not just popping in for a visit." Daniel had to play devil's advocate. "If Weston is associated with the Black Order, he'll know there are agents in the area looking for Chilton."

"That's the beauty of it." She offered him her coyest smile and spread her arms wide to showcase her freckled face and trim figure. "Do I look like a secret agent?"

Daniel's crooked mouth echoed her smile. "Government agent."

Whitney giggled at the correction, selling herself to the hilt. "Whatever. As far as anyone knows, I'm just an heiress who got in trouble back East, and now I'm communing with the horses in Montana. All you tough guys running around here flashing your guns and kickin' butt and saving the day—what do I know about any of that?"

Viselike fingers, steel sheathed in velvet, grabbed her wrist from behind and turned her, destroying the illusion she'd created. "You know enough to get yourself into major trouble." Vincent's grim warning matched the tight set of his jaw. "Spending a couple of days with me and working as Daniel's assistant doesn't mean you know how to work covert ops."

Whitney fisted her hand and tried to pull away, but his grip held tight. That left her best weapon for retaliation. Her mouth. "Don't feel guilty for not showing me the ropes, Romeo. I wasn't on a training mission with you."

His eyes flashed with some unspoken message. A warning. A plea. But she couldn't decipher it fast enough. His eyes blanked. He released her and stalked to the far corner of the room. She should be glad he'd given up the fight. But something inside her made her want to follow him across the room and ask—no, demand—what pains from his past made him shut down like that. What scars made it easier for him to retreat into silence than to share them?

But it wasn't her place to help him. And this wasn't the time to satisfy her curiosity.

Instead, she turned her argument back to Daniel. "When Chilton was holding me at his cabin, there were two phone calls. Obviously he called my father. He gave a rehearsed speech about American greed and corruption, and demanded money and safe passage out of the country in exchange for my release."

She'd spent a long night replaying what details she could remember from the call Chilton had received just prior to her first, ill-fated escape attempt. "I thought he was talking to someone else in the Black Order. But now I believe it was Ross Weston. He'd meet with him first— for a price—and give him the glory of returning me to my father. Think of the PR coup."

Daniel whistled between his teeth. "Negotiating with terrorists? That's quite an accusation. Can you prove it?"

"I'd like to try." She moved a step closer and looked deep into his warm brown eyes, wanting him to understand the painful truth she did. "I know I'm just a pawn in all this. A name. Ross Weston wants a connection to my family. He made that clear time and again when I was working for him. He wanted his trophy wife and political backing all in one package deal. There are only ten days until the election and he's six points behind in the polls. I can play right into his greed."

Daniel reached out and took her hands in his, studying them for a moment before meeting her expectant gaze with his best fatherly grin. "You've thought this all through, haven't you?"

She ignored the black eyes that were boring holes into her back from across the room. "I was on the computer this morning. I've already drawn up a strategy file."

"How would you get in to Weston's ranch?"

"I'd let Chilton kidnap me again." She hesitated a moment at the muffled curse behind her. "I'm still a prized commodity. I'm not sure what the trade is he wants to make with Weston, but I could uncover that, too." She turned her hands in Daniel's so that she could give him a reassuring squeeze. "Throughout all this, you guys are there to back me up. I go in, make nice with the senator, get the evidence we need to prove he's in collusion with the Black Order, then I'm out. You and your men come in and round up everyone, and our mission in Montana is done. Have I left anything out?"

Daniel stood and brushed a kiss across her cheek. "You're a different woman from the one I met in August. Or maybe you're just coming into your own. You've given me a lot to think about."

"I'm serious about this, Daniel."

''I know.'' He released her and headed for the door.

Vincent held it open, though the jut of his shoulder blocked Daniel's path. ''Whitney is no agent. She has no field experience.''

''I have Ross Weston experience.''

Though her eyes had locked on Vincent, Daniel was the one to break the combative silence between them. He smiled over his shoulder at her. ''I'll give you my decision tomorrow morning.''

With a supportive wink, he turned and exited into the hallway. Feeling drained by the whole confrontation, Whitney sank to the desktop. She hugged herself, rubbing her hands up and down her arms, trying to instill physical warmth into her emotional chill. When she heard the soft click, she assumed Vincent had followed Daniel out the door.

But no such luck.

A wall of black appeared in her line of vision an instant before Vincent's large hands replaced her own. With his awkward combination of roughness and gentleness, he kneaded his fingers up and down her arms, giving her his abundant warmth.

''You make me crazy, MacNair.'' His raspy baritone echoed off the books and pine paneling of Daniel's office.

Whitney wrapped her fingers around his wrists to stop the seductive massage. She suspected it might be a ploy to get her to drop her guard, and she didn't think she could resist succumbing to it. ''Good crazy or bad crazy?''

''I don't know yet.''

In a swift move that belied his size, Vincent switched places with her. He sat on the desk. He settled his hands at her waist and pulled her between his legs. His dark gaze melded with hers. He was putting himself at her level, she realized, making an effort to understand. ''Why is this so important to you?''

His heat seeped into her, making her body drowsy with contentment and charged with awareness all at the same time. She balanced her hands on his shoulders and stepped back to put some distance between them.

"What are you doing, Romeo?" She decided to call him on this sudden show of tenderness. "I thought you'd be chasing down Daniel and arguing your side of the case right now."

"I *am* arguing my side of the case." His hands tightened their grip and he pulled her closer, hip to thigh, denim to denim, heat to heat. The blood thickened in her veins as his hands slipped lower. His long fingers cupped her bottom and he lifted her against him. He nuzzled the corner of her mouth, and Whitney found her lips turning, seeking his.

Her pulse raced at the triumphant pleasure of his mouth claiming hers. The sheer size, the mystery, the magic of Vincent surrounded her and pulled her into a spell that robbed her of focus. He stole the need from her and made it his own. Her breasts flattened against the thundering beat of his heart as he held her close. His hands roamed her back, her sides, her bottom, making her feel curvy and feminine and hot to the touch.

He worked even more magic when his fingers slipped up into her hair and he tilted her head back to run his bewitching tongue along her jaw. She felt the heat of him press against her in the most intimate of ways, creating a throbbing ache at the very heart of her. She dug in her fingers and held on to the corded strength of his neck and rubbed against him, wanting the feverish spell to be complete.

"Whit—"

The moan in his throat drew the pad of her thumb and the fascination of her lips to the spot. The bitter tang of alcohol from his aftershave lotion gave way to the salty taste of skin and the earthy flavor of Vincent himself. She slid one hand up to cup the well-formed shape of his head, loving the masculine friction of crisp, short hair against her palm.

She was falling. Fast. Succumbing to the unique sorcery of a man who spoke volumes with his hands and his body and his kisses. A man who said more with a look or a touch than others did with a slew of pretty words. A man whose gruff charm touched her heart, whose loneliness touched her soul.

The conscious admission of those unexpected feelings pierced Whitney's clouded mind. "Vincent—" His name was little more than a ragged gasp for air. She needed to think. She needed to be stronger than temptation. Of the body.

Or the heart.

The hindrance of her thick turtleneck turned the path of his lips back to her face. He kissed the tip of her nose, her eyelids, the hollow of her cheek. He found the pulse beat of passion at her temple and smiled against it. "Is it such a bad thing that I want to keep you safe? It's a habit I picked up recently."

Tender words, spoken with such devotion. Which message did she listen to? The hum of the body that melded so perfectly with hers? The needy clasp of big hands that seemed to find enough curves on her slender frame to hold on to?

Or the words that dictated her actions? The no's that kept her locked away under the guise of protection. A pampered bird in a cage gilded with good intentions was still trapped inside a cage.

Whitney pushed at his shoulders, her mind needing an answer before her body completely betrayed her resolve. Those mysterious eyes, glistening like polished obsidian now, gave her no answers.

He lowered her to the floor, but his hands slipped beneath her sweater and maintained their possessive grasp at her waist. She blinked against the searing touch of skin on skin, and struggled to get the words past the knot of emotions tangled in her throat. "I don't understand you. One minute you're biting my head off, the next you're seducing me. Which is it, Romeo? Are you on my side or not?"

He'd put his body in front of a bullet for her, held her when she no longer had the strength to take care of herself, kissed her as if she was the only woman he'd ever wanted to kiss.

But he refused to let her into his dark, brooding world.

His chest rose and fell beneath her hands in a massive sigh. "You never answered my question. Why are you so set on doing this?" Though he held her as though her thoughts and ideas mattered, he steered the conversation away from himself, carefully avoiding the information she most wanted to hear.

Maybe if she bared a bit of her soul, he'd risk opening up as well. "It's a chance to prove myself. To show you and Daniel and my father I'm not just a flake with a big mouth. I want to be involved with life. I want to make a difference. Like you do."

He released her, his dark eyes shadowed and unreadable as he studied the woven Indian rug on the floor. Their talk must be over before it ever really got started. Feeling the absence of his touch like a winter chill, Whitney hid her disappointment on a shaky breath and backed away.

But before she was out of arm's reach, he caught her by the hand. At first he simply pressed his palm to hers and aligned their fingers, emphasizing how the length and breadth and strength of his hand outmatched her own. Then he slid his fingers between hers, twining them together, all the while studying the shape and scope of her hand like a rare work of art.

A warm liquid honey rushed to her fingertips and reheated traitorous parts of her body that forgot he hadn't yet agreed to her plan. She matched his grasp and willingly let him pull her back to his side.

"First." His low throaty voice was barely more than a whisper. "You are not a flake. You just do your thinking out loud."

It was more observation than teasing, and hope blossomed inside her.

"Second. I do my job, that's all."

"That's not—"

He cut short her protest with a stern glance and pulled her hand between both of his.

"Third." He slipped his fingers down her wrist, pulling back the sleeve of her turquoise sweater. The welts there had receded to pink stripes, but the bruises were rising to the surface, dotting her pale skin with blotches of blue, purple and deep dark red. "What did you prove with this?"

He touched his thumb to the right side of her jaw, and one by one he matched his fingertips to the bruises that ran down her right cheek. "Or these?"

She jerked her chin away from the crude reminder. "Damn you." Her red-haired temperament carried her to the far side of the room. "How dare you." She speared the fall of hair at her temple and raked it across the top of her head before turning on him. "I proved that I'm a fighter. I proved that I'm a survivor. Hell. If I can put up with you for two days, I can survive any terrorist attack or undercover mission."

He stood. "MacNair—"

This time she cut him off, hating herself for falling for his rough-edged charm, believing for a moment that he'd singled her out for some sort of special attention. She'd known it was a trap, but had played right into his old-fashioned, overprotective tenderness anyway. "Are you suggesting I need to lock myself up and never come out? Never do anything to laugh or live or help anyone?"

"Yes. That's what I think you should do."

"That's what *you* would do. Not me."

"Maybe I didn't say it right."

"You made yourself perfectly clear. You're judging me and everything I want to be by your experience." She zeroed in on his position at the desk, never taking her eyes from his stony expression. "Yes, you had some horrible stuff happen to you. Losing your fiancée. Your father's death. I am sorry for your pain. But now you're locked down tighter than that national security you've sworn to defend. And you want me to be the same way?"

She speared all ten fingers through her hair and scattered it into disarray. This had been a loaded conversation from the beginning. She thought that untapped sensitive streak inside him might make him different. But no, he'd prejudged her abilities just like everyone else.

"I know almost nothing about who you are. You don't share your feelings. You don't trust your heart. You touch and you take—you even give—but it doesn't mean anything to you. Maybe the only thing you really care about *is* this job."

Vincent's body shot to rigid attention, reacting to her words but not responding.

"I care about something more. Sure, life's knocked you down a couple of times. But guess what? Bad things happen to other people, too. I had my reputation destroyed, my career stolen from me. I've been abused, shot at, ridiculed. Daniel's divorced. Jewel's going through adolescence. I can go on."

The deadly calm in his expression shifted a bit. But he turned away before she could identify the message there. "Your point?"

Whitney gentled her voice, wondering too late if she had gone too far. "My point is this. There's a difference between you and the rest of us. The rest of us go on with our lives and make the best of it. You're stuck in..." She shook her head, helpless against his brooding silence. "I don't know where you are right now."

She reached out to him. Her hand hovered at his shoulder for an infinitesimal moment. Long enough for her to recognize the rigid set of proud self-defense in his posture and pull away.

"But I know I don't want to be stuck in there with you. I'm going after Weston if Daniel approves it."

She crossed to the door and paused for a moment in the open archway, waiting for a word from Vincent. She didn't expect an apology or words of support. She just wanted a goodbye. Something. Anything.

She got nothing.

A tad of that loneliness he seemed to know by heart reached out and snared her in its cold embrace.

"I don't need your permission or your blessing." She had to do this. For her country. For Montana Confidential. For herself. "So get over it."

GET OVER IT?

How did a man get over fire coming alive in his hands? How did a man get over a woman who spoke the truth and backed up her words with action? How did a man get over Whitney MacNair?

From the shadowed corner of the porch, he watched her kick up dirt and mutter a few unladylike phrases en route to the horse barn. No doubt he was the recipient of at least one of those curses. He deserved it. He couldn't be what she needed him to be. He couldn't say the things she wanted to hear.

All he could do was protect her.

Until he got word from her father that he was to do otherwise, he'd keep her safe and as out of trouble as a mortal man could keep Whitney MacNair.

Whether she liked it or not.

But who the hell was going to protect him from her?

Just like her long, willowy curves and eager kisses breathed life into his battered-up body, her candor was a breath of fresh air to his careworn soul.

Make the best of it, she'd challenged him. Losing his dad had changed his life, made him harder, older. Losing Melissa had been humiliating—a wake-up call that told him the love of his life wasn't really that, after all. He didn't know how to handle the pain, the shock, the confusion life threw his way, so he withdrew to a place where they couldn't hurt him.

But Whitney had met all that, and more, with a smile on her beautiful face and determination to move on to the next challenge life threw in her path. Corrupt politicians. Terrorists. Overprotective fathers. A government agent who didn't know whether to kiss her or throttle her for being so incredibly brave.

The only thing you really care about is this job. Not true. Melissa was wrong, and so was Whitney. He was wrong to forget all the good things, too. He had a loving family. A beautiful mom who had raised a brood of five children almost single-handedly. He was close to his brothers and sisters. There'd always been food on the table and someone around to care about him. And he wasn't always obsessed with the job. Though he studiously avoided any long-term relationships, he hadn't hurt for female companionship over the years.

He'd known women older, wiser, more suited to his personality than Whitney MacNair. But not one had gotten under his skin the way she did. Not one had made him angry and frightened one minute and feverish and alive the next.

Whitney didn't hold back. When she was excited, she hugged. When she was afraid, she fought back. When she was confused, she talked. When she was happy, she laughed.

And when she was in his arms, she turned him inside out with her loving touches and unabashed need.

Oh yeah, she made him crazy all right.

Crazy enough to actually consider letting her have this chance to prove her mettle as an agent. She had something hurting inside her, some pain that drove her to take foolish chances. And while he didn't like her going up against the combination of lethal terrorists and cunning politicians, he didn't like seeing her hurt, either.

"Son of a bitch."

Vincent caught himself the instant his guard lowered. Immersed in his thoughts, he'd lost track of Whitney. He jumped the stairs and headed for the barn after her.

Who the hell was he kidding? She couldn't go after Weston. Letting herself be kidnapped by Chilton when the bruises from her first encounter with the bastard hadn't yet faded was damn stupid. An unacceptable risk.

Yes. Logically, she was a good choice for such a mission. She had the prestige that would attract Weston and blind him to the deception. They shared a history. He couldn't remember all the details of what he'd seen in the paper about her alleged flirtation with the man. He didn't like to think about a man old enough to be her father putting his hands on her.

Vincent stuttered in his stride. He didn't like to think about any man putting his hands on her. He never paused to analyze the fist of jealousy squeezing around his heart as he ducked into the barn after her.

His thick black boots made no noise on the powdery

dirt floor. Though Whitney was no longer in his direct line of sight, he could hear her talking with Jewel and Patrick McMurty. Her energized voice played a familiar rhythm in his ears, distracting him from his confused thoughts. She was so full of life, so ready to laugh—and willing to put it all on the line because she didn't believe anyone took her seriously. "Damn fool woman."

And he was an even bigger fool.

Because he was drawn to her laughter, her energy, as helplessly and hopelessly as a moth drawn to a flame. She was a light in his world that had known darkness for too long.

He wouldn't risk her life. He couldn't allow her to be hurt.

He moved to a spot behind a stall that allowed him at least a partial glimpse of her. Welcome or not, it suddenly seemed imperative that he not let her out of his sight.

He'd make sure that Daniel said no to her plan. That she listened to her boss's final word.

And then—because he was getting to know the utterly unpredictable way Whitney's mind worked—he'd hang around a while longer and keep an eye on her.

Because he had no doubt that even if it was expressly forbidden, she'd try to go after Weston, anyway.

WHITNEY HUGGED her arm around Jewel's shoulders and stood beside her, watching Silver lying on his side in the hay of his stall. His breathing was an audible wheeze, as if a heavy weight was sitting on the old gray's chest.

It was never a good sign to see a horse go down like this, but Whitney saw it as a mixed blessing. Old Silver had lived thirty years, the last few in a great deal of pain from his arthritic hip. Most horses would have been put down after a run-in with a pickup truck. But not him. He was tough. And ornery.

And determined to succeed no matter what obstacles life threw in his path.

While she could relate to his struggle, she could also see the need for his suffering to end. She was sure Jewel wouldn't see it the same way, though.

She looked over Jewel's head to the gray-haired man standing on the opposite side. "Patrick?"

He held his white straw hat in both hands and twisted the brim. He met Whitney's gaze with a slight shake of his head, then looked down at Jewel.

The twelve-year-old shivered, despite the relative warmth inside the barn. But her words were brave. "It's okay, Grandpa. I know it's not good."

He feathered his fingers down the length of his grand-daughter's honey-blond ponytail. "Right now I'm trying to make him as comfortable as I can. But he's old, sweetie. He's nearing the end of his time."

Jewel withered into Whitney's side, acting more like a little girl than the grown-up she was trying so hard to be. "How much longer do you think he has?"

For a moment, there was a slump of age and heartache in Patrick's military-straight posture. "We'll be lucky if he makes it another day, maybe two."

Whitney squeezed Jewel tighter. Moisture burned her eyes and spilled over when she saw the tears already streaming down Jewel's cheeks. "I'm so sorry."

Patrick hugged Jewel from the other side. He reached across and patted Whitney's shoulder, offering her comfort, too. "I have some chores I can do out here. I'll keep watch over him."

Jewel tipped her chin up to her grandpa. "I'd like to stay, too."

As if the sound of the girl's voice triggered it, Silver shook suddenly and lifted his head. Whitney couldn't help smiling through her tears. "I think he'd like that a lot."

Jewel turned and buried her face in Whitney's chest, and Silver settled back down on the hay. Whitney snugged the girl up in her arms and rested her cheek on the crown of Jewel's hair, gladly absorbing the flood of her young friend's tears. She didn't try to offer any comforting words or false promises or mention anything about the hard truths in life. She simply held her, hugged her and cared.

Nearly an hour later, the thundering whop-whop of a helicopter landing on the chopper pad outside stirred her from their sad vigil. Whitney set down the brush she'd been using to groom Dragonheart, the bay Appaloosa she'd adopted as her own on the ranch, and wandered over to the door to investigate. From this angle she had a clear view of the landing area built on the next knoll, away from the house and barn. Daniel sat in the beat-up ranch truck at the pad, waiting for the all-clear to approach the helicopter.

Though the chopper was occasionally used for ranch work, visitors usually meant Montana Confidential business. But Daniel hadn't mentioned anything. He would have called her if he needed her to take notes or call up a file, wouldn't he?

Whitney rolled the kinks out of her neck and tried to ward off a growing sense of unease. Would Daniel think getting kidnapped put her on the disabled list? If he hadn't notified her of an important meeting—even an unimportant one—it could mean he didn't think she was ready to go back to work.

And that meant he wouldn't let her go after Weston.

Fired up by an odd combination of anger at being left out and resignation that she had to prove her worth all over again, she dashed back into the barn. She pulled a bridle over Dragonheart's head and led him out of the stall. In minutes she had him saddled. If no one would invite her to the party, she'd just invite herself.

Grabbing the reins, she stuffed her left foot into the stirrup and pushed up. But before she could swing her right leg over, a pair of hands cinched her at the waist and pulled her down.

"Where do you think you're going?"

Thrown off balance, she stumbled into Vincent's chest. She knew a brief sensation of rock-hard muscle and unyielding will before he set her on her feet and she wriggled away. "Take your hands off me."

She reached for the horse again. This time he wrapped his arm around her waist and carried her down the main aisle of the barn. "You can't leave." His raspy voice was barely a tickle in her ear. "Remember the last time you went horseback riding?"

When he plunked her down on the ground outside, she whirled around. "That's low, Romeo." She swung her arm wide, gesturing toward the helipad. "I just want to see who's here."

The crunch of gravel behind her should have alerted her to the truck's arrival at the house. But she had found a vent for her frustration. "You won't let me do anything else. Why don't you at least let me be the little hostess who greets everyone when they arrive at the ranch?"

Vincent's eyes narrowed, "I want you to be careful."

"Careful? Why don't you just lock me in my room? If you can't trust me to do anything right, you should—"

"Is there a problem?" She recognized the voice before she turned and saw the face. "Hey, kiddo."

Her tirade faded on a harrumph of air. A tall young man in a gray wool suit, with short auburn hair and features much like her own, stepped out of the truck. In a heartbeat, Whitney's frown became a whoop of joy.

"Brian!"

She ran to the truck and launched herself into her brother's arms. He lifted her off her feet and spun her around. She hugged him tight, drawing three months' worth of no family contact out of this one embrace. "God, I missed you."

"It's good to see you, Whit. You look great." She was breathless by the time he set her on the ground. She combed the hair off her forehead and stood still for his inspection. His crisp Ivy League facade slipped a little with concern as he got a good look at her face. And the bruises. "You *are* okay, right?"

"I'm fine. I even kicked a little terrorist butt along the way."

He grinned indulgently, shaking his head. "I remember when you used to hold your own against us, too." The youngest of her four older brothers, Brian had been her confidant and best friend growing up. "They ought to know better than to mess with Whitney MacNair, right?"

"Right."

A tower of black shifted into her peripheral vision, putting an abrupt end to their trip down memory lane. Whitney took a step back. "This is Vincent Romeo. He's the man who rescued me from Chilton. My brother, Brian MacNair."

Brian extended his hand. "We owe you and the NSA a debt of gratitude."

The two men shook hands, an odd meeting of East Coast refinement and Chicago street smarts.

There was no "You're welcome" from Vincent, no "Just doin' my job." Instead, he asked, "Where's Mr. MacNair?"

The stone-faced lawyer that her childhood cohort had become slipped into place. "Detained in Washington."

Whitney's mood crashed and burned.

Her parents weren't coming. Brian was just the messenger—sent to get a visual confirmation that their trouble-some daughter had returned to her hiding place without turning it into a media event. He probably didn't even have a suitcase or any intention of staying over.

The rush of disappointment was bitter as always. But since leaving Washington, she'd gotten enough practice putting on a brave face that she could actually summon a smile. "They're probably up to their ears with Gerry's campaign right now." She tried to explain their absence to Vincent—and rationalize it to herself.

She felt the barest brush of callused fingertips at the small of her back. Should she imagine Vincent's touch was a gesture of comfort? Or an eagerness to hand her over and be rid of her?

"My orders are to deliver her to her father and no one else."

"Correct." Brian turned to Whitney and offered a helpless shrug. At least the fink had the good grace to look apologetic. "We need you to lie low a while longer, kiddo. Dad's pulling in all his favors to find out who leaked the information about where you've been living these past few months. Until we uncover the mole, the NSA has agreed to provide round-the-clock protection for you."

He traded an all-business, man-to-man look with Vincent and pulled a sealed envelope from inside his jacket. "Since we don't know exactly who's involved yet, you're to provide that protection."

He handed the envelope to Vincent and she saw all thoughts of freedom and going after Ross Weston being handed over with it.

"Oh, no, no, no, no, no." Whitney backed up a step. Her gaze darted back and forth between the two men. One dark, one fair. Neither one willing to budge an inch. She pointed a menacing finger at Brian. She couldn't find the perfect word. She swung the finger at Vincent. Damn. She'd suddenly picked up his closemouthed curse.

Frustrated, but without the words to scream, she

clenched her hand into a fist and clutched it to her chest. Her protest finally rose on a painful moan from deep inside her and bit through the shrill articulation of anger.

"I didn't do anything wrong. Not with Weston. Not with Chilton. Not with anyone."

"We're just trying to protect you." She jerked her shoulder away from Brian's placating hand.

"It doesn't feel like it."

She spun her boot in the dirt and stamped into the barn to unsaddle Dragonheart and try to make sense of a world where her fate always seemed to be controlled by someone else. Controlled by a man with power over her. Familial power. Physical power. Or, in Vincent's case, the power to wake her body and touch her wounded soul.

Just once. Just one time, *she* wanted to be the one in control.

But with the ominous specter of Vincent Romeo watching her every move, it wouldn't be anytime soon.

Chapter Eight

"Montana's a huge place, Brian. You didn't even get to see all the ranch."

With her temper simmering on a back burner, and her hurt tucked away in its usual corner of her heart, Whitney had found the strength to play the grateful little sister for the few hours her brother had been able to stay.

While Frank Connolly ran the helicopter through its pre-flight check, she and Brian sat in the front of her red Explorer and talked all around the edict that lay between them. "I'll come back when I have more time," he said.

"After that first Tuesday in November?"

Brian laughed. But Whitney wasn't sure if she was joking or not. She'd grown up in the world of politics. She'd once wanted to spend her life being a part of it. But now she wasn't so sure.

With the same accuracy he had shown when they were kids, he picked up on her mood. "I know this is hard on you. But we can't afford any setbacks. The attorney general's race is close. Gerry has a lead, but it's a small one."

"Don't worry. I already sent in my absentee ballot."

"Your sarcasm hurts, Whit. We're trying to do what's best for the family. The whole family—you included." He reached for her hand on the console between them. She clung to the bit of tangible family support she had left.

"Did you honestly appreciate the press hounding your every move? Your life wasn't your own those first few days after the pictures hit the wire. Remember that photographer who cornered you on the train to Boston? How they camped out at our house in Martha's Vineyard? There were so many on the island ferry that some of the commuters couldn't get home."

"That was pretty lousy," she agreed. She'd just wanted to go home. Hide in her old room. Talk it out with her mom or Brian. But she never got the chance. With her oldest brother's campaign on the line, she garnered the wrong kind of press coverage. So her father called a friend at the Department of Public Safety in Washington, and arranged for her to "disappear" in the wide-open spaces of Montana.

Her father had always been able to get the job done right.

Brian's regret-filled sigh hung in the air. "Life on the frontier here may be slow—but it's safe." She rolled her eyes and the name Dimitri Chilton passed between them. "Sorry. It's safer than it is back East. You're out of the limelight here. And Agent Romeo has been assigned to guard you twenty-four hours a day. Think of him as your own Secret Service man."

Whitney glanced out the window, and saw Vincent standing at the helicopter, chatting with Frank in the cockpit. That explained why he'd hovered around her all through dinner and a quick tour of the ranch with Daniel. Why he'd followed her into the barn to check on Jewel and Silver.

She thought maybe the big guy cared on some level, that his constant surveillance stemmed from feelings more intimate than duty. At least she had hoped that was the explanation for her constant shadow. He'd seemed so hurt when she accused him of caring more about his job than people. She wanted to believe that he just couldn't find the words to express his feelings, even if all he admitted to was a healthy bit of male-animal lust.

Whitney rallied a smile to mask her disappointment. "Great. I always wanted my own Secret Service man."

The helicopter motor began to purr, then it picked up speed and turned into a howl. When the blades beat the air in a full-blown roar, Brian leaned over and kissed her forehead. "We'll find out who leaked your name to the Black Order. I promise."

Not ready for goodbyes and dismissal just yet, Whitney grabbed his arm and slid out the passenger door after him. She raised her voice to be heard over the chopper. "I kissed him on the cheek. I thanked him for a gift that I earned with my hard work, just like I would Dad or any of my brothers."

Brian frowned. He hugged her close and spoke into her ear. "But Ross Weston isn't Dad or one of us."

She'd found that out all too clearly. And way too late to do herself any good. "It was a setup, Brian. He doesn't deserve to be president."

He pulled back, latching onto her shoulders and looking down at her with a protective expression reserved only for big brothers defending their little sisters. "You're preaching to the choir, kiddo. We'll get him."

Her hair whipped into her eyes. She pulled it back and held it at her nape, squinting through the mini-tornado of dust and debris stirred up by the whirring helicopter blades. "Before the election?"

"Just sit tight. We're working on it."

Sit tight and wait for her father and big brothers to take care of her—just as they had her entire life. She loved them for their devotion, but one day they'd have to let her grow up and face the world with its joys and hazards all on her own.

Maybe one day sooner than they expected.

Feeling a sense of finality, a metamorphosis about to happen inside her, Whitney went up on her toes and hugged Brian around the neck. "Tell Mom and Dad I love them. And I miss them."

"Love ya, kiddo."

Whitney pulled away and nodded. They blew kisses once he was buckled inside the chopper. When the helicopter left the ground, she waved and waved until she had to shut her eyes and shield her face from the dust storm. When she could look to see him one more time, they'd already disappeared into the nighttime sky.

"You're disappointed in your family?" Vincent's soft-voiced rasp from the shadows behind her didn't startle her. She was getting used to having him around, even if it was only because he had to be.

She turned, crossing her arms over her stomach, warding off the feeling of abandonment as much as the late-October chill. "It's a fair trade. They're disappointed in me."

"I don't think so." Vincent emerged from the night and strolled up to her. When he reached out, she flinched, unsure that she could resist another spell of his earthy tenderness. His hand hovered in the air until she realized he had something less personal in mind. He pulled a leaf from her hair and cast it aside before burying his hands in the zippered pockets of his leather jacket. "I think they're just afraid."

"They're always worried about me getting into trouble."

"They're afraid you'll get hurt."

So what was *his* excuse for treating her like a recalcitrant child? She thrust her hands into the pockets of her pink suede jacket, mimicking his too-tough-to-care stance. "So. You're stuck baby-sitting me a while longer." She ignored the suspicious narrowing of his eyes and took a step toward him, then past him. She twirled around and backed down the hill, leaving the helipad, her Explorer and Vincent behind her. "Well, guess what? I feel like walking up to the house. So you'll have to walk with me. I'll ride down with Frank or Daniel and get my car in the morning."

She offered him a saccharine smile and a taunting glare. "If you'll let me."

She spun around and headed down the gravel road at a brisk pace.

"Your brother and I are not the bad guys here." She heard him fall into step behind her.

"Depends on your perspective, I guess."

"MacNair, you're being childish about this."

"Because I'm being treated like a child." She planted herself in the middle of the road and shook her fists. Twenty-six years of frustrated freedom shuddered through her body. "You're the biggest, broodiest baby-sitter I've ever had, but you're still my baby-sitter. Dad only hires the best."

His long stride took him past her without stopping. "You don't know what you're talking about."

The gall. Of all the self-righteous, egotistical… Whitney ran to catch him as he turned the corner and followed the road up to the ranch house. "I know exactly what I'm talking about."

Vincent took one step for every two of hers. And just like their climb across Beartooth Mountain, she refused to lag behind. "Our time is running out. In a matter of days, Weston may become President of the United States. If he's in league with terrorists, we can't allow that to happen. If he's responsible for anything that happened to Frank or Court or Kyle, I want him to pay. If he's a threat to you and me and everyone in this country, I have to stop him. More than anyone else, I have the means to do it. You

know it. Daniel knows it. If Weston's innocent, he needs
our help. If he's not, we have to stop him.''

He halted at the base of the back steps, not even breaking a sweat from the quick, hard hike. ''And if you die
trying, what does that prove?''

Whitney paused on the step above him, flushed from
anger and exertion. ''That I tried.''

Damn him and his patronizing, all-knowing taunts. Her
father was investigating a Washington connection to the
Black Order. And with the recent bustle of agents in the
war room, she had no doubt that Daniel and Montana Confidential were looking into Weston's innocence or guilt.

Why couldn't she contribute something, too?

Damn Vincent for not understanding. Damn everyone
for not understanding.

She marched on up the steps and into the house. Daniel
would be lodged in his office or the war room at this hour,
and the McMurtys were out in the barn with Jewel. So
Whitney stomped up the stairs to her room, intending to
punctuate her dramatic exit with a solid slam of her bedroom door.

Behind her, she heard an unexpected thump instead of
a satisfying click. She turned and saw the toe of a black
boot blocking the doorway. Whitney threw herself against
the door and pushed, but it was no use. Vincent was there,
an immovable force as always.

She let the door fly open and shoved at his chest. ''Get
out.''

But with humiliating ease, he seized her by the shoulders and half lifted, half pushed her inside the room. He
set her down and closed the door behind him, turning the
lock with an ominous click.

''I'm not letting you out of here.''

''Let—'' Her hands settled defiantly on her hips. ''Letting me?'' She stormed across the room, putting the four-

poster bed and a gulf of misspent feelings between them. She pulled off her jacket and threw it onto the bed, throwing down a gauntlet of challenge. "Who's the kidnapper now?"

"Dammit, Whitney—" Saying her full name was shock enough. But to see him throwing up his hands in surrender startled her into silence. Subdued, but wary, she flipped on the lamp beside the bed. The light illuminated him up to his waist, leaving his face in shadow. But his black eyes gleamed with a light of their own. "Try to see this from someone else's point of view."

"Whose?"

"Mine." She waited for the lecture about knowing her place and being smart enough to stay there. "I care. I care about—"

His words died. Not much of an argument. But enough to intrigue her. "About what?"

The silhouette of broad shoulders rose and fell with a deep breath. He unzipped his jacket and stepped into the light. But with black hair, unreadable eyes and that black stubble shading his jaw, he was still a dark outline against the creamy-white door. A mystery she couldn't define.

"You want to see my orders?" He reached inside his jacket and pulled out the white envelope Brian had given him at his arrival.

"I can't do that. They're top secret."

"Look at them." He tossed the envelope onto the bed. She hesitated a moment, expecting some kind of trap. The kind where she dived in, headfirst, without thinking, and got herself into trouble. So she thought about it. Then curiosity won out over caution and she picked them up. At least now she understood the breach in protocol. The orders with the presidential logo were still sealed.

But Brian said he'd been assigned to her.

Whitney clutched the envelope in her hand and searched

for an explanation. "I don't get it. If guarding me isn't your job, then what are you still doing here?"

Vincent saw the speculation crease her forehead into a frown, and knew he had her complete attention. He wasn't here because of some authoritative order. He was here because of her. He needed to be here. He needed to know she was safe. He needed to know she wouldn't put her life on the line for family or country or any other thing he could take care of for her.

And he needed her to understand that.

While he struggled for words to explain the unique bond he thought they shared, she moved to the corner of the bed and hugged the bedpost, waiting for him to go on. For a fiery-tempered redhead, she could be incredibly patient.

"I'm not leaving." He took off his jacket and hung it over the back of a chair to emphasize his point. Whitney hugged the bed a little tighter. Maybe it was the holster and gun hanging off his left shoulder. Maybe it was the uninvited man in her room that made her uncomfortable.

"You can't change my mind." He nodded. She'd certainly made it a challenging task. Logic hadn't worked to talk her out of this crazy idea about going after Weston. Sweet talk, such as he could manage, hadn't worked. He even doubted the locked door on her room would stop her.

That left convincing her her own way. He had to talk.

"I want to show you something." He reached inside his front right pocket and pulled out a worn brown leather wallet. He cradled it in his hand and traced the circle that had imprinted itself into the cover over the years. A calming sense of power radiated from the leather into his veins. He had to do this. He couldn't think of any other way to reach her.

He opened it slowly, taking care not to damage the fraying hinge. He pressed his thumb to the name engraved on the silvery shield inside. *Romeo*. "It's my father's badge."

"You carry it with you?"

"Whenever I can." On certain missions he left it in a safe-deposit box to keep from damaging or losing it. Otherwise, it was as much a part of him as his gun or his own badge.

Whitney inched her way closer, thoughts of independence and protest pushed aside for the moment as curiosity took over. "May I see it?"

His father had been a powerful influence on his life. When he put the badge into her hand, he prayed that his father was with him now. He needed some sort of inspiration to guide him through this.

"I'm trying to tell you about my dad. How it felt to lose him." He wrapped his hand around the opposite bedpost, self-conscious to see it gesturing in the air. "I don't want to feel like that ever again. It hurt so bad." He spread his hand flat against the front of his shirt. "The weight on my chest. I had headaches all the time. The counselor said I just needed to have a good cry. But I couldn't, you know. My brothers and sisters needed me. Mom needed me. I had to be there for them. I had to be the man."

"You never cried?"

He shook his head. "Had to grow up. Had to deal with it."

"How?"

He looked over to Whitney, anxious to know if he was making any sense. She held the badge reverently between her hands, listening without a word. But she was looking up at him in such a way that the soft glow from the lamp caught and reflected in her eyes. A sheen of moisture sparkled amongst the quicksilver there. Something inside him tightened, then did a crazy flip-flop that left him short of breath.

"I moved past it by trying to make sense of what he had done. Understanding the gift he gave that girl. He reunited her with her family. Saved his partner's life that day, too.''

Whitney blinked. Tears squeezed out and trickled down her cheeks. He felt those tears deep inside him. He felt the salt prick his own eyes, the pain well up from his soul. Those tears were his tears. The ones he had never shed.

"I was so proud of him. I *am* proud of him." He reached out and clasped the badge, swallowing both of Whitney's hands within his own for a moment before replacing the wallet in his pocket. "I carry it with me to remember what kind of man he was. To know what a good man should be. I'm trying to keep you safe. Like he would. I'm trying to be that man. For him."

"You don't want anyone else to hurt the way you did." His gaze locked on a crystal teardrop that clung to her auburn lashes. "Do you still hurt?"

She blinked, and that tear joined the others staining her sweet, translucent skin. Something inside him unclenched and freed itself.

For an instant in time he was too shaky to stand. But then Whitney walked up to him and wrapped her arms around his waist. He stood there mute. Amazed. The damp warmth of her tears soaked through his shirt and burned his skin. What had he done? How could just talking about…? How could a simple plan backfire so completely?

And then Weston and terrorists and presidential orders didn't matter. Finding a release of his own in her free-flowing tears, Vincent caught her up in his arms and hauled her in as close as a man and woman could be without being one.

She laughed. She argued. And now she cried as the mood possessed her. She was so open. So honest. So in tune with the humanity he had somehow lost along the way.

And because she could feel those things, he felt them,

too. He buried his nose in the crown of her clean, baby-sweet hair and rocked her from side to side. She wept for him and he held her close. He allowed a bit of her emotional courage to nudge open a dark corner of his soul. The light swept in and surrounded his heart. Vincent breathed easier as a huge burden lifted from his chest, carried away by Whitney's tears.

Some time later—moments, maybe minutes, maybe more—his strength spent, and her tears drying on her freckled cheeks, it was Whitney who spoke. "Thank you for sharing that with me. I know talking about personal stuff isn't easy. Talking isn't easy for you, period. It means a lot that you did."

He needed to say something, to thank her for the gift she had given him. He'd meant to use his father's example to persuade her not to put herself in danger. To see the pain losing someone could cause—even if the reasons for sacrifice were noble. But as always, Whitney turned the tables on him.

But Whitney seemed to understand his confusion. With her arms still forming a protective circle around him, she leaned back and offered him a beautiful tear-smudged smile. "I think he'd be very proud of the man you are."

Vincent slipped his hands up to frame her face. "Thank you."

And then, because he had no more words, he bent his head and kissed her. Her skin felt cool between his hands, her lips soft beneath his. It was a gentle kiss. A healing kiss.

With the tip of his tongue he found each dry tear along her cheeks and jaw and beside her eyes. He soothed each wound with his lips.

And as her cool alabaster skin heated beneath his touch, the kiss became something more.

He plunged his fingers into the silken fire of her hair

and guided her mouth back to his. She opened beneath him and welcomed him, inviting him in with the same incendiary passion with which he claimed her. Their tongues mated in an impetuous dance. Joining. Retreating. Tasting. Then gliding together once more.

A fuse ignited within him as her hands began to move. She drew circles on his back, pressing into him with palms and fingertips. She found a sensitive spot near the base of his spine. She came back to it time and again after the first shudder. She touched him through his shirt, then snuck beneath to tease the spot with her fingernails, sparking convulsions of shimmering heat that zapped straight to his groin.

"Whit—" He begged her to stop. Begged her not to stop.

She laughed seductively beneath his mouth, torturing him with thoughts of her hands all over him, skin to skin, touch to touch, fire to fire. Her hands slid down, cupped his buttocks and squeezed, drawing him closer to her feminine heat. Closer to her elusive spirit. Closer to her generous heart.

A defensive wall crumbled within him and he felt himself swell with need, with desire, with a thing much too complicated for him to name.

Instead of analyzing the new emotions kindled by her adventurous hands, he mimicked her moves, skimming the sleek curve of her hips and clasping a handful of her sweet little butt. With something like a growly laugh himself, he picked her up and leaned back, throwing her off balance.

"Vincent!" Her squeal of delight became his as she snaked her arms around his neck and held on for the short ride to the edge of the bed. He set her on her knees facing him, letting her tower over him for a change. At this particular level, with her hands braced on his shoulders and

her hair falling down around his face, he was afforded a
most exquisite view.

"Say it again," he breathed, before catching the tip of
one small breast in his mouth. Beneath a layer of silk and
a whisper of lace, the feverish peak beaded against the
stroke of his tongue. Her instant response stoked the flame
already burning inside him. "Say my name."

Her fists butted against his shoulders, then raked in
handfuls of his shirt. "Vin—" He suckled at the delicious
curve, loving the hiss of breath in his ear. "Vin—"

So this was the way to silence her. He smiled at her
struggle and turned to explore the other breast. Her long,
supple fingers clutched the back of his head and held him
there, demanding the same attention he was more than
happy to deliver.

She pressed kisses to his forehead, nuzzled and nipped
around the shell of his ear. While his fingers worked the
buttons of her blouse, her hands slipped beneath the neckline of his shirt, pushing it aside to brand his skin. She
moaned in frustration as the material caught in the band
of his holster. He moaned along with her and shrugged his
shoulders, encouraging her to rip the damn cloth if that's
what it took to have her hands on him. Her fingers
kneaded, but the leather refused to budge.

Then all at once, she pushed herself away. Vincent
sucked in an almost painful rush of air. He was a man on
fire, and the means to cool the throbbing heat had suddenly
been denied him. But like a lifeline to conscious thought,
he anchored his hands at the curve of her waist, not yet
willing to surrender his hold on her entirely.

The lack of oxygen in the sweltering room seemed to
affect Whitney, too. She raked her fingers into her hair and
dashed it back behind her head into wanton disarray. God,
she was a wild, wonderful beauty. Sexy, yet innocent.
Young, yet instinctively wise to the touches and tastes that

could make a man ache until he forgot everything but the thought of making her his.

Vincent pulled himself back from that brink and watched her passion-drowsy eyes come into focus. Her tongue darted out to lick her kiss-swollen lips, and his body pulsed in rhythm to the unconscious movement.

But it was the downcast turn in her quicksilver gaze that cooled the inferno still raging in his veins. Her sure fingers were now working the cotton of his shirt, tucking it beneath his holster, straightening it around his neck, smoothing the puckers against his chest.

"Vincent—"

He captured her hands between his and stilled their nervous tidying up. "What?"

"This isn't just..." For a woman who had just heated his blood into molten fire, her fingers were like ice. Her gaze dropped to their hands as he began to rub them and give back some of her warmth. "This isn't just some really crazy way to keep me in line, is it?"

And then her eyes met his. That same caution he'd seen when her brother said that her parents weren't coming to see her after her kidnapping haunted her eyes. That bracing for disappointment clouded her gaze and triggered his considerable protective instincts. "Are you on duty right now?" she asked. "Or are you here because this is where you want to be?"

Only Whitney MacNair would stop the most passionate chemistry lesson of his life to have a conversation. But she needed to talk. She needed to understand. She needed to believe that she was the reason he was here.

He needed her to believe it, too.

Apparently the sealed orders hadn't been enough to convince her that he'd stayed in Montana by choice. That he couldn't quite trust himself to let her loose on the world without him. Whitney had given him a gift earlier. Making peace with his father's death had been a long time coming. It had taken her openness and generosity to lead him toward that light.

He could do no less for her.

Vincent released her entirely and walked to the door, needing the distance between them to think clearly and say what needed to be said. When he turned around, she had sunk onto the bed, sitting with her legs curled under her. She'd crossed her arms beneath her breasts. Her blouse gaped open. The white silk of her bra had become a translucent sheath beneath his wet mouth, hinting at the coral tips inside.

The fever inside took hold of him again. But he was made of stronger stuff. "You are so beautiful." Words seemed weak. He needed to show her how he felt. Linking his gaze to hers, he unstrapped his gun and laid the holster on her desk. He pulled his badge from his pocket and set it beside his father's. "I'm off the clock as of right now. I'm here because I want to be here. With you. Whitney."

He waited.

The shadows in her eyes gradually lightened from doubt to hope. But he didn't blink, didn't move until she lifted her arms and reached out to him.

"Well." Her tenuous smile became a temptress's invitation. "Seeing how you have the night off..."

With a precision of movement, Vincent peeled off his shirt and gathered her into his arms. Their lips touched and the conflagration reignited between them.

Soon, the fire blazed out of control. In a flurry of grasping hands and flashpoint kisses they tumbled, skin to skin, onto the bed. The delicate mounds of her breasts seared his chest. Her hair fanned across the pillow, a visual flame that drew his hands and his lips to its irresistible fire.

No words were spoken, no promises made.

But when Vincent buried himself inside her, he crossed

a line. Her legs wrapped around his hips, her fingertips wicked down his spine, and drove him straight to the edge. Her consuming heat detonated around him and there was no turning back. She bathed him in fire and he finally, willingly, surrendered his control. He caught his name in her mouth and demanded her kiss as he found his own release.

Whitney's light blazed through him, surrounded him, became a part of him. She brought sunlight to the shadowy recesses of his soul, and cracked open the lonely confines of his heart.

Afterward, his body replete with the gifts of her body and spirit, Vincent crawled beneath the covers and tucked Whitney close to his side. Using his shoulder as her pillow, his beautiful fireball of energy promptly fell asleep.

Those same tender feelings that had snuck around his defenses in the cabin up on Beartooth Mountain kicked in. He lifted a handful of her red-gold hair to his nose and inhaled the sweet female scent of her. How could one skinny bit of a woman turn his life so completely inside out in just a few short days?

As he, too, drifted off toward sleep, he thought of his father's brave sacrifice. He thought of Melissa Stamos and her claim that the dangerous world of an agent and a personal life would never mix. He thought of Dimitri Chilton and his thugs manhandling Whitney, stripping her of her dignity and hunting her down like prey when she dared to escape. He thought of Ross Weston, a man of power and mystery whose presence in Montana raised suspicion amongst every man on this ranch.

He thought of Whitney, willing to die for a misguided need to prove her worth to the world.

Vincent pressed a kiss to the crown of her hair and wondered if he had just made the biggest tactical error of his life.

"WHAT ARE YOU DOING?"

Sleep made Vincent's voice crackle at a deliciously low pitch.

Whitney grinned with the secretive smile of a woman well loved and scrolled the cursor to the next page on her tiny computer screen. "Shopping."

She sat at the desk with her legs tucked up to her chest and her laptop resting on her knees. Whitney huddled with plenty of room to spare inside Vincent's discarded shirt.

The only light in the room came from the screen itself. But it glowed brightly enough to illuminate the ripples and hollows of Vincent's warm olive skin as he sat up in bed. The sheet and blankets pooled around his hips, exposing the broad expanse of crisp black hair that spread across his chest and curled in a narrow trail down to his... Well, she had discovered firsthand where that path led.

She combed her fingers into her hair and let it fall across her cheek, hiding a blush of remembered passion.

"It's three in the morning."

"That's the beauty of Internet shopping. Whenever I get the urge, I can indulge myself."

"How often do you get the urge at 3:00 a.m.?"

Whenever she couldn't sleep. Whenever nightmares plagued her. Whenever she couldn't resolve her mind to what her heart told her to do.

"I'm shopping for you, in a way." She needed to talk, needed to focus on a silly, mindless project like this. She didn't want to think anymore about the horrible guilt that had awakened her in the protective circle of his arms. "I'm trying to decide whether you're more the satin camisole kind of guy, or if you'd prefer the sheer-peignoir set."

"I don't think either one is me."

She giggled at his dry humor and scrolled to the next page. "It's for me, Romeo. Of course, there's a baby-doll set. Ooh. Here's a sweet little teddy. One hundred percent cotton.''

"I like you naked."

Whitney jumped in her skin at the deep, rich voice right next to her ear. She'd been so intent on ignoring his slumberous charm that she hadn't heard him climb out of bed.

And now he stood right beside her, a magnificent sculpture of classic male proportions. A living, breathing work of art.

Helpless to do more than stare at the controlled precision of his movements, she made no protest when he closed the laptop and set it on the desk. He scooped her up from the chair and carried her back to the bed.

He made good on his word and stripped his shirt off her. When he lay down beside her, Whitney felt the faint stirring of guilt edge its way in between them. She flattened her hands against his chest. "Romeo—"

"Vincent," he insisted, peppering her nose and cheeks with featherlike kisses. "When it's serious, call me Vincent."

"This kind of serious?"

Whitney dug her fingers into his shoulders and pushed. Together they rolled over. She landed on top, straddling him in the most intimate of ways. His hands settled at her waist, binding them together. She felt his power beneath her. His brawny strength. His illusory control. His beautiful onyx eyes gazed up into hers, patiently waiting for her to speak.

But now, when it counted most, she didn't know what to say.

So she took a cue from the pro himself. Maybe she didn't need words to express everything she was feeling. A tremulous fear shuddered inside her. And then she listened to her heart.

She leaned over him, letting her hair fall forward. The

curls teased his nipples. His lips compressed as he struggled to lie still, and Whitney smiled. In this, at least, he would let her follow her own will.

He was a chained beast, docile beneath her for now. From her superior position, she trailed her hair along every part of his body, generating a teasing friction that soon had him squirming beneath her. She followed the same trail with her hands, feeling the quiver in his flanks as she stroked down his sides.

The beast was gathering strength beneath her hands, responsive, yet restrained each time she touched him. A muscle jerked here. His fingers clenched there. She heard her name on a low, guttural growl in his throat. A raspy caress that hummed along her sensitized nerves.

As Vincent stirred, she grew bold. She leaned over farther and traced the same pattern with her tongue and her lips, tasting the salt on his skin and inhaling his musky scent. His hands squeezed her hips and anchored her tight as he rose against her.

Whitney squeezed her eyes shut and rode the broiling heat that pooled at her very core. Her breath came in stuttered gasps as she strove to regain equilibrium. Somehow, in the midst of her seduction, she had become the seduced. The wild animal had freed his spirit and now she was the one to be tamed.

Vincent's hands were on her breasts, her buttocks. He wove his fingers into her hair and pulled her mouth down to his. He rolled her beneath him and entered her swiftly, his mouth claiming hers in a fierce kiss.

"Vincent—"

She breathed his name as he swept her into his hands, his mouth, his unleashed need. He drove into her once, twice, again. She sailed to the stars and then drifted slowly, sweetly back into his strong, sheltering arms.

With her body still humming with the aftershocks of

loving him, Whitney curled against his chest and pretended to doze.

Sleep couldn't claim her. The same thoughts that had haunted her dreams earlier refused to subside.

Vincent had given her this night to feel special, this night to feel loved. She hoped she had given him the same gift in return.

Because there would be no more nights after this one.

When the threat of Dimitri Chilton and the Black Order had ended, when Ross Weston had been proved to be a traitor or a patriot, he'd have no reason to stay and protect her. He'd return to Chicago, to his fatherless Italian family that meant so much to him, to an important job that didn't involve baby-sitting an impetuous, headstrong heiress who drove him crazy.

Whitney squirmed at the notion of being cast aside again. Thinking she stirred in her sleep, Vincent feathered his fingers into her hair and gently massaged the nape of her neck. She melted into him, imprinting his unpolished brand of tenderness in her memories to last for all time.

Come morning, there'd be no tenderness.

In just a few hours she'd have to betray the fragile trust that had blossomed between them.

Only now, she wasn't just afraid of putting her life in danger.

She'd be risking her heart, too.

Chapter Nine

How did one go about getting kidnapped, anyway?

Whitney's morning wasn't going according to plan. Last night she'd left her Explorer at the helipad, away from the house and barn, and managed to drive away from the ranch without being followed. She'd stopped at the Old Firehouse Gym to shower and change into jeans and an olive wool blazer.

But now what?

She took a sip of her diet cola and looked at the antique Regulator clock hanging behind the counter of the soda fountain where she'd stopped for a drink. Nearly 10:00 a.m. Her time was running out.

She hadn't thought much beyond how she could get away from the ranch undetected. She'd made record time driving up Highway 89 into Livingston, even calculated the location of the highway patrol so she could slow down without being ticketed. She didn't need the authorities running a check on her. Daniel had the means to track down such a report in the war room. He'd pinpoint her location in an instant, and then she imagined a fleet of cars, maybe even a couple of helicopters, swarming after her.

Because she had no doubt Vincent, with Daniel and the other Montana Confidential agents in tow, would be coming for her like a herd of riled-up big brothers out to stop a forbidden date with destiny.

She had to find Dimitri Chilton before they found her.

Her short life as a secret agent would be over before it ever got started. "Looked good in the trench coat, but couldn't get the job done."

"Excuse me?" The teenage girl working on the other side of the polished pine counter interrupted her thoughts with a polite smile.

Whitney needed to stand out in a crowd not get lost in one.

"What's the deal with all the tents and trailers outside?" As usual, nervous impatience prompted her to talk.

She picked up her cup and climbed off her stool. The Robin's Nest soda fountain was part of a souvenir shop inside a restored train station. One end of the station was now a formal restaurant. The main concourse had been turned into a museum. Whitney had chosen to hang out at the gift shop because its two entrances allowed her to be seen by both the traffic on Main Street and the tourists wandering in and out of the museum.

Not that anyone seemed to be looking for her at the moment.

The girl followed her over to a display of signs made of old barn wood. "With the political rally for Senator Weston at the high school, there's lots of folks driving into town. Every vendor with something to sell has set up shop, hoping to cash in on the extra customers. We opened early this morning ourselves."

A long strip of land between the railroad tracks and the street served as both park and parking lot. This morning it was bustling like a carnival. "When is Senator Weston supposed to show up?"

"Not until tomorrow night. At the high-school auditorium. It's the only place in town big enough to hold everyone. Our band will play. The choir will be there.''

''You play in the band?''

The girl nodded. ''Clarinet. If you want to come, though, you need to have a ticket.''

''Don't worry. I'll have an invitation.'' One way or another, she'd find a way to check out Weston.

She pretended an interest in the amusing and philosophical sayings carved into the signs, and the girl moved on to help another customer who'd just walked in. His black coat clicked all Whitney's senses into alert. She slipped around to the back of the display to get a look at the man. Too tall to be Chilton. Too skinny to be Vincent. She breathed out a sigh mixed with relief and frustration.

This was getting her nowhere.

Trading goodbyes with the teenager, she stepped outside to try her luck in the open-air market.

She strolled past the funnel cake stand and stopped to watch a cooking demonstration at the next tent. She hovered at the back of the crowd, raised her hand and asked a question—making herself seen and heard.

Nothing.

She tossed her soda into a trash receptacle and made a few purchases. Some homemade fudge to send to her mother. A set of handwoven place mats she didn't need. At every stop she chatted with anyone who was willing to have a conversation. All the while she kept scanning the crowd, looking for men dressed in black clothes.

After a half hour without success, she sat on one of the park benches and pulled out a piece of fudge to sample, herself. Surely one of Chilton's men would be out looking for food and supplies, or scouting for the next easy target to bargain with. Someone was bound to notice her out on her own—away from the Lonesome Pony and her big, brooding bodyguard.

Thinking of Vincent made the sweet chocolate in her mouth taste bitter. He would never forgive her for sneaking out in the dark before dawn.

She'd half hoped he'd wake up and snatch her back into his arms, growl one of his decisive no's and keep her in her place. But days without proper sleep, and a night full of physical exertion had left him snoring softly on her pillow.

Sprawled across her bed, naked to the waist with his legs tangled in the sheet and his dark head cradled against the wrinkled pillowcase, he seemed vulnerable to the cruel realities of the world he conquered by day. She'd curled her hands into fists, resisting the urge to cover him up, to climb back in beside him and shield him with her body.

The tough guy had opened up to her last night—shown her that he was much more than a crackerjack agent or a skilled lover.

He had a heart.

He didn't quite know what to do with it yet, but he had a heart. His feelings for his father had been difficult to express. But for her sake—because he thought it would make her stay—he'd struggled with those words and emotions he hated so, and showed her that he cared.

Whether that caring stemmed from his sense of duty or the craving they shared for each other, she couldn't say. She still had much to learn about Vincent Romeo and his secrets.

But now she'd never have the chance to learn them.

He'd been hurt by one woman already. She doubted he could forgive another for abandoning him.

Having lost her appetite entirely, Whitney wadded the fudge back inside its paper and stuffed it into her bag.

Waiting didn't sit well with her. She rose to her feet and searched the park for an inspiration. She would not botch this self-assigned mission. Now that she'd added

Vincent to the list of important people she'd disappointed, she couldn't afford to fail.

She couldn't just drive up to Weston's ranch. According to the locals, he wasn't due to arrive in Livingston until tomorrow. If she walked up to his front door, he'd be suspicious of how she knew he was already in Montana. Chilton had to be the way she got to him.

And then the inspiration hit in the form of an eager young man who handed her a brochure.

The campaign tent. Volunteers handing out Vote for Weston stickers and discussing pamphlets filled with the senator's plans to "Take back America for Americans."

Of course. Why hadn't she thought of that before?

A frisson of anticipation shivered along Whitney's spine. She took a deep, steadying breath and hurried over to the booth. Someone there would recognize her name, if not her face, and report back to their chief. If Weston knew she was here, *he* would put Chilton on her tail.

"I knew I recognized you. You're the lady in the photographs." The same young man who had given her the campaign brochure circled her and sat on the edge of the folding table beneath the tent. His awestruck rendition of spotting a celebrity captured the attention of the two women sitting behind the table. "Are you still a Weston supporter?"

Whitney laughed and lied through her teeth. "Of course I am. That was all a misunderstanding. I worked for the senator because I believe in what he stands for. I still do."

"Do you think it's smart for the senator's mistress to be seen at his campaign stops?" Though asked without the leering undertones of the reporters she'd encountered in Washington, the question made her cringe.

"I'm not..." No. She had a role to play now. She couldn't afford the luxury of defending herself. "I just happened to be in Livingston today. I thought I'd stop by and see how preparations were going for the rally tomorrow.''

''Big doin's,'' the young man promised. As he launched into a blow-by-blow account of the senator's arrival by train and parade to the high school through town, Whitney tuned him out. Instead, she focused on how the two women at the table stared at her, questioning her, condemning her.

Whitney stood tall and smiled beneath that scrutiny, until a new awareness assailed her.

She was being watched.

A ripple of unease cascaded down her spine. The two ladies continued to cast glances her way while the young man prattled on.

But this was something different. Someone different.

Adding a few un-huhs from time to time to keep the man talking, Whitney scanned the area, moving just her eyes. Had Chilton spotted her? Or was this crawling sense of dread a reaction to being identified as the fallen woman who had set Washington on its ear a few months earlier?

''...and then, of course, he'll move on to the capitol in Helena, where he's scheduled to give another speech. It's his last tour of the home state before Election Day.''

A palpable danger hummed in Whitney's ears, tuning out the rest of the campaign spiel. She turned her head now, openly searching the faces in the crowd, looking for a man in black whose conscienceless eyes promised suffering and death.

She spotted a familiar face. The humming became a deafening roar as the blood pounded in her veins. At the far end of the park, a sun-weathered, sandy-haired man stepped out of the gift shop where she'd bought her soda less than an hour ago.

Daniel Austin.

That unruffled air of cool authority was evident even at this distance. He slipped his tan Stetson onto his head, tipped it to the two ladies that walked past him, then lifted his head with a subtle nod. Whitney turned and followed the direction of his gaze across the busy street.

Court Brody.

Whitney didn't wait to see if anyone else from the ranch had come to town. They were all here somewhere. Looking for her. Saving her from her own foolishness.

She spun completely around. They hadn't spotted her yet. She breathed in through her nose and out through her mouth, calming herself, weighing her options, making a plan.

"Miss MacNair?"

She tapped the young man on the arm, calming his concern. "If you'll excuse me, I have to go."

"Take some brochures."

She grabbed the handful he gave her and fanned one open. Burying her face behind it, she walked back toward the benches, away from Daniel. The speed of her pace created a breeze that lifted her hair and blew it around her shoulders.

"Damn." The brochures flew from her hands as she grabbed for her hair. Subtle. "Double damn."

She remembered Vincent's insistence on her wearing that itchy black cap on the mountain. Her hair was like a red flag to a bull, he'd explained. She had to hide it if she didn't want to be noticed.

Right now she didn't want to be noticed.

Beating down the urge to run, Whitney ducked into the next tent. Indian blankets. Throw rugs.

Scarves.

She pointed to a three-foot square of lightweight, mustard-colored wool. "This is lovely. How much?"

She paid the inflated price and wrapped the scarf around her head, tying it tight beneath her chin and pulling it around her face to mask the style and color of her hair.

Hunching her shoulders, she zipped from tent to tent, making her way toward her Explorer and the sunglasses she kept in the console between the two front seats. She couldn't drive away with Daniel and Court so near, but she might be able to sneak inside for the glasses to complete her disguise.

Whitney rounded the last tent and froze.

Vincent.

He paced back and forth beside her car like a caged animal. Tall and dark.

And angry.

She could see the heat of the emotion shimmering in his eyes. He surveyed the parking lot as he paced. His fingers splayed at his hips, revealing the bulge of his gun beneath his leather jacket. So much strength. So much power. So much control.

What would he do if she showed herself right now? Greet her with that stoic disinterest of the man she'd first met? Or swallow her up in his arms and celebrate her safe return?

Vincent stopped pacing. Whitney held her breath.

Like the feral animal he was, he tilted his nose into the air and sniffed. Thirty yards separated them. Did he sense her presence? Did he know he was being watched?

His shoulders rose and fell, and Whitney sighed along with him. Then, in the flash of an eye, he pounded her window with the side of his fist.

Whitney jumped in her boots, feeling the jolt all the way to her heart.

She backed up a step, hugging the flap of the tent. Hiding herself and her shame and regret from his view.

"What have I done?"

Whitney collapsed in on herself, hugging herself, unable to stanch the guilt that reared its head and clutched her in its painful jaws. She backed away another step.

She smelled the spicy sweat an instant before she felt the jab in the back of her ribs.

"Good to see you again, Miss MacNair." The false guise of civility in Dimitri Chilton's accented voice couldn't mask the threat behind the gun in her back.

Was this what success felt like? This heart-stopping chill that stunted her breathing and made her stomach clench to keep from crying out loud?

"What do you want?" she asked on a croaky whisper.

"Come with me." He slipped his hand around her waist beneath her jacket, pulling her against him in a crude mockery of an embrace. "Do not make a scene, or some of these very nice people might get hurt."

This was what she wanted, right? This was what she had to do. Her gaze strayed back to Vincent, silently crying out for help, silently warning him away.

Dimitri's lips brushed against her ear. "Including your friend there. He has already cost me three men." He pressed the gun into her back, hard enough to bruise the skin. "It would be my pleasure to get rid of him."

Whitney turned her head, trying to look over her shoulder. He wouldn't kill Vincent in broad daylight, would he? Not with all these people around?

Turning was a mistake. It allowed him to see the fear in her eyes.

Chilton laughed the devil's laugh, right into her ear. "Walk with me. Like we haven't a care. My associate is parked in the street."

Powerless against the gun at her back and the threat to Vincent's life, Whitney let him guide her across the marketplace. Vendors and patrons she had chatted with earlier paid no heed to her as they strolled past, step in step, like an army marching to its doom.

She focused on breathing. She focused on staying sane.

She focused on why she had wanted Chilton to find her in the first place.

In a matter of minutes, he had her stuffed in the back seat of a nondescript blue Ford. Whitney slid to the far corner as he climbed in beside her. He tapped the back of the front seat and gave a command in a language she couldn't understand. The driver nodded and pulled into the flow of traffic. At the next intersection he stopped and a third man climbed into the passenger seat. After a few more turns, they pulled onto the highway and headed out of town.

Whitney huddled in her corner, clutching her bag of souvenirs in front of her and reciting the reasons over and over in her mind why she thought becoming a hostage again was a good idea.

"What, no vile words of protest, Miss MacNair? No kicks to the face?"

Whitney responded to his taunts with a disjointed observation. "You're not wearing black."

Chilton's eyes narrowed, as if she had actually surprised him with that one. "Excuse me?"

Other than the lethal-looking black steel handgun that rested on his lap, he looked like any other citizen of a small Montana town in his jeans, denim jacket and black felt hat. It staggered her comprehension to see how easily these cold-blooded killers could blend in with the American landscape.

It was then that Whitney realized she was in way over her head. She didn't have to feign fear and ignorance this time. "You know my father won't pay a ransom. What do you want with me?"

Chilton leaned toward her. With the coldest excuse for a smile she'd ever seen, he lifted his gun and touched the tip of the barrel to her temple. Like a loving stroke straight from hell, he drew the gun along her cheekbone to the corner of her mouth. "Not a damn thing."

Whitney squeezed her eyes shut to block out the hideous caress. But Chilton enjoyed his game far too much for her to escape so easily. He put the cold steel right beneath her chin and forced her head back. Whitney snapped her eyes open, obeying his command to pay attention. "But someone else is willing to pay a very high price for you."

"I'M GOING WITH YOU, and that's final."

"You screwed up, buddy." Frank Connolly's accusation resonated deep in Vincent's bones. He returned his attention to the ten-inch army knife he was strapping to his leg. "She was on your watch, and now she's gone."

Vincent stood off to one side of the command center located in a secret room beneath the Lonesome Pony's ranch house, and watched Frank, Court Brody and Kyle Foster gear up for an unsanctioned mission into the Absaroka-Beartooth Mountains. They had an impressive storehouse of weapons to choose from. Swiss double-action Sig-Sauer pistols. Uzi submachine guns with twenty-and twenty-five-round magazines. Smith & Wesson .38's. Not to mention the two grades of plastique explosive Kyle stuffed into his backpack.

"You're taking all that?" Vincent questioned. Other than refilling his ammo supply, he'd packed nothing besides the contents of his nylon duffel bag.

He had nightmare visions of all that firepower playing out. They might bag Chilton and his men, but what about Whitney? He kept having flashes of her lying on the floor, bleeding.

Just like his dad.

Pale and helpless and bleeding to death.

Because it was the right thing to do. Because she had

to prove something to herself and to these men, and maybe even to him.

"There has to be a better way."

Court Brody, once an outsider to the group himself, pointed out a more logical argument. "Your orders say to take out Chilton by whatever means necessary. I've seen what the man can do. Believe me, this is necessary."

Vincent's new orders from the president had been simple and to the point. But he didn't give a crap about them right now.

His first priority was the same as Montana Confidential's.

Bring Whitney home.

He'd known she was gone the moment the sunlight hit his face and woke him that morning. The bed was cold. Her scent had faded on the sheets and on him.

And in the hollowed-out dent of the pillow beside him where she had slept, she'd set his father's badge.

The message she'd left him had been excruciatingly clear.

Bait.

Despite the tears she'd cried, despite the passion they'd shared, despite the way he'd dropped his guard and shared part of his past with her—she'd left him.

Alone and cold, she'd left him.

She'd set herself up as bait to draw out Ross Weston's connection to the Black Order.

To prove to the world what kind of hero she could be.

A combination of unwanted emotions twisted deep in his gut. Was he angry with her for using him like that? Was he angry with himself for thinking he could trust her?

Or was it just stone-cold fear that he wouldn't find her in time that nestled around the unfamiliar ache in his heart?

Unused to dealing with the emotions Whitney stirred inside him, Vincent shut them down entirely. He buried them in that neat, orderly place inside him where feelings didn't matter. He dug a deep hole and hid them away where they couldn't get in his way. He had a job to do. And, by damn, if he had to take on every man in this room to get that job done, he would.

"MacNair's my responsibility." He braced his feet in a defensive stance, preparing to do battle against impossible odds to have his way. "You need me. Or do you want to give Chilton more time with her while you track down Weston's hideaway?"

Daniel, who'd quietly sat in front of a computer monitor while the rest of them argued their point, finally stood and joined the divisive clash of titans.

"Look. She's already in. We can't change that." He picked up a stack of printouts and tossed a set of papers to each man. "We hope that she's okay, and play it like she was one of us."

"She *is* one of us," Frank insisted.

Daniel spared him a glance and held up the papers in his hand. "Montana Confidential was formed to uncover and destroy the Black Order, to eliminate the threat of terrorism on American soil. Whitney's the only one who seems to remember that."

The coiled tension in the room subsided a notch as each man retreated into himself.

"I read her plan. Brief yourselves on it. It's solid. She's our inside man on this assignment now. We don't jeopardize that by bickering among ourselves. Now let's get out there and give her some backup."

The others assembled the last of their gear as if Daniel's dictate was the final word on the matter.

"That means you, too, Romeo."

Vincent nodded. He slipped his bag onto his shoulder and prayed to God that Whitney could fool Chilton and Weston as completely as she'd fooled him.

LONG BEFORE they turned off the main highway, Chilton had forced Whitney to lie down on the back seat. Using her own scarf as a hood, he covered her face. He bound her wrists together with something hard and leathery. A belt, perhaps.

Blindfolded in such a way, she breathed in her own stale air. The hood was hot and suffocating. She knew the moment they turned onto the gravel road that wound up into the mountains. However, the driver had never learned the wisdom of driving slowly on gravel. Whitney felt each bump, jolt and curve in her head and stomach. Her sense of balance went haywire. Her head pounded, and throwing up that bit of fudge she'd eaten earlier seemed like a very real possibility.

But she didn't dare sit up to steady herself, didn't dare complain. Chilton's gun seemed to always be stroking her shoulder or hair, keeping her in her place.

When the car finally lurched to a stop, Whitney tried to steady her spinning head. She had to get a grasp on her location, had to prepare herself for playing along with this undercover game she'd volunteered for, wherever it might have taken her.

She could be anywhere, she realized. Back at Chilton's cabin. In the middle of nowhere beside a ditch that would become her final resting place. She prayed that when she opened her eyes, this would all look familiar.

Wraparound porch. Stone house. Metal outbuildings.

She prayed she had figured this out right. Maybe her instincts were off. Maybe she'd put the pieces together wrong. Maybe Chilton wasn't taking her to Ross Weston, after all.

When she screwed up, she did it big time. And when she was a success... Oh hell. When was the last time she'd gotten anything right on her own?

She heard the distinctive click, slip, smack of weapons

being checked and loaded. She'd learned to recognize the action by sound, after spending time with Vincent. It was a cold sound, a deadly sound. Maybe more frightening than the gunshot itself, because of the ominous import of what it promised. Two car doors slammed in front of her, and Whitney knew the driver and the guard in the front seat had gotten out. To stand watch or to assassinate her, she couldn't tell.

Oh God, oh God, oh God. How could Vincent live in a world like this? How did a man survive this kind of torturous uncertainty day in and day out?

There's a time to run, a time to fight and a time to shut up.

Whitney added a time to think to Vincent's list of crime-fighting advice.

The weight on the seat beside her shifted and the door opened. She welcomed the rush of crisp mountain air that swept over her body, cooling the gagging heat and clearing her mind of the paralyzing panic.

She had to gather her wits. She had to…

"Get out, Miss MacNair."

…think faster.

Sitting up was a dizzying task in itself. But when Chilton dug his talons into her upper arm and dragged her across the seat, she lost all sense of up and down in her crazy, off-kilter world. She would have landed on her knees in the gravel, but Chilton jerked her upright, wrenching her shoulder. Whitney cried out as she fell against him.

In the next heartbeat she felt his breath on her skin through the scarf. "Shut up."

The dirty little whisper pressed against her ear and she obeyed.

He released her for an instant and she sucked in half a breath of cool air. But before she exhaled, he snatched her by the leather strap at her wrists and tugged. She grit her teeth against the cut of the band in her tender skin and followed, stumbling over her own feet on the gravel, led like a sacrifice to the slaughter.

She managed to stay on her feet long enough to feel the change in terrain beneath them. Now she was on something hard and flat, a sidewalk or paving stones. Did Weston's ranch have a path leading up to the broad porch? She couldn't remember.

When Chilton stopped, so did she. She squeezed her eyes shut, cocked her ear, fine-tuned her senses and tried to determine what was going on around her before she fell victim to it.

She jumped at the unexpected pounding of fists on wood.

Moments later she heard the slip of a dead bolt and the turn of a doorknob.

"Yes?" The clipped question held no trace of an accent.

She didn't dare cross her fingers for Chilton to see, but in her heart she prayed.

"I wish to see him." Chilton's condescending order was easy to identify.

The silence that followed lasted a lifetime.

The next voice she heard was Chilton's. "I have a delivery for you."

"What have you done to her?"

Whitney bit the inside of her lip to keep her breath from whooshing out in a noisy celebration of success.

Ross Weston.

She knew that charm-filled, resonant, patronizing voice by heart.

"She is more trouble than she is worth. I hope you know that."

In a face-off of evil versus evil, neither Chilton nor Weston wanted to back off. "I know all I need to."

"It is time to complete our bargain."

Weston's impatient sigh was audible to her own ears. "Untie her first."

With all the callous care she expected from him, Chilton loosened the wrist strap and pulled it off. She wiggled her fingers as circulation returned to her cold, numb hands, and prepared herself for the performance of a lifetime— the unveiling of Whitney MacNair, grateful little rich girl.

She squeezed her eyes shut against the glare of the clear afternoon sunlight as Chilton pulled the hood from her face and let it hang around her neck.

Whitney blinked her eyes open and looked straight into Dimitri Chilton's cultured sneer. She staggered back a step with a gasp of fear. She breathed in a reviving lungful of crisp autumn air to clear her head and play her part.

She turned and saw the terrorists on the porch, weapons hanging loosely in the crook of their elbows. She looked toward the door and saw four Secret Service types in dull blue suits flanking the tall, stately man in the open doorway.

Then she lifted her gaze to the man who represented everything that had gone wrong in her world.

She squeezed out a few tears, just for effect, then ran up the stairs and threw herself into his arms.

"Ross!"

Senator Weston folded his arms around her and pulled her close. There was something more territorial than comforting in the kiss he pressed to the top of her hair.

"You're safe now, Whitney. I'll keep you safe."

While she snuggled against his barrel chest, he lifted his head and barked orders to the men in suits beside him. "Take their weapons. Pay them what we discussed and hand over their travel papers. Then get rid of them."

Whitney pushed some space between her and Weston's suede vest. She tipped her head back and offered up an innocent smile. "*You* negotiated my freedom? How? Why?"

His white teeth gleamed down at her with the promise of future explanations.

But the smile stopped when he gave one more order. "Escort them over the border yourselves. I don't want to see their like in my country again."

Chapter Ten

The next hour played out like a skewed scene from an Agatha Christie parlor mystery.

Clinging tight to Weston's arm, Whitney followed him into his study at the head of an entourage that included two professional bodyguards who answered to Jordan and Buck, a reserved Native American woman in a maid's outfit, and Ross's campaign manager, Warren Burke.

The room itself was massive, the size of a small apartment. Behind folding walnut doors lay a room straight out of one of Ernest Hemingway's safari stories. It was an eclectic mix of heavy wood furniture covered in animal-hide prints and leather. Row upon row of bookshelves and cubbies had been built into the side walls and filled with impressive gold-foil editions of books that looked as if they'd never been read. A stone hearth and fireplace filled the wall opposite the door. And hunting trophies of various sizes, from all parts of the world, had been stuffed and mounted on the walls or set out on display.

It was a room filled with power and wealth and secrets.

Weston pushed open the doors with grand ceremony and ushered everyone inside. Standing in the middle of the room was a fiftyish woman wearing an impeccable Chanel houndstooth wool suit with strands upon strands of gold chains hanging around her neck.

If she was startled by the sudden influx of guests, she didn't show it. Whitney hardly recognized her when she turned and looked at the senator. The woman gave everyone else a disinterested glance, but lingered a moment at Warren Burke's expressionless face.

A deep sigh lifted her shoulders before she stepped forward to greet everyone.

Weston pulled Whitney along with him to the center of the room. "You remember my wife, Margery."

"Mrs. Weston."

Whitney smiled and shook hands with the superficially beautiful woman. Her perfect nails and perfect upsweep of too-blond hair played well on television. But in person there was something brittle and forced about her welcoming grace.

"I can't believe you brought her here." The shock and hurt on Margery's face was diluted by the vodka she held in her left hand. But she smiled anyway and asked, "How is your mother, Whitney?"

"Busy with Gerry's campaign in Massachusetts."

Her heart went out to the sad, used-up woman. Apparently Whitney hadn't been the only victim of Weston's lust for power.

Everyone who wasn't carrying a visible weapon sat at Ross's request. The two guards stationed themselves inside the door. Ensconced on a leather sofa, Whitney sat on something that felt suspiciously like real leopard skin and kept an eye on the moose that watched her from above the stone fireplace while drinks were served.

She was dying to ask just what kind of arrangement he had made with Dimitri Chilton. What kind of payment had the terrorist agreed to? What was the going rate for her life these days?

Was this the only way the Black Order could get out of the country?

Somehow, she doubted it. There had been too many of them. One died. Another took his place. They had a stronghold or a pipeline somewhere. They didn't need Ross Weston's influence to get out of the country.

So what *did* they need from the senator?

And what had he asked for in return?

Her?

Common sense as well as modesty told her that she alone wasn't worth the price of the innocent lives that had been lost or destroyed along the way.

Frank Connolly's plane had been sabotaged. He and his wife, C.J., had been stranded in the mountains with a hit man from the Black Order on their heels. Court Brody had infiltrated a local militia to expose the Black Order's influence on the group. His identity had been revealed and he was nearly killed. Kyle Foster had dealt with a bomb threat at the capitol and nearly lost his own life to a lethal virus the terrorists created to poison Helena's water supply.

Carl Howard had died trying to save her. Jewel, an innocent child, had been attacked.

And for what? For what?

This was clearly Ross Weston's room, a blend of cultured wealth and violence.

Not unlike Dimitri Chilton.

Did the two men have more in common than their personalities?

The answers were here in this room. Some instinct, deeper than female intuition, stronger than logic, told her the answers to all her questions were here. Inside the big teakwood desk. On his computer. Hidden behind one of the cabinet doors.

Here was where she'd find the evidence to implicate Ross Weston.

Now how did she go about finding it?

"Whitney?" She blinked her eyes into focus and realized she'd been staring at Weston. With one foot up on the hearth, he rested his elbow on his knee and stoked the fire burning there. "You all right? We were just talking about our next step."

Play the game, MacNair, she reminded herself. *Play the game.*

She cleared her throat and stood. "The next step should be calling my father and telling him I'm all right."

Margery saluted her husband with her empty glass. "Yes, Ross. Why don't you call Gerald, Sr. and tell him his little girl is safe with us."

Weston straightened, ignoring his wife's embarrassing sarcasm. "I want to wait until my men have taken care of the problem. There's no sense raising Gerald's hopes until we know for certain the Black Order is no longer a threat. I want his gratitude, not his wrath breathing down my neck."

Right now Whitney wanted nothing more than to call her father and share her suspicions about Weston. Though she'd been hurt that he'd sent Brian to check on her instead of coming himself, he could earn a huge number of brownie points by destroying Weston's career for her.

Satisfying as the prospect might be, that was personal, vengeful thinking. She had a job to do, a part to play.

"So are we hostages here?" she asked.

Even Margery perked up at that question. Warren brought over the crystal decanter of vodka and refilled her empty glass, soothing Margery's flare of concern. "That's an unfair question, Miss MacNair."

Warren Burke's pointy nose reminded Whitney of a weasel. He was attractive, she supposed, in a plastic-toy-doll kind of way. Tanned features. Blue eyes. Hair that went through a weekly trim and was coated with enough hair spray to withstand a winter blizzard.

He definitely spoke the party line. "The senator is doing what's right, not only for you but for the country."

Whitney held her tongue. Didn't anybody give a straight answer in this house? She turned back to Weston. "So are we hostages or not?"

"Absolutely not." He moved toward Whitney and cupped his hands beneath her elbows, holding her in a friendly embrace. "Think of this as a safe house. We're well guarded, well stocked, secluded. It's a perfect place to wait until Chilton's men have been disposed of."

"What does that mean? 'Disposed of?'"

He tapped his finger on the end of her nose and Whitney nearly gagged. "You're worrying your head with details that don't concern you. I've taken care of everything."

"Dimitri Chilton concerns me." She decided to push his buttons, see if she could force some useful information out of him. Whitney stepped back and held out her wrists, exposing the bruises and scrapes Chilton had inflicted on her. There was no way to reveal the internal wounds he had scarred her with. There was no way a man like Ross Weston could ever understand that kind of hurt. "I want the FBI or the state police or somebody to arrest him. Put him on trial. Make him pay for his crimes."

"He will pay." Ross gathered her hands in his. The move reminded her of Vincent, the way he always protected her. Listened. The way he tried to understand even when he had no clue. Her skin crawled at this mockery of a good man's brand of comfort. "You know my stand on foreigners in the U.S. They live by the same rules we do, or they go home. And if they dare to bring their politics into my country, then I will deal with them."

Whitney snatched her hands away. "You're talking about stump speeches. Winning votes. You're too casual about all this. Dimitri Chilton has killed people."

"Trust me. I stopped him."

She'd rather trust a rattlesnake. Damn his callous ego. She wanted answers. "You can't just stop a terrorist by paying him off and shipping him out of the country."

"I'm a powerful man." He dismissed her concern by walking away. He sat behind his oversize desk and pushed a button on an intercom panel. "One day soon you'll realize that."

Whitney followed him to the desk. "What's to keep them from coming back?"

"I'll explain it when you're ready."

"I'm ready now."

Ross smiled that bright false grin of his. "I've always liked your spirit. But later. You're tired now." Right on cue, the maid appeared in the doorway. "Alysia. Take Miss MacNair up to the green guest room. Show her where to freshen up."

"Yes sir."

"Rest for now, then join us for dinner."

"But—"

"Later, Whitney. I promise."

He traded some secret with her that she didn't understand. But he wouldn't let her question it. He'd already called Warren over to evaluate something he'd pulled up on the computer.

Whitney nodded an excuse to Margery and followed Alysia's long black braid up the grand staircase to her room.

So much for her first foray into gathering intelligence. Frustrated as she might be, she hadn't completely lost hope. She'd heard Daniel say that a mission wasn't always accomplished in one strike. At least she'd gotten herself behind enemy lines where she could do some good. She'd play along with the senator's egomaniacal hero plan for now. Later, she'd find a way to get into his study alone and dig up the proof she needed to connect him in a premeditated plan with the terrorists.

She only needed to do two things. Find out what Weston had done with Dimitri Chilton. Then find out what had brought the two together in the first place.

Getting out of this mess with her head still attached to her neck didn't sound like a bad idea, either.

WHITNEY DISCOVERED two things after she finished her shower and started to dress.

There was no phone in the plush guest room where she was staying.

And Ross Weston still remembered her dress size.

According to Alysia, her own clothes had been taken to the laundry room, leaving no option but to slip into the clingy off-white sweater dress. Matching hose and shoes had been provided as well.

"This is sick." She surveyed her appearance in the adjoining bathroom's full-length mirror. Whitney felt like a package, wrapped up and put on display in a department-store window. The dress fit her beautifully, hugging the curves she had and skimming past her more angular features. The color set off her hair and complemented her fair skin. The two-and-a-half inch heels on the strappy pumps had probably been chosen to show off her long legs.

"What a sick man."

A year ago, four months ago, even, she would have accepted Ross Weston's gifts. She'd worked her butt off for the man, putting in long hours, racking her brain, calling in family favors. She'd earned the bonuses. Just as any other employee earned compensation for a job well done.

But the senator hadn't meant to reward her for her hard work. He wanted to buy her favor. He wanted to woo her. He wanted to dress her up like his own little plaything and put his hands on her in any sneaky way he could.

A shudder crept through her and Whitney snatched at the sleeves, pulling the material away from her skin. "Idiot."

She'd been stupid and trusting and naive.

But no amount of tugging and straightening and redressing could erase the feeling of being bought and sold from her skin.

No wonder her father, her brothers, Daniel and Vincent were so overly protective. With her impulsive judgment, she was a menace to herself.

But no more.

She had gotten herself into this mess—no, she had dived headlong into this mess. This time, she would get herself out.

She'd still play the part Weston wanted her to. His golden girl with the young, firm body and connections to one of the most influential men in American politics. But now, at least, she understood the game.

Whitney eyed the clock beside the bed. Dinner was at six. She had a good twenty minutes before she had to make an appearance.

The house was huge, bigger inside, it seemed, than outside. To her knowledge, the four men who'd taken Chilton and his thugs away hadn't yet returned. That left Weston, Margery, Burke, the maid and two bodyguards to avoid. Whitney had slipped in and out of parties with bigger guest lists before. Avoiding those six should be a piece of cake.

She removed her shoes and carried them with her down the stairs so as not to make noise on the wooden runners. On the first floor, she heard Warren Burke talking on the phone in a small office that had been assigned to him. She'd expected the household to be bustling about for dinner, but no one else seemed to be on the premises. Even the doors to Weston's study stood slightly ajar. The room was dark, except for the flickering shadows given off by the dying fire. She listened outside for a moment. Nothing.

Loving her luck, Whitney checked the hallway, saw it was clear, then quickly slipped in between the folding doors. In the moment it took for her eyes to adjust to the dimmer light, she realized she wasn't alone.

Alysia stood behind the senator's desk. She quickly closed a drawer when she heard the door move.

"Alysia?"

The maid's stoic eyes revealed nothing except the glow of embers in the fireplace. "May I help you, Miss MacNair?"

Was it proper agent etiquette to ask someone why they were snooping in a drawer when she had come there to do the same thing?

Whitney wasn't ready to trust anyone. Her instincts told her to cover her appearance. The same old excuse seemed to be a good one. "I was looking for the senator. I was curious to know if he'd contacted my father yet. I'd really like to place that call."

Alysia nodded. "I'll tell him you're looking for him. If you'd like to wait here, I'll rebuild the fire."

"That's all right." Maybe she could buy herself some time alone, after all. "I'll just turn on a few lamps."

"Very well." With a polite nod, Alysia glided from the room.

Seizing the moment, Whitney dropped her shoes on one of the couches and hurried around the desk. She tried the drawer that Alysia had been in, but the thing wouldn't budge.

"Locked." So how had the maid gotten into it?

A quick check through the other drawers revealed nothing that would put the nation's welfare in jeopardy. Stationery. A bottle of aspirin. Writing utensils. A hodgepodge of mementos from the University of Montana at Bozeman.

Keeping an eye on her time, Whitney grabbed the letter opener from the top of the desk and pried it into the keyhole of the locked drawer. "Dammit, Vincent, how would you do this?"

Thoughts of her big, brooding rescuer inspired her to keep trying. Just as quickly, thoughts of her betrayal rushed in, zapping her will to continue.

How one man could keep leaping into her thoughts time and again, she didn't know. She only knew she missed his gruff presence, always around somewhere, annoying her, protecting her, loving her.

Loving her?

Whitney sank into Weston's oversize chair and analyzed what her heart was trying to tell her.

Vincent Romeo couldn't possibly love a flaky handful of trouble like her. He could make love. Oh yeah, he could do that real well. But he probably didn't understand the emotion any better than she did. She only knew that she wanted...that she wished...

A drawl of hushed laughter outside the door cut short Whitney's brief detour into hopeless speculation.

"Oh my God," she breathed.

A time to run, a time to fight, a time to shut up.

"Definitely time to shut up and hide." She slapped her fingers over her mouth and ducked beneath the desk, desperately wishing her nervous words wouldn't get ahead of her brain.

She poked her leg with the letter opener she still clutched in her fist. Nothing should be out of place. She climbed out, dropped the letter opener back into the pencil holder on top of the desk, and... *Yikes!*

Halfway across the room, standing out in mismatched glory against black-and-tan leopard spots were her shoes.

Whitney reached out helplessly, but it was too late. The door slid open and she slipped beneath the desk and held her breath.

The woman's laughter entered the room first. "Warren, that's hardly an appropriate thing to say."

Margery.

There was the click of the door, the shuffle of footsteps, then Warren Burke answered on a laughing whisper. "You like it when I say inappropriate things."

Whitney flattened her back against the inside wall of the desk. Did kissing make a sound? The few beats of silence were punctuated by Margery's slurred laugh. "I don't know how I'd survive this godforsaken wilderness without you. If Ross wins this election—"

"He'll win," Warren promised.

"That's what I'm afraid of." The sudden sadness in Margery's voice touched Whitney's conscience and filled her with pity. "If he wins, there'll be no divorce. And I don't know how much longer I can keep living this lie."

"I'll always be here, Margery." Whitney heard that kissing sound again. A sigh, perhaps. Maybe a hum of pleasure. Then Warren broke it off. "I have to go. We'll walk in separately for dinner."

"Of course."

The door opened and closed once.

So the wife and the campaign manager were having an affair. Hardly anything worth reporting. But her stomach clenched with angry resentment at the discovery. Why had she, the innocent victim, been burned by scandal, while the couple really having the affair went unnoticed by the press?

Why the hell had she ever wanted to get into politics, anyway?

The door opened a second time. Whitney waited a few seconds longer before crawling out from beneath the desk.

The clock gave her only a minute to get to the dining room without raising suspicion.

She checked her pulse as she dashed across the room to get her shoes. Did all agents develop high blood pressure?

"There you are. Alysia said you were looking for me."

Or maybe an agent's heart stopped beating often enough that pulse rate wasn't a problem.

With her shoes still dangling from her hand, Whitney fixed a smile on her face and turned to greet Ross. In another time and place, he might have looked handsome in his western-cut suit of fine gray wool. But Whitney saw the corrupt man he was inside. She smiled, all the same.

"Thanks for the dress."

He nodded toward the shoes in her hand. "Is everything all right?"

"They pinch my feet a bit. I'll have to break them in."

"Did you want a drink?"

"No, I—" *Dammit, Whitney, think.* She'd lied to Alysia, and now she had to lie her way out of this. The phone on the desk offered her the perfect escape. "I'm just worried sick about Mom and Dad. There's no phone up in my room. Can't I call them?"

"I put you in that room so you wouldn't be disturbed. I can't imagine what you've gone through with Chilton. But I thought the opportunity for complete rest would be what you needed."

What she needed was a confession of collusion from him, preferably brought about by intense, painful torture. "I want to call home."

"I'll have a status report after dinner. I promise I'll explain everything then. After that, you can call your father." He reached out and stroked her cheek, a gesture of comfort she found eerily reminiscent of Chilton's taunting caresses.

Whitney froze the smile on her face but moved away. Weston followed. He walked up right behind her and clutched her shoulders. He nudged aside her hair and whispered into her ear.

"Be patient with me. I have plans for this country you can't imagine. I want to make us strong again. Powerful."

"We're the most powerful country in the world."

He turned her in his arms and shook his head. "We're losing our respect. We're getting weak. I intend to reverse that course. With your father's backing, with you at my side. You'd make a beautiful first lady."

Whitney laughed, hoping that was a joke. "Senator, you already have a wife."

His bright eyes narrowed to searching slits that held no laughter. "I can take care of that."

The implication of his words chilled Whitney all the way to her bones. Maybe she'd overplayed her hand. Maybe Vincent was right, that it was a mistake for her to think she could deceive such a ruthless man.

But it was too late to back out of the charade. She was on her own. And come heaven or hell, success or failure, she would have to see this game through to the end.

Since bolting from the room and running into the mountains wasn't an option, Whitney did what she thought was impossible. She braced her hand on Ross's shoulder and went up on tiptoe to kiss his cheek. Judging by the satisfied gleam in his sparkling blue eyes, the action pleased him.

Leaving him that little taste to lure him along in her game, she smiled. "I look forward to our talk later."

"YOU THINK she's in there?"

"Yes." Lying on his stomach on the ground beside Daniel, Vincent adjusted his night-vision goggles and surveyed Weston's ranch one more time. He wanted a glimpse of red-gold hair. He just needed to see her.

He and Daniel had taken up point at the very same spot where Whitney had thrown her arms around his neck and he kissed her. She'd been worried about him getting hurt. Worried if he was coming back to her in one piece or a body bag.

Now it was his turn to worry. At last he understood Melissa's fear about a relationship with an undercover agent. This scared the hell out of him. Whitney could be a prisoner in there. She could be hurt and unable to call for help. Even if she hadn't tipped her hand to anyone thus far, she'd be living moment to moment, making snap decisions, doing things that she normally wouldn't do. One wrong move could get her killed.

If it hadn't already.

Daniel shared that fear. His every move on this operation had been careful and discreet. "I want a visual." He called the order over the shortwave radio each man wore. "Who's in position?"

Vincent handed Daniel the goggles and pulled the black stocking cap he wore down over his face. "I know my way around the compound."

Daniel grabbed his forearm. Out of respect alone, Vincent paused to listen. "Your face has been ID'ed. You're strictly backup on this."

"By Chilton's man." Vincent nodded toward the layout of buildings. "If he pops up again, I'll take him out."

"Not good enough. If you raise a ruckus, Whitney could get caught in the crossfire."

A cold, antsy fury simmered beneath the surface of Vincent's skin. This wasn't just about retrieving the one hostage who had gotten away from him. It wasn't about proving himself on the job to these men. "I know I'm not DPS, but I'm better than you think."

"I don't care if you're 007. You stay put." Daniel turned his head back to the microphone on his shoulder. "Kyle. Report."

"There's no activity outside. Not even a guard posted. Does anybody else think that's a problem?"

"Chief?" Court Brody called in. He'd been searching outside the immediate perimeter of the compound, keeping an eye out for unexpected company.

"Yeah, Court."

"I got four John Does in a ravine stuck inside a blue Ford sedan. They've been hit execution style."

Daniel's curse was echoed by Kyle and Frank, who sat back in the van with the radio and tracking equipment. "Please tell me it's Chilton?"

"Negative," Court replied. "Three Caucasian males. One African-American."

"Son of a bitch."

Vincent reacted to the news with the same fearful implication of the other men. Chilton might not be at the ranch with Weston, but he was still around. The fact that no one knew his present location made him that much more unpredictable. And unpredictable meant deadly.

"Romeo!"

Vincent was already halfway to the house when Daniel summoned him. He had no intention of turning back until he saw Whitney with his own eyes.

In one piece.

DINNER HAD BEEN a creepy affair, with five-star food and stilted conversation. Afterward, Margery excused herself to go to bed. Ross made a promise to talk to Whitney as soon as the mysterious call he kept referring to came in. He and Warren went to Warren's office to work on tomorrow's speech. The guards left to eat in the kitchen, and Alysia began cleaning up.

Whitney said her good-nights and headed up the stairs. But she had no intention of hanging out in her room.

She still hadn't put on her shoes, so she was able to

move around the house without a sound. She saw Margery close her door, found Alysia on a cell phone in the kitchen talking to her family. The two guards were just starting their main course. And the senator and Warren were deep in conversation.

Whitney wasted no time returning to the study. She didn't know how to pick a lock, but she did understand the rudimentary idea behind a crowbar. This time, when she picked up the letter opener, she jammed it between the drawer and the desktop and pried the damn thing open. The small chip of wood that splintered off wasn't noticeable unless you looked at the drawer straight on, and somehow she didn't think the senator spent as much time crawling around the desk on his hands and knees as she did.

She wasn't sure what she'd expected to find inside, but maybe something more suspicious than a couple of file folders marked Correspondence and a box of computer disks. She was still new at this spy business, and since she didn't know exactly what to look for, she skimmed through each folder.

The letters were copies of responses to lobbyist requests, and personal letters to business associates asking for campaign contributions. Nothing in particular jumped out at her so she moved on to the computer disks, all the while keeping an eye on the clock and the door. She'd allowed herself thirty minutes this time. There were scads of dishes to wash, lots of food to eat—and the senator liked to talk.

"Why can't there just be a file marked Black Order?" Whitney asked herself. "Because Weston isn't a stupid man," she answered her own question. "But he does have an ego. Wouldn't he want proof of his great work?" Though she kept her voice at a whisper, she deepened the pitch to mock Weston's pompous tone. "How I saved America single-handedly."

Montana.

Well, it wasn't as obvious a title as *Deal with the Devil*, but it made more sense to her than any of the account disks she'd seen thus far.

She checked the closed door once more and turned to the computer. Just maybe…

The ding the computer made when she booted it up rang through the room like an alarm bell. Whitney jumped back in the chair, then lurched forward, hugging herself around the monitor. Her panicked response came too late to muffle the sound. When her pounding heart receded enough for her to hear her thoughts again, she shook her head at her foolish reaction. "Must be a trick to that, too."

With the computer up and running, she slipped the disk in and scrolled through the menu. Names of towns, mostly—Helena, Butte, Livingston. A few she didn't recognize—Wayne, Vogel. And then she saw a file that caught her eye

Sons and Daughters of Montana.

Could that be anything other than the militia group the Black Order had supplied with weapons and explosives?

She'd filed a dozen reports on that mission herself. The potential for discovery hummed in her veins.

Whitney clicked on the file. A list of names. She recognized the group's leader, Joshua Neely. She scrolled down and found Charlie Korbett. Wasn't that Court's brother-in-law?

When she clicked on the next page, the humming stopped. A cymbal-clanging brass band started up inside her as she focused on one tiny asterisk and the name beside it.

Court Brody.

Beside Court's names were three capital letters. FBI.

And underneath, the words *second installment—pd.*

"Oh my God." Her first words were little more than a thought. "Oh my God."

Proof.

She slipped her fingers into the hair at her temple and raked it over the top of her head.

She'd found proof.

Ross Weston knew Court Brody had been with the FBI. Someone had tipped that bit of information to the militia and blown his cover.

"Oh my God."

Now what? Did she look for more? Was this enough?

"Warren, if the kids want to come up to me afterward, let them come. We've scheduled two hours, and the speech is short."

"Kids don't vote, Senator."

"Their parents do."

The conversation in the hallway ended Whitney's speculation. She was getting good at this scrambling-to-hide part. She shut off the computer and grabbed the disk, then straightened the contents of the drawer and closed it.

The doorknob turned. Damn. Didn't anybody around here believe in privacy?

She searched for a pocket to hide the disk, but the clingy dress had none. Her shoes? Too far away. With the incriminating disk burning her hands, she hid it in the only place she could think of that wouldn't show.

By then it was too late to run, too late to hide.

"Whitney? I thought you'd retired for the evening." Senator Weston closed the door behind him and turned the lock with an ominous click. "What are you doing in here?"

Chapter Eleven

Standing with her back to the door bought her a few precious seconds to cross her arms and reach up to pinch some color back into her cheeks.

How did she explain why she was hanging out in his study? And more importantly, what excuse did she come up with for being at his desk?

Her knee butted up against his overstuffed leather swivel chair. Whitney clamped down on the inside of her lip. It wasn't much of an idea, but it was the best one she had.

She plopped down into the chair and spun around, arms outstretched, head tipped back, legs snugged together in the most ladylike fashion. She was appropriately flushed and breathless when she stopped herself. "I can't believe all this is yours."

The double play of flirty innocence and admiration of his wealth fed into the man's weak spot—his ego. The suspicious frown on his face softened into a self-effacing smile.

"Well, it's nothing like your parents' estate, but it gives me the roomy feel of Big Sky Country."

"Don't be so modest. I know this isn't the only property you own. I've been to your home near Mount Vernon. Remember?"

He unbuttoned his suit jacket and stuffed one hand into

the pocket of his slacks with the panache of a sixty-year-old *GQ* model. "Ah, yes. That was the environmental bill we were putting through that weekend, wasn't it?"

She'd been editing the document and lining up key support from lobbyists and fellow senators. *He'd* been lounging by the pool and taking long lunches. Though she refused to put on a swimsuit and join him, he'd insisted she and another aide work outside with him. The sunshine had freckled her skin, and his laissez-faire attitude had riled her temper.

She'd earned a pair of Kennedy Center tickets with that project.

What a naive, idealistic fool she'd been.

No more.

Tonight she had to beat the senator at his own manipulative game.

She ran her fingers along the top of the desk, admiring the fine wood and working up the nerve to lie through her teeth. "I always enjoyed working for you."

Whitney almost scooted away from the purposeful stride that carried him across the room. He spun the chair to face him and leaned over her, bracing his hands over hers on either arm of the chair. "There is something between us, isn't there?"

She cringed beneath his searching eyes. She was covered in cashmere from neck to wrist and down to her knees, but those bright blue eyes made her feel exposed. The plastic disk wedged against her thigh suddenly felt like metal on fire.

"I'd better go."

She tried to stand, but Ross refused to back away. If anything, his face moved closer to hers. Whitney pressed her back into the chair, buying herself as much breathing room as she could.

"I'm so sorry you got caught in the scandal. I know it

was hard for you." Surely this wasn't an apology. "But we weathered it just fine. Didn't damage my ratings in the polls one bit. You know, it hurt me, too, to see you suffer. But maybe it was all for the best. You're here with me now."

In what way was humiliation in front of an entire nation for the best?

She had to get out of there before her gag reflex kicked in and she told him how she really felt. "Ross, it's getting late. I really should be turning in."

He took her hand and pulled her to her feet. "My power is about to skyrocket," he promised as if it mattered to her. If she thought he was merely helping her up, she was mistaken. His fingers tightened around hers and he led her to one of the matching leather sofas. "I want you to be a part of that again."

Whitney frowned in confusion. "You want me to come back to work for you?"

Ross pulled her down at his side. His left hand settled on her knee. Alarm bells went off in Whitney's head. How friendly would the senatorial scumbag want to get before he let her go?

"I want you…" His significant pause was emphasized by sliding her skirt up her leg, leaving nothing but silk stocking between her knee and his hand. "…to be at my side."

Whitney crossed her legs, escaping his hand and protecting the disk from any further forays. "Do I understand you correctly?"

He twisted then, laying his left arm across the couch behind her shoulders. "You could be first lady." He kept moving closer and Whitney lifted her hand to his chest in an automatic gesture of self-defense. His right arm settled across her lap and he put his lips right up to her ear. "You'd like that, wouldn't you?"

His hot, moist breath swirled around the cup of her ear. She squeezed her eyes shut against the sickening stroke of his tongue on her lobe. But when his hand moved to cup the outer curve of her thigh, her eyes shot open.

A sharp jab to his nose or Adam's apple would get him off her.

It would also completely blow her cover.

That left her words. She flattened both hands against his chest in a mild protest. "Ross, we shouldn't."

"No. Not yet. Not right away. But in a few years' time, no one will notice. I'll put you where you belong. Right by my side." His hand moved higher, hiking her skirt with it. His thumb slipped to the inside of her thigh. Another inch and he'd find a stab of hard plastic instead of soft woman.

Pushing hadn't worked. Protests hadn't worked.

Whitney swallowed her pride and turned her mouth to his. Surprised by the bold gesture, Ross smiled against her lips. It was a smug smile of triumph that made the kiss all about him as he took what she offered.

Distracted by her response, Ross allowed her to push his hand away from dangerous territory. Instead, he loomed over her, forcing her back into the cushions, grinding his mouth against hers. Her nostrils filled with the stench of his expensive cologne. She tasted brandy on his tongue as he forced his way inside.

A flare of out-and-out panic erupted in Whitney. She stiffened her arms and shoved at his chest. "Ross—"

He lifted his head as if he'd been struck. But his body still pinned hers against the sofa. Caught beneath a glare of predatory displeasure, Whitney hurried to soften her rejection.

"It's a tempting offer, but—"

"But what? I'm offering you the world. In time."

He made it sound as if he was doing her a favor. The arrogant, groping bastard!

A bit of the fire that had convinced her to go after Weston in the first place creeped in and replaced the icy chill in her veins.

"If you want me, you'll have to earn my father's approval." Ross's eyes narrowed at the mention of Gerald MacNair, Sr. "And he would never support a candidate who has been linked to terrorists. This afternoon, on your front porch, I saw you wrap up a deal with Dimitri Chilton. How do you explain that?"

"I made a deal to save your life."

"Behind the government's back?"

The hand that had trapped her from behind moved around her shoulders and settled at the base of her throat. For a moment, she thought he meant to strangle her. Whitney held her breath, afraid to look away from his eyes, afraid to move, afraid to stay.

But then, with something like an indulgent laugh, he pulled away entirely and stood. He straightened his vest and buttoned his jacket, donning his good ol' boy persona. Whitney sat up and slid away from him. She picked up her shoes and started to put one on. Then the idea to clench it in her fist and brandish it as a weapon should he put the moves on her again seemed to make better sense.

The man she had feared moments ago vanished behind a polished white grin. "What if I told you that I've rid this country of the Black Order?"

"They've been killing people across the state for the past three months. How—?"

"Tomorrow night, at Livingston High School auditorium, I will be giving a speech that will guarantee me the White House." He puffed up with arrogance and pride. "I'll tell the country that I, Ross Weston, have saved America for Americans."

"I did what no government agency could do. I ended the Black Order's reign of terror."

"What do you mean?"

He flashed his white teeth in a smugly triumphant smile. "The Black Order has been in the country for months. An insidious little foray across the Canadian border at first. But their threat has grown. They brought hit men. Insurgents. They've tried to destroy our superior way of life." He paced the room, taking stage even though she was his only audience. "These terrorists have tried to poison our water system. Blow up this state's capitol. Influence our greatest scientific minds. They've murdered the men and women who make America the proud country she is."

Whitney clutched her shoes tightly to her chest. The urge to put as much distance between herself and Weston was as strong as the desire to accuse him of being a greater threat to their country than the Black Order.

The proof of his collusion burned against her thigh and deep in her heart.

Though her stomach twisted into knots beneath the strain, she managed to keep her voice calm and even. "And what exactly will you tell the people at the rally?"

"That I saved them." His blue-eyed gaze looked beyond her to some distant point in the past. "I saved you. I saved Governor Haskel. I saved my country."

He shook his fist, and she could imagine his picture in the papers, on the TV screens, shaking that same fist, giving this well-rehearsed speech. The vision of this madman running the country was as unacceptable as the idea of surrendering democratic rights to the whims of a terrorist. Whitney stood and eased toward the door. His delusions of grandeur frightened her almost more than Chilton's hands-on violence had.

Absorbed in his own glory, he didn't seem to notice her eagerness to escape.

She didn't get very far, though. There was a terse knock at the study door. Ross crossed the room to open it.

In the hallway stood Warren Burke. His perfect coiffure had a lock out of place. It fell across his forehead and pointed toward eyes that were bright with alarm. "There's a call. You'd better take it."

Was this the report he had mentioned earlier? The one that would explain his "arrangement" with Dimitri Chilton?

But apparently Whitney's snooping was done for the day.

Ross grasped her shoulder and bent his head to press a kiss to her forehead. "Believe in me, Whitney."

One of the security guards—Buck, she thought—materialized through a doorway and escorted her up to her room while Ross and Warren disappeared into Burke's office.

WHITNEY TOSSED her shoes onto the bed, stripped her clothes en route to the shower and stood under the pounding spray until the water ran cold.

It seemed no amount of scrubbing and soaking could get the dirty feeling of Ross Weston's hands off her skin.

At last, exhausted by the mental games she'd played all day, she turned off the water and stepped out. She wrapped herself up sarong-style in a white fluffy towel and moved out to the vanity area of her bedroom suite. Though she'd rinsed her mouth a hundred times in the shower, she fixed a toothbrush and tried scouring the senator's taste from her mouth. Rinse and spit. Rinse and spit. Seemed she couldn't spit far enough and often enough to erase all the lies—Weston's and her own—that had contaminated her sense of honesty.

She attacked her hair next. She picked up a big flat brush and ran it through her tresses. Every convenience had been provided for her—clothes, toiletries, makeup—almost as if she'd been expected.

"Oh no." The brush clattered into the sink. "Oh no." She clasped her hand over her mouth to stem the useless tears that burned sudden and hot behind her eyes.

He *had* been expecting her.

He hadn't seized any opportunity by arranging for her release from Chilton. He'd arranged to have her kidnapped in the first place.

His own little prize. His own little trophy to ensure and celebrate his trip to the White House.

Anger welled up as quick and intense as her fear had. "You son of a bitch."

She grasped the rim of the sink and leaned over it, her breath coming in short, stunted gasps. She concentrated on settling the retch in her stomach. She breathed in deeply through her nose, pursed her lips and exhaled a long-drawn breath of air. She needed to calm herself, she needed time to think.

That was when she became aware of the presence in her room. The skin-tingling sensation that she was being watched. And by something more wary, more intent than that glassy-eyed moose in Weston's study.

Whitney sifted a fall of hair between her fingers and combed it back over her head as she straightened.

She saw him in the mirror first, a shadow among the shadows of her room. Big, brawny, dressed in black from head to toe.

With beautiful onyx eyes that glittered with a fierce emotion and reached across the distance to touch her very soul.

There were no words. He never used many to convey what he was feeling. He simply reached out to her.

Whitney hesitated. She turned to see if his welcome was real. If he was more than an illusion concocted by her needy heart. And then she flew across the room and was swallowed up in the haven of Vincent's arms.

She wrapped her arms around his waist and snatched handfuls of his jacket within her fists. She buried her nose in the open vee of his coat and drank in the clean familiar smells of leather and wool and man.

He lifted her onto her toes and squeezed her tight, wrapping her up in his body and scent, stamping her with his imprint—leather and hardware, tender hands and callused skin, hard muscle and a heart beating a life-affirming staccato beneath her ear.

"Vincent. Vincent." Shudders of unspent anger and pent-up fear shook her body. But he held her with scorching need and exquisite care.

He nuzzled his nose into the damp hair at her temple and kissed her there. He rocked her back and forth ever so gently, never saying a word.

He held her like that for a moment out of time, long enough to become aware of the press of a zipper against her breast, the bulge of his holster beneath her arm, the possessive squeeze of his hands along her waist and bottom. And when his fingers moved up to frame her face and feather into her hair, she tipped her head back and welcomed the gentle claim of his mouth on hers.

Like an instantaneous crackle of electricity, tender possession gave way to greedy passion. His tongue plunged in, forever erasing the taste of any other man. Whitney wound her arms around his neck and lifted herself into his kiss. As her palms savored the delightful static of crisp hair at his nape, her towel gave way. In an instant, she was bare-skinned against leather and denim and the pressing need of his hands. His electric touch gave her new life, new strength and a feverish heat all her own. Those gifts he gave her in abundant supply.

His forgiveness, however, might be a long time coming.

With that thought to sober her, Whitney tore her mouth from his and buried her face beneath his chin. His breathing sounded as labored as her own as she tried to regain her equilibrium. How could she want one man so much? Need him to feel complete? How could she hurt inside so much at the thought of causing him pain?

When the current between them subsided, it was Vincent who finally pulled away. He picked up the towel and wrapped it around her again. She took over the job of tucking it in at her breast and holding it there, crossing her arm in front of her to secure herself inside the dubious armor of fuzzy cotton.

She sifted her fingers through her hair and held a loose ponytail at her nape. "How did you find me?"

"I knew where you'd be."

Those spare words, the intense scrutiny, were unnerving. Whitney sought a way to distance herself from the doubts she knew lay there between them. Brooding strength and garrulous beauty were an odd combination to begin with. She'd blown her chance to share something more than passion with Vincent when she'd left despite his wishes that morning. He'd taken a huge risk by talking about his past, and she'd repaid his effort by leaving him.

Passion would turn into resentment, eventually. And she didn't think she could stand the thought of Vincent Romeo hating her.

That left only the mission. Maybe she could redeem herself in his eyes by turning this into a success.

Tucking the hair behind her ear, she scouted through the clothing strewn across the floor. She picked up one particular bundle and handed it to him. "Here. This is for you and Daniel."

"Panty hose?"

"There's a disk inside with a file that shows a connection between Weston and the Sons and Daughters of Montana. He knew Court was working undercover with them. I think he's the one who revealed his identity.''

Vincent's curse added an air of normalcy to their hushed conversation in the darkened bedroom. ''Should I ask why it's in your hose?''

''No.'' Too sharp an answer. It hung in the air and demanded an explanation. Whitney shrugged off the memory of Weston's leering eyes and groping hands. ''I didn't realize this kind of work would be so creepy.''

She probably didn't know the half of it, judging by the grim lines creasing along Vincent's unshaven jaw. ''Where's Weston now?''

''Last I knew, he was on the phone, taking some important call. I think it was about having Chilton deported. He sent four security men with Chilton and two other Black Order guards this afternoon with travel visas and enough cash to get them on a plane to Agar.''

''Four?''

''Yeah. You know, dark glasses, blue suits, wires sticking in their ears.'' Vincent's utter stillness absorbed the room's atmosphere, chilling her. Goose bumps of alarm prickled along her skin. ''What?'' Whitney hugged her arms around her body. ''Dammit, Romeo, talk to me. What?''

''Court Brody found four dead men that fit your description up in a ravine.'' Her knees weakened at the senseless waste of more lives and she sank onto the bed. She didn't need Vincent to tell her the implication of those four murders. ''Chilton's still out there somewhere.''

''And Weston doesn't know it.'' She latched onto his sleeve, demanding he listen as she thought out loud. ''He thinks he's got it all under control. He has this master plan he believes is going to make him a hero and carry him right to the White House. If Chilton shows up again—at the house here, or at the rally in Livingston—there's no telling what he'll do.''

Vincent took her hand and pulled her to her feet. ''I can take you out of here right now.''

Whitney dug in her heels. His offer of safety was tempting, but she couldn't. ''That would be quitting with the job half done.'' She knew Vincent understood that kind of commitment. He was the living, breathing essence of dedication to his work. ''I have to stop him. He's vulnerable now. If Weston's deal with Chilton has gone wrong, he'll be scrambling for other options. He'll say or do something to incriminate himself, and I'll be right here.''

His dark eyes glittered as he stood there, unmoving, studying her from head to bare toes, and back to her face.

''Then here.'' He reached into his jacket and pulled out a tiny silver box he pressed into her hand. She recognized the microphone from their first visit to Weston's ranch. ''Take this.''

She curled her fingers around his reassuring gift and felt the strength of his protection wash over her like a healing balm. Now she wouldn't be alone against the devil. She'd have Vincent watching over her like before. And this time, she didn't seem to mind.

''Frank Connolly will record everything at the other end. The five of us are all linked with mikes.'' Vincent's efficient, businesslike explanation sounded like words of love to her. But she knew he didn't fully believe in such things. ''I'm not giving you the earpiece, that could be detected.

''But I'll hear every word you say.''

''Every word?'' Whitney clutched the miniature mike to her breast and gave him a wry smile. ''You really want to listen to everything I have to say?''

She was teasing. He wasn't.

''Yes.'' He reached out with the tip of his finger to lift a stray tendril of hair and tuck it behind her ear. ''I'd better go. If I overstay my welcome, someone will get suspicious.''

Whitney followed him to the window, and wondered only briefly how he had scaled the wall to the second floor. As soon as he raised the sash, a woman's voice could be heard down below on the side porch.

Vincent pushed Whitney back against the wall beside him, hiding her in his shadow. Whitney pushed against the arm at her waist, but it wouldn't budge. She settled for closing her eyes and training her ears to the pitch of the voice. ''That's Alysia, the maid.'' But she couldn't make any sense of the words. ''What's she saying? I can't—''

Vincent clamped his hand over her mouth and pulled her into his arms, trapping her with her back to his chest. The barest vibration of wary tension transmitted from his body to hers. She got the message. She held herself perfectly still until she heard the beep of a cell phone being disconnected down below. When the soft footsteps faded away, she pulled at his hand and he released her. ''Arabic?''

Vincent nodded. ''Something about moving a timetable to tomorrow morning.''

''Ross is hosting a brunch for the local dignitaries before the parade and speech at the high school.'' A new piece had just been added to the puzzle. ''She's not Native American, is she. She's—''

''One of Chilton's people. Hell. Weston's not running this show after all. I wonder if he knows that yet.'' He rubbed his hand along his stalwart jaw and shook his head. ''You're sure you don't want to just get out of here and let them all kill each other?''

''That almost sounded like a joke, Romeo.'' She reassured him with a determined smile. ''I'm strong enough to do this. I'm stronger knowing you're here.''

His dark eyes pinned hers. "We're all here. Daniel and the others. We're following your plan."

Something close to shock lifted her tired spirit. "You're using my idea?"

"It's a good one. The perimeter's secure, like you requested. The detection units are in place."

Daniel was using *her* plan. Would they follow her contingency plan as well?

"If Chilton shows up to talk—"

"We'll let him through. Use him to trap Weston. But I guarantee you—" Vincent took one of her battered wrists and held it up to the moonlight streaming through the open window "—he's not getting back out of here alive."

The raspy tone of those powerful words thrummed through her. He carried her hand to his chest and pressed it flat against his heart. How could this man not know about love when his emotions ran so deep? How could he not believe in it when he showed such caring?

"You give the word and we'll be here. Don't be a martyr and give it too late." She knew he was thinking of his father. Maybe it hurt him too much to love. Maybe opening himself to that remembered pain was the one thing that frightened her tight-lipped hero. Maybe together, she could help him rediscover the joy that went along with loving, too.

"Vincent. About this morning—"

He pressed a finger to her lips and hushed her. "We'll talk about that later."

"Promise?"

"Just do your job, MacNair."

He speared his fingers into her hair and covered her mouth in one quick, soul-stealing kiss.

Then he turned and slipped out the window. He dropped onto the porch roof without a sound and disappeared into the night.

Whitney stood at the window a while longer, watching the darkness that was so like him, so much a part of him. The darkness could be a frightening thing. But there was peace there, too. Comfort. The darkness was where dreams began and ended.

And it was where she'd found the man she loved.

A cold north wind whisked through the window and chilled her bare skin.

She loved Vincent Romeo.

How else could she explain the fever his touch ignited in her? How else could she explain the relief and joy at simply seeing him again? How else could she explain the horrible fear squeezing around her heart?

She thought she'd wanted this assignment to prove her competence to her father, or Daniel—or to shove it in the faces of Ross Weston and the rest of a world who saw her only as a scatterbrained princess attached to a powerful name.

But maybe there was something more in her drive to put Weston and Chilton behind bars. She *did* talk too much. She was impulsive and emotional, and had silly hobbies like shopping and riding horses.

Maybe she wanted this so badly because she needed to feel worthy of all the overprotective big brothers and fathers in her life. She needed to feel worthy enough to earn Vincent's love.

The revelation made her feel ancient. She closed the window and shut the curtains, then crawled under the covers still wrapped in her towel.

Vincent hadn't placed an inordinate amount of faith in her, he just expected her to do her job. Clinging to that matter-of-fact confidence in her abilities, she hugged the microphone he'd left her tight in her fist. Come morning, she didn't intend to disappoint him.

ROSS WESTON'S GIFT to her the next morning was a figure-hugging pantsuit in nubby charcoal wool. Whitney pinned the tiny microphone beneath the collar of the sleeveless blue turtleneck she wore, pulled on the jacket and fluffed her hair so that it fell across her shoulders.

"I hope you guys can hear me."

More than anything, she wished she could hear a friendly response. A *good-luck, kid* from Frank. A *be careful* from Daniel. Even a *shut up and do your job, MacNair* from Vincent.

Those last imagined words made her smile. "Don't be talking about me behind my back."

She leaned closer to the vanity mirror and applied some copper-tinted lipstick. She smacked her lips together and threw her shoulders back, approving the final look. Irresistibly attractive and blissfully naive was a hard combination to achieve. Hopefully, Weston would buy the blend of strong colors and a schoolgirl pout. "Here goes nothing."

With her hand on the doorknob, she paused, speaking freely to Vincent and the agents of Montana Confidential one last time. "Remember, Romeo—when I give the signal, you'd better be there."

She closed her eyes and imagined a raspy *I will.*

Whitney needn't have worried about the impression she made on Ross Weston. The glib senator was clearly distracted the moment she walked in.

They were again in the study, with the usual cast of characters. Weston, Margery, Warren Burke, the two guards and Alysia, along with some visitors. Whitney slipped a glance at the black-haired woman, ostensibly busy filling the buffet table set up in front of one of the picture windows. Had she alerted Chilton to the senator's schedule that day? Were there submachine guns hidden beneath the tablecloths? Or had she simply called in to verify that she would keep watch on the senator?

Whitney had a gut-tingling feeling that nothing would be simple this day.

When he saw her in the doorway, the senator broke away from the couple he was chatting with. "Whitney." Despite a glare from his wife across the room, Weston slipped his arm behind Whitney's waist and introduced her. "This is Whitney MacNair from the Massachusetts and Washington MacNairs. This is, um, the mayor..." Weston paused. He couldn't remember their name.

Though she enjoyed watching him suffer the minor embarrassment, Whitney was here to play a part. She extended her hand the way her mother had taught her and completed the introduction herself. "Mayor Hunt. It's a pleasure to meet you."

"Miss MacNair." She could tell by his callused grip and natural smile that Glenn Hunt was a man of the people, the type of man who should be in politics. He turned and introduced his wife, Sue.

Whitney smiled in genuine recognition. "I believe we work out at the same gym."

Okay, so this politicking part was second nature to her. Keeping her eye on unfolding events and getting Weston to talk was not.

Weston left her chatting with the Hunts and went over to Warren Burke by the desk. The two men bent their heads and whispered. The flushed glower on Ross's face indicated he hadn't heard what he wanted to.

She excused herself and went to pour a cup of coffee. She put the cup to her lips and whispered into the mike. "He's agitated about something."

"Good morning, Whitney." The pointed voice startled her. "Always talk to your coffee cup?"

"Margery."

Mrs. Weston made no effort to hide the silver flask she pulled from her pocket to doctor her coffee. She also showed no real interest in Whitney's reaction. "My husband didn't come to bed last night. Not that that's all that atypical, but I don't suppose you know where he was, do you?"

"No."

A hand at the small of her back startled Whitney a second time. She decided to set her cup and saucer back on the table before she spilled it. "Whitney. Dear." Ross stepped between the two women, embracing them both. "Governor Haskel's plane has been delayed. He won't be joining us this morning. To help out, I thought I'd drive on in to the Bozeman airport to meet him. I want to talk with him before this evening's festivities." He dipped his head and smiled at Margery. "You don't mind staying and entertaining our guests, do you?"

"That's what I'm here for, isn't it?"

He leaned over and pressed a kiss to his wife's forehead. Then, for no good reason, he kissed Whitney goodbye as well. Then, with a quick nod to Warren, the two men headed for the door.

No! Success slipped through her fingers as Weston slipped out the study door. "They're leaving."

"It happens all the time," Margery answered, thinking the comment had been meant for her. "You get used to it."

There's a time to run, a time to fight...

Definitely time to run.

Without a backward glance, Whitney darted through the door after Weston.

"Ross!"

Warren held their coats in his hand just outside his office. Slowing to a walk, Whitney gave Ross a breathless smile. "I wanted to ask if you found out anything last night."

Weston frowned. "About what?"

"You said you were going to get final word on Dimitri Chilton so I could call my father." She spotted the phone on Warren's desk and went on in. She turned the phone box to face her, lifted the receiver and kept right on talking as she began to dial. "He must be going out of his mind. Please, just let me call him and tell him I'm okay. Then you can talk all about your terrorist-elimination plans later."

A rough hand snatched the receiver from her ear. A rougher hand grabbed her above the elbow and pushed her away from the phone. "Ow. Let go."

Ross Weston's perfectly tanned skin blotched as blue veins of fury popped out on his forehead. "I said you could call when I'm ready."

He slammed down the receiver and she jumped in his punishing grasp. This was it. This was her chance to push him into revealing the truth. "Don't you have the Black Order under control yet?" It was an attack on his power, a taunt at his ego. "I thought you shipped them out of the country."

"I had them killed." His bright white teeth nearly spat the words in her face. The coolly suave senator had disappeared behind a frightening temper. He spun around and dragged her through the door after him. "But until I have verification from my men, I can't announce a damn thing. Neither can you."

"Jordan has the car out front." Warren made the announcement as a matter of course without showing any reaction, concerned or otherwise, about his boss physically abusing one of his guests. "We'll move you to a safe house until Chilton is located."

Warren shrugged into his coat and opened the front door.

A neat bullet between the eyes crumpled him to the floor.

Dimitri Chilton pushed aside the man with the smoking pistol and smiled in the open doorway.

"How rude to leave your guests unattended. Why don't we all go back inside and rejoin them."

Chapter Twelve

Weston's hand locked on her arm as Chilton and his men stepped over Warren Burke's body and forced them back into the study. There were screams and startled curses and curt commands as everyone was herded to the sofas and chairs in the middle of the room. A blow to the head rendered one guard unconscious. Alysia the maid had the other on his knees with a gun to his temple.

"Not yet." Whitney whispered the urgent request into her microphone. Right now, Ross Weston was just a bully and a hostage himself. She needed time to prove he'd been working with Dimitri Chilton from the start.

But fraying tempers and hidden agendas left her with very little time to spare.

Perched on the edge of a sofa, practically in Weston's lap, Whitney jabbed him in the ribs. His surprised *oof* and a sharp twist of her arm were enough to free herself from his grasp.

She let her father's Irish temper color her cheeks. "Let me guess. Your plan's not working out the way you hoped."

"Shut up."

Whitney shook her finger at him. "Oh no, no, no, I'll tell Daddy."

Weston shoved her away and stood. "Don't you have any brains, woman?"

Oh, so he really thought she was a flake, did he? He wanted her body and her last name, and to hell with the person she was inside. "Enough to know who has the real power in this room."

Before he could sputter an answer to that one, Chilton was there with his gun. He jammed the barrel into Weston's stomach and grinned with heartless satisfaction. "Shall I let your constituents tear you to pieces? Or should I take that pleasure all for myself?"

Foolish and bold, Ross batted the gun away. "I gave you everything you asked for."

Glenn Hunt, who shielded his wife behind him on the sofa, spoke up. "You two know each other?"

Chilton ignored the question. "You tried to kill me yesterday. Was that part of the agreement?"

"What agreement is that, Ross?"

Weston gathered his wits and leveled his glare at Whitney. "This is none of your business."

"If I'm going to die for it, it sure as hell is." Whitney glanced around the room. Maybe she could feed other pertinent information to Vincent and Daniel. "I see three rifles in this room, four handguns, and—" she pointed at Chilton's leg, to the leather sheath she knew he carried inside his boot "—I know this guy carries a big knife because he's used it on me before."

Margery muttered something like a swooning sound and collapsed against the sofa. She wasn't out for the count yet, though. "Ross?" Her voice was weak and trembly. "What's going on?"

"Shut up, Margery. I can get us out of this."

Chilton threw his head back and laughed out loud at that one. When he was done, he had his gun pointed right at Margery's forehead. "And just how will you do that?"

Weston flashed his bright white teeth. "Go ahead. With her out of the way, I'll be free to marry Whitney and earn her father's endorsement."

"Excuse me?" Whitney's protest went unnoticed.

"Think of the sympathy vote." Ross's smile was a cold, conscienceless smirk.

"You bastard!" Margery's curse earned a silencing slap across the face from Chilton. She huddled into Glenn Hunt's shoulder and whimpered with fear.

"I am tired of playing games with you." Chilton grabbed Weston by the shoulder and forced him to his knees.

But even with a gun at his temple, Ross never blinked. "You can't kill me. You'll have an international incident on your hands. You'll never get out of this country alive."

Time!

Don't be a martyr.

Whitney heard Vincent's warning inside her head. But it was too soon! She couldn't call for help until she had her proof.

Her pulse pounded in her ears. Think, Whitney! Think!

"I have no intention of ending your life. You're too valuable to me." Chilton nodded to his men. "Line them up.

"I want you to see the kind of destruction you are responsible for. I want you to understand what I will be holding over you each time you think about saying no to me. Each time you think of sending your men after me with guns instead of money."

Margery screamed. Someone grabbed Whitney by the arm, dragged her over to the desk and forced her down onto her knees next to the others.

"Ross, if you can stop this, you have to." She pleaded on deaf ears. "If you reneged on the deal, make it right."

"What do you know about the deal?"

The temperature rose as tempers frayed. Whitney took a deep breath. Now she was down to winging it. "Two years ago you went on a goodwill mission to the Emirate of Agar. You hired the Black Order to come to the U.S."

"You bitch." Weston tried to stand.

Chilton shoved him back to his knees and swung his gun around on Whitney. "What do you know about that?"

"It's the oldest con in the book. You hire someone to cause trouble. Then you clean up the mess and you're branded a hero. People shower you with gifts, money. Votes."

Weston pounded his fist in his hand. "I am known for my antiterrorism stand."

"So why did you bring them into the country?"

Weston fell for the second oldest con in the book. He admitted his guilt. "To become President of the United States!"

Whitney's heart pounded over the pall of silence in the room. She stared into the black steel void of the gun barrel pointed at her face. Then she looked up into the darker void of her kidnapper's eyes. "So, Dimitri, you agree to murder people for a couple of years and then leave the country when this guy tells you to?"

Chilton's throaty chuckle was the voice of evil itself. "You're half-right. But why surrender a good thing? If extracting information from a senator is beneficial, think of what I can 'negotiate' from the president himself."

Weston turned his blotchy red face up toward Chilton. "You're the one who reneged on the deal. You asked for information and I delivered. I gave you Dr. Birch and that FBI agent. I got you into the Quinlan Research Institute, so you could get your hands on their biological weapons.

"I asked for two things in return. Whitney MacNair, and a speedy departure before election time."

Triumph surged through Whitney, renewing her

strength. She was about to nail the last plank into Weston's coffin.

"It was *your* idea to have Chilton kidnap me?"

"Yes." Dimitri answered the question for her. He shifted his attention back to Weston. "But you called in someone to rescue her."

Even Ross had the good sense to watch his mouth when Chilton pressed the gun to his head. "Her father did that behind my back. I tried to stop it. I told you everything I could find out."

He didn't even bother to deny the accusation. Whitney squeezed her eyes shut and sent up a prayer of thanks for that bit of good news. Her father hadn't abandoned her entirely. He'd sent Vincent to her.

"Did you?" Chilton paused to note Whitney's reaction. "Are you sure you weren't hoping that agent would kill me?"

"You were supposed to bring her to me so I could hand her over to her father. *You're* the one who screwed up."

Chilton raised his fist and backhanded Weston across the face, knocking him to the floor. Whitney caught her breath and sat back on her heels, jarred by the force of the blow. Chilton leaned over Weston, who nursed his bleeding mouth with the back of his hand. "I do not screw up. That is an American phrase. It is an American excuse."

Chilton grabbed Whitney by the front of her shirt and yanked her to her feet. Thrown off balance, Whitney clung to Chilton's fist for an instant in time and prayed Frank Connolly had recorded every word. Dimitri pulled her face up to his, forcing Whitney to breathe in his sweaty stench. "Where is your boyfriend now, Miss MacNair?"

"You mean Vincent?" *When it's serious, say my name.* He'd made the request in the throes of passion. She prayed he understood her secret cry for help now. She pointed to the door. Honesty always was the best answer. "Just outside?"

Chilton muttered some foreign obscenity and slung her to the floor. Whitney's head glanced off the edge of the desk. A shower of pain exploded behind her temple and her world spun into a nauseating swirl of bright lights and floating animal heads.

She staggered to her elbows and knees and clutched at the pain. Her vision cleared long enough to see the blood in her cupped hand.

And the tiny steel microphone that had slid several feet across the hardwood floor.

Whitney's gaze collided with Chilton's hateful black glare.

He crushed the mike and all her hopes beneath the heel of his boot.

"Kill them!"

And then came the fury of crashing glass and splintering wood. Tiny explosions of thunder erupted all around her. Black storm clouds streamed into the room. That damn moose was struck by lightning and crashed down to earth. Whitney covered her ears and sank to the floor, sucked helplessly toward oblivion.

"Get up!"

Whitney screamed her way back to consciousness as a jolt of electricity ripped across her scalp. Chilton had her by the hair, jerking her onto her feet. He snaked his arm around her waist and buried his gun into her ribs, half carrying, half dragging her toward the open door.

"Whitney!"

She squinted through the chaos, focusing her eyes on the raspy call.

A shadow walked straight toward her. Tall. Dark. Deadly.

"Fight him," it said.

She obeyed the command the way she would obey her own heart.

Whitney fisted her hand and rammed her elbow back.

Chilton's grip slackened. Whitney stumbled. A thunder-clap exploded, loud, in her ears.

Dimitri Chilton slumped to the floor. A dead man.

Whitney fell, but she never hit the floor. Strong arms caught her and swept her against a wall of safety and warmth.

"I've got you, Whit." She turned her face to the comforting smells of leather and wool and let the blackness take her away from the pain. "I've got you, sweetheart."

WHITNEY CAME TO in a bright white room. Pain sheared through her head as she opened her eyes to the light. She quickly closed them and tried to move away from the brightness, but her head felt like a squared-off bowling ball and wouldn't budge.

"Hi."

She pinched one eye open and saw Daniel Austin standing beside her bed with a grim expression of fatherly concern. The poor man needed a shave. That scruffy, worried look just wasn't him. He needed to smile. Daniel didn't smile nearly enough.

"Hospital, right?"

Daniel's fingers brushed against hers, and she latched onto his easy, comforting grip. "The doctor wanted to keep you overnight for observation. You have a few stitches and a concussion."

"Did we get the bad guys?"

Daniel squeezed her hand. "We sure did. Chilton and his men are dead. Weston's in custody."

Had she done her job? She hadn't failed, had she? She didn't want Daniel to be disappointed in her.

"I got enough information to put him away?"

"Everything we need is on tape. You did a nice job, Whit."

One little tear of relief found its way down her cheek and onto the pillow. "Thanks."

And then she saw his smile. "But you try another stunt like that without telling anyone first, and I'm gonna cut off your catalog supply."

Whitney laughed, then cringed. The sound reverberated through her skull. She pressed her palm to the gauze pad at her temple to still the vibrations.

Daniel bent down and kissed her cheek. "I'm glad you're okay. I'll get out of here so you can rest."

Whitney nodded and watched him leave. Her line of sight took in a bright array of color. As her eyes adjusted to the light, she focused in on the bouquets of white and yellow daisies, bright pink tulips, roses of all kinds. The cards had been stacked on the table beside her. Frank and C.J. The McMurtys. Kyle Foster's family. Court Brody and his wife. Her parents. Her brothers.

"A lot of people think you're something special."

A shiver cascaded through her at the dark, raspy voice. It was a release of a breath she hadn't realized she'd been holding.

She rolled over and found the tall, broad shadow of a man she'd been searching for. "Romeo?"

He took her right hand between both of his and sat on the edge of the bed beside her. He looked even worse than Daniel. His dark stubble couldn't mask the deep lines of strain beside his mouth. She reached up to brush her fingers across the dark shadows beneath his eyes.

"You saved my life. You killed Chilton."

Vincent brushed his fingers through her hair, gently lifting it from her face. "He's never going to hurt you again."

The deep-pitched break in his voice touched a hurtful place inside her. This man cared about her pain and suffering. The astonishing depth of his compassion never ceased to amaze her. He'd risk his life, his hurts, for her.

How could she make him see he could risk his heart, too?

Whitney wrapped her hand around his and held on tight. She didn't want to let him go. But it had to be his choice to stay.

"Thank you for being there for me. It means everything that you believed in me."

He nodded as if his commitment to her safety was no big deal. Like letting her fight her own battle for once wasn't a gift beyond measure.

"You got grit, MacNair."

Whitney nodded. She held tight to his hand and drifted back toward slumber.

Maybe that was the best he could do. It wasn't a declaration of love, but it spoke of his faith in her. It spoke to her heart, the way she wished Vincent could. Maybe she was hoping for something that just wasn't there. She and Vincent shared a mutual physical attraction, but maybe he was a man who couldn't give his heart away anymore. He'd been hurt too often.

A relationship between the two of them was probably doomed to fail, anyway. She'd keep getting into trouble, and her moody giant would eventually get tired of rescuing her.

She loved him, anyway.

VINCENT STUCK two fingers beneath his collar and loosened the tie that was cinched around his neck. If it wasn't for his boss's insistence, he'd have never agreed to come to this fancy party. But good PR with the president was nothing to sneeze at, and if attending this damn reception at the White House would earn him a few days off, then he'd do it.

Just like any other mission.

This one did have a few perks, though.

Whitney reached up and straightened his tie. "Either wear it right or take it off." She smiled in that mischievous way that put him on guard and turned his insides to mush. "You just helped make the world a safer place for democracy. I don't think the president's going to care if you take it off."

He caught her hands and held them against his chest. "I want to fit in."

"Don't tell me big bad Vincent Romeo is afraid of a few dignitaries and cucumber sandwiches."

"I am not afraid."

Her quicksilver eyes that hid nothing from the world narrowed with concern. "You've been jumpy all day. Is something going on?"

Vincent breathed in deeply. Yeah. Maybe the biggest mission of his entire life.

She looked so beautiful. With all that red-gold hair tumbling around the shoulders of that elegant blue dress. Tall and fresh and full of life.

He'd nearly lost that life.

That light.

She'd been released from the hospital three days ago, but she still wore a gauze bandage that masked the stitches in the hairline at her temple. Chilton had had her in his hands, using her as a shield while bullets were flying. There'd been so much blood on her. Head wounds did that, he knew, but it was her blood.

He'd nearly lost her.

And all he could think to say was, *You got grit, MacNair.*

"Romeo?"

She shook him slightly, pulling him from his deep, regretful trance. She could do that for him. So easily. Time and again. She had more guts than any man he'd ever served with. She met what life threw at her head-on—fists flying, mouth running, heart hoping.

He wanted that sunny, golden personality to be a part of his life. He didn't know how much he needed her sunshine until he'd almost lost it forever.

Melissa had once told him that a relationship with an agent would never work.

He'd make it work. With Whitney.

He just had to tell her how he felt.

And today was the day he planned to do it.

He felt her tender fingers on his face, checking to see if he was all right. "C'mon. You're looking a little green around the gills. Enough making nice with these people. Let's say goodbye to my folks and get out of here."

She led him by the hand to her family's table. He'd met all the brothers, sized them up, passed inspection himself, he thought. Whitney was a carbon copy of her mother, Rose MacNair, though her personality came from her father, Gerald, Sr.

Brian was monopolizing the conversation with one of the congressmen Vincent had met earlier. "Without Montana Confidential to stop him, Weston would still be trading secrets. My baby sister saved lives."

Whitney slipped her arm through Brian's. "Do I hear music swelling in the background?"

Brian patted her hand and kissed her. "You're a hero, kiddo. And to think all along I thought you were just an annoying little brat."

She smacked his arm. The friendly interchange reminded Vincent of his own family gatherings. Maybe their backgrounds weren't so different, after all.

After shaking hands all round and accepting a kiss from Rose, Whitney dragged Vincent right up to the man himself, Gerald MacNair, Sr. He reminded Vincent of an Irish boxer, red-haired, compact, tenacious, and smarter than he'd like anyone else in the room to believe.

Something about Gerald's command of himself made Vincent stand a little taller himself. "Treason is a high crime." Gerald was detailing his own personal plans for Ross Weston. "He'll have no political career, ever. He won't be able to sell his story from prison. He won't be able to practice law. And if he has any money left over after Margery's done divorcing him, I'll sue him on behalf of the people of Montana for the emotional hardship he caused by inviting a terrorist organization to conduct their business on American soil."

Vincent admired the man's thoroughness. "Sir, I don't think I'd want you breathing down my neck."

Gerald slid a pointed look toward Whitney, who sat at his side. "I don't have to, do I?"

Whitney rolled her eyes and stood while Vincent stuttered for an appropriate response. "Smooth, Dad."

She kissed him on the cheek, rescuing Vincent from the "what are your intentions toward my daughter?" conversation.

He wanted to have that conversation.

He wanted to have it with Whitney first.

WHITNEY RODE with Vincent in silence up the elevator at the Wardman Park Hotel.

His silence was nothing new.

But this mood swing was.

She'd seen him angry. Frustrated. Passionate. Hurt. Caring. Deadly.

But she'd never seen him nervous.

She'd made a conscious decision at the hospital that she would accept whatever relationship he wanted to offer her. For whatever length of time. They'd agreed to travel together to Washington for the president's reception honoring their defeat of the Black Order. They'd shared two fabulous days together, seeing the sights, making love, holding each other.

She hoped it wasn't ending tonight.

Had her family scared him off? She couldn't imagine anything scaring Vincent.

Was he looking for a way to let her down easy? Perhaps the thrill of being with her was only related to the high-stakes tension of the job, and now that the job was done, the thrill was gone.

Had he decided she was just too much work? That he didn't get enough in return from her to justify a long-term relationship?

Completely depressed and utterly miserable, Whitney followed him down the hall to their room.

"Close your eyes."

"What?"

Vincent wasn't one to play games. What was going on with him today?

"Humor me."

"Okay." Whitney squeezed her eyes shut and waited while the key card buzzed and clicked in the lock. Vincent opened the door, and with his hand at the small of her back, guided her inside.

The door closed behind her. She breathed in an over-powering sweet smell and frowned. Or no, was that smoke? "Romeo?"

"Open your eyes."

Whitney did.

Her jaw dropped open in mute shock. Vincent Romeo, man of silence, was trying to tell her something.

In every corner of the room, from the vanity counter to the window shelf, were roses. Dozens of them. Hundreds. Rich red bouquets in crystal vases.

And on any flat surface where no rose could fit, there

was a candle. Tall ones. Fat ones. White ones. Blue ones. In candlesticks and sitting on plates. Each one flickered with a beckoning light. They alone illuminated the room.

"Romeo?" Should she read something into his room decor?

He took her purse and jacket, and peeled off his coat and tie. He disappeared into the bathroom for a moment, then came out with two champagne flutes filled with a clear sparkling liquid. He stopped and pressed a button on the radio, and soft, dramatic opera music filled the air.

Whitney pressed her lips together and tried to translate the unspoken message.

Did he think he needed all this to prove that he cared?

A tumble down the slope of Beartooth Mountain had been a romantic enough setting for her.

"Romeo?"

He handed her one of the glasses and clinked hers in a toast. "It's just sparkling water. The doctor said no alcohol for two weeks."

She took a sip along with him and found herself strangely without words. She walked to the window and sniffed the roses there. So many. So beautiful. It nearly overwhelmed the senses. "This is really something."

He moved up behind her, slid his arm around her waist and drew her against his chest. She closed her eyes as he nuzzled her hair. This was what she needed. It was all she wanted from him.

She sank back into his strength and tilted her head for his lips to explore her neck.

He sniffled right in her ear, breaking the mood. But she wanted it back.

Whitney turned, took his glass and set it on the corner of a table with hers. Then she met his dark, hungry gaze and held it as she walked into his arms.

At first they simply stood together, swaying a bit with

the music. Vincent's hands began to roam and she followed his lead. She tested the breadth of his shoulders beneath the crisp white cotton. She ran her fingertips along the smooth column of his neck.

He skimmed her back, captured her waist, caught and squeezed her bottom.

He sniffled again.

Whitney leaned back and frowned. She made note of the pink tip of his tan nose. "Are you okay?"

"I just want you to know how I feel." He turned his head and sneezed. "I want tonight to be special."

She framed his clean-shaven jaw between her hands. "I always feel special when you're with me."

She pulled his mouth down for a kiss and he willingly obliged. She thanked him for the romantic gesture, then turned the kiss into something more.

Whitney rose up on tiptoe, pressing her mouth into his, demanding more. She wrapped her arms around his neck, rubbed her fingers into his short hair. Then she held on and let herself slide against him. He was hard and straight and unyielding. Her breasts flattened, her hips caught fire.

His hands splayed at her waist, his long fingers curving toward her bottom. He lifted her again, pulling her close, re-creating the same glorious friction between them.

His mouth left hers to explore her cheek and jaw and neck. Her feet hit the floor, for only a moment. He lifted the sweater she wore up over her head and tossed it onto the bed. Then she was in his arms again, silk against cotton. The music played. The aroma of roses filled her senses. The light from the candles flickered against her skin like the teasing caress of Vincent's tongue.

He slipped the strap of her camisole down her arm and continued his exploration across her collarbone to the point of her shoulder. "You're like fire in my hands," he praised her, supping on the swell of her breast where skin and silk met. "Cool, creamy skin. Sets me on fire."

Whitney shuddered at the power of his words. She needed him to know that he kindled that same fire in her, that he made her just as crazy. With breathless determination, she unbuttoned his shirt. His mouth caught hers and linked them together as they pushed the cotton off his chest and down his arms.

With the shirttails still hanging from his waist, he gathered her to him. Claiming her with his mouth. Branding her with his heat. Healing her with his touch.

Communicating his love the only way he knew how.

He sneezed.

The unexpected sinus explosion startled them both.

"Romeo?" Was he sick? Did he need her to get some medicine or a doctor?

"No." He ignored the sneeze and the next few sniffles and returned his attention to her face. Each freckle that had annoyed her so over the years became a tempting target for his lips and tongue. Tickling, teasing…

He stopped.

More startling than that sneeze, his sudden stillness alarmed her.

His lips froze beside the bandage at her temple.

And then he walked away from her. Walked clear to one end of the room and back. Leaving her standing there, chilled. Alone. Clutching her arms in front of her feverish body.

"Talk to me, Vincent," she pleaded. "Please talk."

He swiped one hand across his jaw then came back to her at the center of the room. Not close enough for their bodies to touch, but close enough to feel his heat and frustration. And something more.

Whitney waited.

Vincent slipped her camisole straps back into place. He

straightened her hair around her face. Then he touched his fingers gently to the cut at her temple.

"You shouldn't be a part of the life I lead. People get hurt."

The regret in his voice broke her heart. She caught his hand when he would have pulled away. "I would have gotten hurt, anyway. But I would have gotten killed if you hadn't been there to save me."

Vincent pressed her hand between both of his and sniffled. "What about when I go out there to save somebody else? What if I turn out like my dad? I can't put anybody through that."

"That's not your choice."

He frowned at her vehement response.

"If someone—" she sought her words carefully "—cares about you, she'll find a way to live with the danger. Some people are stronger than others, stronger than you think."

I'm strong.

"You don't know what it's like to lose somebody you love, Whitney."

She was afraid she was about to find out.

Vincent released her and crossed to the window. A twinge of Whitney's temper kicked in at his refusal to listen to her.

"Listen, Romeo." She twirled around to face him.

But her argument died on her lips. Vincent sniffled again. And then he sneezed. "Damn." It sounded as if he was cursing through a wad of cotton. He sneezed again. And again. And again.

"Vincent!" Whitney ran to his side, grabbed him by the shoulders and turned him. His eyes were glossy with fluid, his nose was turning redder by the minute, and when he spoke, she could tell his sinuses were swollen and full.

"These are the same symptoms Brian has when he gets around cats. You're allergic. I think it's the roses."

"I dote tink so."

She couldn't help laughing at his stopped-up voice. It was a belly laugh. A cleansing laugh that shook her shoulders and flushed her cheeks with warmth.

Big bad Vincent Romeo was allergic to roses.

She slipped her hand around his neck to apologize, but the laughter was still there in the lilt of her voice. "I'm glad you're human like the rest of us."

"Oh yeah?"

"Vincent!" Her laughter died in an instant. Not because of his teasing dare, but because of the flames that shot up the curtain behind him. One of the candles had gotten too close.

She jerked him away from the growing blaze and spun around, searching for help. Resourceful as always, Whitney grabbed the two wineglasses and tossed the sparkling water on the blaze. It dampened the curtain but didn't put out the fire.

"Get out of here!" Vincent yelled. The sprinkler system kicked on, dousing the room with water and triggering the fire alarm. He pulled the bedspread from the bed and tried to suffocate the flames.

Whitney had a better idea. She pushed her soggy hair off her face and ran to the bathroom to fill the ice bucket with water.

"Move, Romeo!" She shouted the warning above the high piercing tone of the alarm.

Vincent turned. She tossed. She saw too late that he had put the fire out. The water splashed with ignominious glory into Vincent's face. It ran down his jaw and dripped onto his naked chest.

He looked up and squinted against the pulsing shower of water from the ceiling spigot, staring at it as if the wonders of the world could be explained by that silvery metal disk. He smoothed his hair back with the palms of his hands and shook off the excess water before he finally spoke. "Nothing's simple with you, is it?"

Whitney clutched the bucket in front of her. She'd seen that look in his eyes before. Pure black. Intense. He moved toward her and she backed away a step. He wouldn't hurt her, she knew, but this was going to be the part about not getting anything right. About being a danger to live with.

"Vincent..."

And then the sneezing attacked him again. His shoulders shook with the force of his reaction. One mighty man laid low by a bit of rampant pollen.

Whitney laughed. "I'm not afraid of you."

"Why not?" Vincent advanced.

She stood her ground. "Because I love you."

The words shocked them both into stillness. She hadn't meant to say them. She didn't want to put that kind of pressure on him.

But she felt them. In every cell of her body.

So she said them again.

"I love you."

And then the most astonishing thing happened.

Vincent smiled.

This was no gentle curve of the mouth, no half-formed grin.

This was an ear-to-ear, devastatingly handsome, melt-her-down-to-her-very-toes kind of smile.

"Vincent?"

But of course, he didn't tell her what his reaction meant. Instead, he pulled his leather jacket from the closet and draped it over her shoulders, snapping it at he neck and pulling the front together to add a protective layer of warmth over her sodden silk camisole that suddenly revealed everything. Before she could thank him for the tender gesture, he scooped her up in his arms. She fell against his chest and held on to his neck. The ice bucket landed on the floor and hope landed in her heart.

He carried her to the door and opened it. "Where are we going?"

He took her past the neighboring guests who had gathered in the hall to investigate the alarm. He gave a brief explanation to the security guard, bypassed the sealed elevator, and headed straight for the stairs. He had no shirt, and she wore only her skin-hugging camisole and skirt beneath his jacket. But he stood tall, confident, strong.

Mysteriously determined.

He pushed open the door to the stairwell. He carried her in to the landing and they were all alone.

"Vincent, dammit, what are you doing? People are staring at us."

"Shh." His mouth covered hers in a silencing kiss.

He came up for air and carried her down a flight of stairs. Whitney scrambled within his grasp. "You're not dumping me out on the street, are you? I'm sorry about the fire and the water and the roses and the whole thing, but it—"

He kissed her again.

By the third floor he let her breathe again. Her argument was a little more subdued, but no less sincere. "It was a wonderful, romantic gesture. I'm sorry I ruined it for you, but where are you taking me?"

Those black eyes met hers, clear and dark as the midnight sky. "I'm going to ask the manager for a new room where I can make love to my girl all night long."

Whitney blushed all the way to her toes and inside her heart. The portent of his words stoked a fire deep in her belly and made her cling to his shoulders in a grasp that would never let go.

"Okay."

It was all she needed to say.

Chapter Thirteen

Patrick McMurty cussed all the way out to the barbecue pit with his wife, Dale, close behind, giving instructions and ignoring every last thing he said. "The first of November is too damn late in the year to have this thing fired up."

Dale smiled, the spirit in her trim body every bit a match for her husband's tall, lanky frame. "You're the only thing that's all fired up. Now, c'mon. I said I'd help."

Patrick had started the fire last night before Whitney and Vincent had arrived back at the ranch for the final debriefing on Montana Confidential's mission. Whitney perched on the top rail of the corral, scratching Dragonheart's nose and spoiling him with a couple of carrots.

She'd come here three months ago, hating this place before she ever arrived. It was a life sentence back then. A punishment for being the ultimate screwup in a family and a city that didn't tolerate screwups.

She gazed up at the snow-studded mountains that lined either side of the valley. There were no people here, she'd despaired. No places to shop. Nothing worthwhile to do.

But she'd found a family here. Daniel Austin and the others. The McMurtys. Vincent.

She'd found a purpose.

It was enough to care. About people. About work. She'd

learned pride and satisfaction doing things as mundane as typing or cleaning tack. She'd learned what was important to her. Not the shopping. Not the prestige of a political career.

Her country.

Her friends.

Her heart.

Those were the things that mattered.

Dragonheart butted his nose against her leg, demanding her attention. She apologized for running out of carrots, then gave him a good rub down the center of his face. "Okay, boy. You matter, too."

She looked back at Frank and Dale, and saw the silver-haired cowboy lean down and give his wife a kiss. Then Dale curled her arm through Frank's and they huddled together, watching the beef grill over the coals. Their bickering no longer alarmed her as it had when she first arrived. It was just their way of talking. After forty some-odd years of marriage, their way of talking must work.

"Molly!"

Kyle Foster's crisp voice shouted an order that his three-year-old daughter dutifully ignored. She had a running start ahead of Kyle and his dark-haired wife, Laura, as they left the barn.

"Horsey!"

Whitney laughed and jumped down to scoop up the bundle of energy into her arms. "Yes, it is." She leaned closer to the railing so Molly could touch Dragonheart's nose.

"Toft!" Molly snatched her hand away in a startled giggle when the horse snorted in response to her petting.

"You tickled her."

"Here. I'll take a load off your hands." Kyle swept Molly into his arms.

He put his lips to her cheek and snorted a zerbert against

her skin, delighting his daughter. She grabbed Kyle's face between her chubby fingers and shouted again. "Horsey!"

Laura Foster possessed the cool serenity that reminded Whitney of her mother. But there was no doubt in Whitney's mind that she adored Molly and had found her perfect match in Kyle. Something about the way they were always holding hands gave them away. "Will you be staying in Montana long?" she asked.

Whitney shrugged her shoulders. "As long as it takes. There's still some paperwork to wrap up."

Kyle pulled his gaze away from Molly. "Paperwork nothing. We're going to get you out in the field again."

Whitney beamed beneath his praise. "Thanks, Kyle."

"Oh, Jewel was looking for you in the barn."

Her smile faded. During her trip to Washington, the inevitable had finally happened. Silver had succumbed to old age and pneumonia. Whitney felt guilty for not being here when Jewel had needed her. The twelve-year-old had lost much more than a horse. She'd lost a prized friend.

"I'd better check it out."

She breathed deeply and braced herself as she strolled to the barn. She found Jewel cleaning out one of the stalls. Whitney grabbed a pitchfork to lend a hand. "Hey, champ."

"Hi, Whit."

She'd try regular conversation first. "Did you talk to Charlie Korbett yet? He came with his sister to the barbecue." Charlie's sister, Sabrina, had recently married Court Brody, an old flame and father of her sixteen-month-old son.

"He hasn't talked to me yet."

"That could be because he's outside playing horseshoes, and you're in here mucking out stalls."

"I don't feel like playing."

"Maybe you could just go watch. I think he's kickin' Court's butt out there."

Jewel sighed with all the drama of an adolescent. "You know, there's no one to talk to when you're not here."

"I can't be here twenty-four hours a day, champ. But there are lots of people around here who care about you."

"I know. But Gramps is sad about Silver, too."

Whitney moved the wheelbarrow to the next stall. This wasn't exactly how she'd planned to spend her day, but if Jewel needed her... "I don't just mean Frank and Dale. What about C.J.?"

Jewel wrinkled up her nose. "Frank's wife?"

Whitney shook her head. Was she ever this age? Okay, so maybe a couple of weeks ago. But she got over it. "You know she cares about you. Look at all the times she's tried to talk to you, invite you places. She doesn't want to come between you and Frank's friendship. She wants to become another friend."

"Maybe." Jewel was weakening. "But she doesn't know anything about horses."

"I'll bet she knows about losing something you care about."

Jewel gave the idea some consideration. "She doesn't have any parents, does she?"

"No."

"That's gotta be tough."

After a few minutes of working in companionable silence, Whitney thought they should get out into what was left of the sunlight. "C'mon. I told Dale I'd help with dinner, and it's almost four o'clock."

"She's gonna let you cook?"

Whitney stuck out her tongue. "I get to help set the table."

Jewel took both pitchforks and hung them up. Whitney disposed of the wheelbarrow. She hugged the girl to her side and they walked out of the barn together. She was glad to see that Jewel's smile matched her own. But then the girl stopped and pulled away.

"You're not going up to the house?"

"No." Jewel's blond pigtails were already flying out behind her. "I'm gonna go beat Charlie. Hey—tell Frank and C.J. to come on out."

Whitney waved at Court and Charlie. She found Sabrina on the porch swing, rocking the baby to sleep. She tiptoed over. "How's he doing?"

Sabrina shook back her long brown hair and grinned. "Just like his daddy. Plays hard 'til he drops. Then falls to sleep as soon as his head hits the pillow."

Whitney turned at the footsteps running up behind her. Court squeezed her shoulder and pressed a kiss to Whitney's cheek as he circled her. "I heard that."

In one fluid movement he slipped onto the porch swing beside his wife and tipped her chin up for his kiss. Then, like the proud papa he was, he scooped his son into his arms and cradled the sleeping boy on his shoulder.

He thumbed back at the horseshoe pit. "I thought I'd give young love a shot. They don't need an old guy like me hanging around."

Sabrina grabbed his knee and turned for another kiss. "Don't sell yourself short, cowboy."

Whitney silently excused herself from the ongoing debate.

She found Frank and C.J. Connolly in the kitchen. C.J. was brewing a pot of tea, and in her very proper British accent was regaling Frank with the history of this particular leaf. The former military pilot sat on a stool, leaning toward her across the counter, drinking in every word.

Whitney averted her face, squelching the urge to point out to C.J. that Frank was watching her lips. He inched his way closer and closer while C.J. chatted, until he raised up on his elbows and kissed her.

"Yes. Well." C.J. tucked her straight blond hair behind her ear and gave him a stern look. Tough-guy Frank curled his lips into something like a pout and C.J. laughed. She cupped his cheek and kissed him back.

By the time Whitney cleared her throat to make her presence known, there'd been a great deal of kissing and laughing.

C.J. blushed and Frank sat back on his stool. "Hey, kid. You need something?"

"Jewel's invited you both out to play horseshoes."

"Really?" C.J. pressed her fingers to her lips. Her expression was a blend of doubt and hope. Frank reached across the counter and squeezed her hand in support. "You're sure?"

Whitney shrugged. "I can't make any guarantees, but I think she's seeing you in a new light."

"Frank, let's go." C.J. led Frank into the dining room and Whitney followed.

"I thought I had table detail." She nodded toward the dining-room table which had already been set for fifteen, plus high chairs for the two little ones. She counted the place settings again. There was one for each Montana Confidential member and his family—or her guest. Plus two more. "Are we having company?"

Frank nodded. "Sheridan and Jessie Austin."

Whitney clapped her hands together. "He called them?"

"He thought since the job was done out here, he'd take a shot at reconciliation."

"Yes!" This was great news. Seeing his ex-wife and his son would be the best antidote for the weary frowns Daniel had been sporting lately.

Daniel was wearing a path on the rug in his office when Whitney opened the door. Her heart went out to this man who commanded authority. This man who had taken her under his wing and stuck by her even when he hadn't wanted the job.

"You look fine." Whitney walked in and straightened the collar of his blue plaid western-cut shirt. "This look suits you."

"She said she'd be here at four." He checked his watch. "It's four-ten."

"Give her time. Not everybody drives like I do."

"Thank God for that." He resumed his pacing. "What am I going to say to her?"

Whitney planted herself in his path. "What do you want to say?"

Daniel raked his fingers through his hair. "That I'm sorry. That I made a mistake. That I'm a different man now than I was when I left her."

"That all sounds good."

"How do I know if she even feels anything for me still?"

Whitney smoothed the lock of hair that had fallen across his forehead. "She's coming all the way from Maryland to see you. She feels something."

"But where do I start?"

"Tell her you love her. Then take it from there."

Five minutes later, he bolted out of the house and down the steps to greet Sheridan and Jessie. He hurried around the car and opened the door for a gently pretty woman with shoulder-length, chestnut hair. There were hushed words between them.

And then Daniel wrapped her up in a fierce embrace. The woman stretched up on tiptoe and clung to him. A young boy, about Jewel's age, climbed out of the car and ran around to join them. Daniel reached out and pulled the boy into their hug.

The whole Confidential team and their families stood on

the porch and watched with unabashed curiosity and approval. Whitney's eyes grew hot and misted over. "That's Sheridan and Jessie, I take it?"

Frank winked. "That's them."

Whitney felt suddenly alone amongst all her friends. "Has anybody seen Vincent?"

"So, Romeo. What do you think of the place?"

After everyone had eaten their fill of slow-roasted barbecue, potato salad and corn on the cob, and done enough talking to do any family reunion proud, Daniel asked Whitney and Vincent to go down to the war room with him.

Vincent traced his fingers along the keys of a satellite cartography system, admiring it like a restored vintage Harley. Whitney found out that he'd disappeared down here for the afternoon. He was a man who liked his gadgets, after all. "Quite a setup. I'm impressed with the technology and support."

"Good." Daniel propped his hip on the corner of a desk and crossed his arms. "I have a proposition for you."

"You're not gettin' me to move to Montana. The fresh air's nice, but I'm a city boy."

Daniel laughed. "Then I've got just the thing for you." Vincent's gaze sharpened as Daniel grew serious. "The Department of Public Safety needs a man to outfit a Confidential agency in Chicago. With your NSA training and connections to the city, I thought you'd be the perfect candidate. You interested in the job?"

Vincent went still. That utterly quiet kind of still that sucked the energy from the atmosphere and put Whitney on alert.

"Yes." Daniel stood, ready to shake hands and call it a deal. But Whitney knew better. Vincent hadn't moved yet. "On one condition."

Daniel gave an affable shrug. "I think the DPS is willing to be flexible. What is it?"

"That Whitney goes with me. As my wife."

Whitney sank into the chair behind her. The breath she held whooshed out and left her light-headed.

Vincent came to her and took her hand. She followed as he sat back on a desktop and pulled her into the vee of his legs. His hands settled at her waist in a familiar possessive grasp. He looked her in the eye and said simply, "I love you."

Whitney was only marginally aware of the elevator door closing behind Daniel. She stared at Vincent's lips, wondering if they had formed those three words she just heard. She looked into his eyes, dark pools of midnight glass that always told her the truth.

She ran her fingertips along his cheek and jaw, then settled them onto his lips.

"I love you." He said it again. Twice. Vincent talking. Not a fluke.

She felt the words with her touch. Heard them in the rasp of his voice. Felt them in the depths of her soul.

"I know you love me."

She threw her arms around him and hugged him with all the strength she possessed. She rubbed her cheek against his five o'clock shadow and flattened her palms against his hair. She absorbed his heat into her skin and his clean, leathery scent into her nose.

She sensed his confusion and leaned back against the brace of his hands. "I figured it out a while back. You confirmed it in D.C. with that whole rose fiasco." Whitney opened up her heart and let it shine through. "Even though you're a man of few words, your eyes and actions have told me you love me time and again."

Those same beautiful eyes caressed her face. He twirled a finger into a lock of her hair and tucked it behind her ear. "If you know so much, MacNair, why didn't you tell me? You like doing that."

She splayed her fingers across his chest, pressed them flat against the beat of his strong heart. "I just wanted you to realize it for yourself. I wanted you to choose to love me."

"Oh, I do, MacNair." His fingers slipped into her hair and pulled her close. "I do."

He punctuated his promise with a kiss that stole her willing heart.

"You think your family's going to accept me?" he asked after a while, still tasting her freckles with his lips.

"I think so. Anyway, I'm a big enough girl to make my own decisions. I love you. I want to marry you and move to Chicago. I want to fight by your side against injustice in this world and I want to have your babies."

"Not at the same time."

She laughed at the gruff command, knowing he protected so well because he loved her.

"Besides," she teased, "think of the shopping there!"

She laughed in delight, watching him shake his head. "There's Water Tower Place. Marshall Field. Neiman Marcus—"

Vincent silenced his woman with a kiss.

HARLEQUIN®
INTRIGUE®
and
DEBRA WEBB

invite you for a special consultation at the

For the most
private investigations!

SOLITARY SOLDIER
January 2002

**Look for three more COLBY AGENCY
cases throughout 2002!**

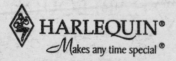

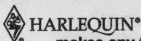

TRUEBLOOD, TEXAS

Coming in January 2002...

THE BEST MAN IN TEXAS

by

Kelsey Roberts

Lost:

One heiress. Sara Pierce wants to disappear permanently and so assumes another woman's identity. She hadn't counted on losing her memory....

Found:

One knight in shining armor. Dr. Justin Dale finds himself falling in love with his new patient...a woman who knows less about herself than he does.

Can the past be overcome, so that Sara and Justin may have a future together?

Finders Keepers: bringing families together

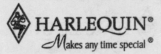